The Fall Out

BOSTON REVS THREE OUTS BOOK 1

Jenni Bara

The Fall Out

Boston Revs Three Outs Book 1

Copyright @ 2024 Jenni Bara

Line Copy and Proof Editing by VB Edits

Final Proofreading by Jeffrey Hodge

Interior formatting Sara Stewart

Cover by Cheslea Kemp

ISBN: 978-1-959389-12-5 (ebook)

ISBN: 978-1-959389-14-9 (paperback)

Jennibara.com

DEDICATION

To Britt, he's yours.

But not just because you called him first...

although you did.

Playlist

Banana Pancakes - Jack Johnson

One of Them Girls - Lee Brice

My Stupid Mouth - John Mayer

Hanging By a Moment - Lifehouse

You're My Better Half - Keith Urban

How You Remind Me - Nickelback

More Than Friends (feat. Meghan Trainor)- Jason Mraz

Someone You Loved - Lewis Capaldi

Chasin' You - Morgan Wallen

You and Me - Lifehouse

Drunk on Your Love - Brett Eldredge

Don't Happen Twice - Kenny Chesney

19 You + Me - Dan + Shay

Feels Like Home - Chantal Kreviazuk

BOSTON REVS
BASEBALL CLUB

REVS | METROS
APRIL 1ST | 6 PM

LINEUP

COACH: TOM WILSON #49

1	KYLE BOSCO #29	RF
2	JASEPER QUINN #16	1B
3	EMERSON KNIGHT #21	3B
4	ASHER PRICE #5	C
5	HENRY WINTERS #44	2B
6	EDDIE MARTINEZ #30	SS
7	COLTON STEWART #23	DH
8	TRISTIAN JENNER #27	LF
9	MASON DUMPTY #22	CF
P	CHRISTIAN DAMIANO #35	P

B

CONTENTS

Avery
1

MARCH

"Which lucky man will be the one to help Avery get over another jackass?" My best friend Wren craned her neck, searching the crowded bar. She paused to inspect each male in the room, studying them with eyes so dark they were almost black. She assessed them, one by one, like she was at work at Boston's most prestigious auction house, and they were pieces of art she'd been tasked with appraising.

"Please, let's make this more awkward." I took a sip of my beer and studied the surface of the round high-top table, where two wineglasses and one brown bottle sat between us. Wren and Jana were Chardonnay girls, but I'd take a Bud Light over wine any day. Luckily, they didn't hold it against me any more than they did my lack of interest in makeup or nail polish.

"No blonds," Jana chirped, encouraging Wren's endeavor instead of helping me stop the madness. "I veto *all* the blonds."

Because Joe the jerk was a blond. I picked at the corner of the blue label and forced the anger that had started to simmer inside me to cool. Not even a month ago, I found out my boyfriend was an utter ass. At first, I was sad, sure, but now I kept circling back to pissed off. At myself, at him, at my dad's career choice. All of it.

This afternoon, my best friends decided it was time I moved on, so they'd dragged me to this bar to enact their half-cocked plan. I wasn't on board. Although Wren and Jana were my people, they were insane. In the best ways most of the time, but *other times*, they were just crazy.

I tended to attract that. Big personalities liked the calm that was my typical mood. I'd known Wren since she moved to Boston in middle school, which meant I'd spent most of our high school years keeping us out of the trouble she found.

I met Jana on my first day at the Boston Zoo. She was in the advertising and marketing department. She loved coming up with the next amazing idea, but sometimes she forgot her ideas depended on the animals' cooperation. Which usually led her to begging for my help. Within weeks of meeting her, she became the marshmallow fluff to the peanut butter and jelly sandwich Wren and I had long ago become. In reality, *they* were probably the jelly, the fluff, *and* the peanut butter. *I* was the boring white bread.

"Redheads are out." Wren sipped her wine, still scanning for a non-blond, non-ginger that she deemed worthy.

"But gingers are freaky. Why are we banning them?" Jana brushed a hand through her strawberry-blond curls, pushing them off her face. Peering over her shoulder, she pointed a long pink nail at an auburn-haired guy with a ponytail at a high-top two tables over. "I like that guy for her."

I slunk back in my seat, hoping he didn't notice her pointing right at him.

"No. She needs a tall, dark, and handsome."

As I'd predicted, their too-loud voices attracted the man's attention, and he turned our way.

"Sorry. Girls' night," she mouthed before turning back to us. "She's always going for blonds or gingers. And they all suck."

I wouldn't say *that* was what I'd done wrong over the years.

"I think—"

"No." Wren cut me off with a shake of her head, sending her brown bangs floating around her face. "You don't get a say. Your picker is broken."

"Picker?" Jana asked.

At the same time, I scoffed. "*Broken.*"

Jana gave me the side-eye and pursed her bright red lips. "You suck at picking out good guys. We can all agree on that." She patted my hand, her watch clicking against my silver charm bracelet. "I just don't think I'd call it a picker."

So I'd had a few bad boyfriends. Okay, maybe more than a few. That didn't mean some rando in this bar would fix the issue.

I rolled my eyes and slumped farther onto my stool. "I very much doubt you'll find the perfect guy by pointing one out in a crowded bar and sending me home to sleep with him."

"No attachment," Wren corrected. Her dark eyes cut into me harshly. "So don't spend the night. Sleeping, *cuddling*? That shit will cause you to catch feelings." She scrunched her nose and shuddered.

I let out a long sigh in response, and Jana rolled her eyes at me.

Why was the idea of feeling something for the guy they wanted me to sleep with so appalling?

I didn't get a chance to ask before they went on.

"Plus, we're not looking for perfect. Hot but a complete self-centered asshole would work. We don't want you to really *like* him." Jana tapped the wooden table with her nails.

"Right. You just need a man to break the loser spell." Wren glanced around again, chin lifted high. "Like that guy." She pointed at two men standing at a ledge not far from our table.

Okay, yeah, the guy with black hair was hot in an Adrian Grenier kind of way. But he was definitely younger than I was. Maybe twenty-three? And way too smiley. God, didn't it hurt his cheeks to smile that big?

The guy he was with had more of an edge. His strong jaw was clenched tight and dusted with a five-o'clock shadow. His deep brown eyes were narrowed when they met mine, and I fought the shiver that tried to race down my spine. As he took me in, they softened, along with his expression, and he slid his teeth over his full bottom lip, like maybe he was interested. But then his focus shifted a fraction, to where

Wren was still pointing at him, and a veil fell over his face. In an instant, his glare was back.

I yanked her hand down. "Can we not point?" My face flamed, and thanks to my pale complexion, it would be obvious to anyone in a ten-foot radius.

My friends, who loved to torment me until I blushed, laughed.

"Don't make a scene." I buried my face in my hands. "I'm seriously not hooking up with anyone tonight. Can't it just be a girls' night?"

"Too late. They're coming this way," Jana said.

I groaned into my hands. I loved my besties. I did. But I wasn't sleeping with a random guy to break my loser spell, regardless of how brilliant my friends thought their plan was. Even if I was willing to consider it, I wouldn't pick the broody dude who was probably headed our way so he could yell at us.

To break the spell, all I needed to do was pay more attention. Learn to stay away from the guys who were more interested in getting to know my father than me. Find a man who listened when I talked. One who didn't perk up when I mentioned my last name.

When the heat in my cheeks had cooled a fraction, I sat up again. Immediately, my focus landed on the two guys who were closing in quickly. Part of me wanted to panic. To get up and bolt out the door. But the odds were in my favor, weren't they? There were two guys and three of us. And in this trio, I was consistently the one who could fade into the background. So that's what I'd do. Then I'd make a quick escape.

Christian
2

"ARE YOU GOING TO BE A DICK?" Emerson Knight, my teammate, dragged me across the bar toward the three women pointing at us. Normally, being pointed at like I was a spectacle gave me the urge to run in the other direction, but the gorgeous blond was…intriguing. She wasn't showy like the women who flanked her. They were dressed to attract every male in the bar, but she was all big blue eyes, long silky hair, and perfect skin. Even the way the deep red blush crept up her cheeks was cute. And although I wouldn't tell my teammate that her smile hit me like a massive kick in my gut, I couldn't deny I was interested enough to buy *her* a drink.

"I'm never a dick," I gritted out.

His response was simply to laugh. We'd met in AAA ball and had played together for three years, so at this point, he knew me.

Emerson and I shared an apartment in Boston like we had in upstate New York, and tonight, he'd dragged me out for a drink at the bar around the block. Though I had no interest in being social, I had to admit it wasn't a bad idea. I could use the distraction to release some of the pressure building up inside me over my first game as a starting major league pitcher.

Tomorrow. Nerves clawed up my throat, but I locked my jaw and stomped that shit down. Winning was about confidence.

"Come on, Dragon. Boston won't be like Florida."

Spring training in Florida had been unreal. In the minors, there were usually women around, but the intensity was nothing compared to the ball bunnies who flocked to spring training. Aggressive and in my face, and that wasn't for me. I wasn't the type of guy who fucked just anyone. If there wasn't chemistry, then it wasn't worth my time.

"Pretend we're still a pair of nobodies in the hills of New York. They might not even watch baseball. Just 'cause they were pointing doesn't mean they know us." He ran his hand through his hair. "I'm hot as fuck. Women tend to see me, whether they know who I am or not."

I snorted. Emerson was something, that was for sure.

Although he was a few years younger than me, we'd both been called up to the major league baseball team in Boston this year. He'd been brought up as the Revs' new third baseman just before spring training had begun, and I'd gotten the call two weeks into it.

I'd always thought that if this day came, I'd be living the dream. And I supposed I was in some ways. But damn, I was desperate for a night where no one was focused on how I threw the ball or said the wrong thing to a reporter. If one more person told me it would help if I stopped giving them dumb sound bites, I might break something. Dad told me to brush it off. And I was working on letting shit go. But I didn't make it to the MLB by being a quitter, so it wasn't easy.

"How about we don't talk baseball at all? It could be fun. All three of them are smoking hot." He elbowed me.

He was practically skipping next to me. Like a happy little puppy. If a rainbow unicorn mated with the Energizer Bunny, the result would be Emerson Knight.

I grunted at him, which he took to mean I was unhappy.

"Stop with the pissed-off vibe."

I huffed in response, giving him side-eye. Just 'cause I didn't shit rainbows all the time didn't mean I was mad. "No baseball. We don't play it. We don't follow it. We aren't even fans of the fucking sport."

"Okay." He smiled. "I'm a garbage man."

I stumbled over my own feet and gaped at him. "*Why?*"

He shrugged, his entire being practically sparkling at the fucking idea. "It sounds fun." He whacked my arm three times in his normal lack of personal space. "We can collect the stuff that people throw out. Wanna be a garbage man too?"

Why in God's name would I want to hoard other people's trash?

"No." I tossed both hands in the air. "Not at all."

He chuckled, but he didn't seem surprised by either my exasperation or my answer.

I came out tonight to relax, not *lie*. "We're not making up careers. I'd rather say I'm unemployed than talk about a job."

"Hmm." With a shrug, he spun to face me and walked backward to the table. "Women like men with jobs, so if it comes up, you're better off collecting garbage with me than pretending to be unemployed." He smirked and turned around again. "Hey, pretty ladies."

This was going to be a disaster. Especially since the gorgeous blond had her head bowed and was studying her ballet flats, clearly not interested in our company, while the women I didn't want to deal with were watching me like I was their next conquest. Not happening. There was not a single spark of interest in my body for either of them.

"Hello there." Smirking, the redhead held up her wine and tipped it our way. "Aren't you two looking happy"—she waved the glass at Emerson first, then turned to me—"and pissed, all at the same time."

I frowned but didn't bother with a response. No, I was too busy watching the woman who'd piqued enough interest in me to drag me across the room.

As if my attention were a physical caress, she lifted her head and focused on me. Like a tranquil lake in the afternoon sun, her eyes sparkled. I wanted to dive in and get lost in them. Fuck, I sounded like a bad poem. I blinked twice but couldn't shake myself free of the spell her gaze had put me under. And she didn't look away from me either.

"Don't worry about Dragon." Emerson moved in, knocking his IPA against the wooden surface as he claimed the spot between the ginger and the brunette.

He could have them. I stepped closer to the blond. Her mouth turned up slightly on one side, the hint of movement making my chest pinch.

"My friend is just generally constipated."

Stomach lurching, I whipped to the right and glared at my team-mate. *I was what?*

He smirked at me. "I can't help that you have to deal with constant constipation."

"Wow, what an opening line." The brunette laughed.

I still hadn't found words.

"He refused to let me tell you I was a garbage man, so there wasn't much else I could say."

"Holy hell," I snapped.

The two women flanking my teammate laughed.

"I'm just going to…" The blond pointed toward the hallway near the back. The sign above it read *Restroom*. "I'll be back."

Based on the way she averted her gaze, I was pretty sure she was planning an escape from the man she now thought had issues taking a shit. How very attractive.

I might kill Emerson tonight.

Before I could stop her, she slipped away. I tracked her as she went, unable to pull my gaze from the light denim covering the perfect peach-shaped ass. A crop tank top and jeans weren't high fashion, but damn, she made it look like it was. Her blond hair was pulled into a ponytail, the curled ends hanging past the light blue top that clung to her. Heads turned as she moved through the space, and I wanted to follow behind her just to rip each of the fucking guys' eyes out for thinking they had the right to stare at her ass.

"Dragon?"

I turned.

"I'm Wren." The brunette leaned in. With one arm resting on the table in front of her, the move caused her breasts to lift and push up into the deep scoop of her red shirt.

I kept my focus trained on her face. She wore too much makeup for my taste.

She tilted her head to one side, her dark hair falling over her shoulder. "Do you believe in sex without commitment?"

I clenched my teeth. There was no good answer to that question. Did I? Sure. I was a moody asshole with a short fuse. People got sick of me as fast as I got tired of them. But I wasn't a fucking a trophy for women to brag about. And since I'd made it to the majors, I'd discovered how many women were interested in just that. Saying that aloud, though, made me sound like a pompous dick. At least that's what my teammates had told me the last time I mentioned it to a woman.

Plus, the only woman in the bar who piqued my interest had fled the moment I approached. So I didn't bother answering the question. I didn't plan to stick around if the blond woman didn't come back quick.

I scowled.

"Dragon's more like a good scotch than a beer." Emerson took a sip of his drink.

"Perfect." Wren smirked.

Her friend, though, only frowned.

Wren bumped her with an elbow. "He means Dragon here." She patted my hand.

On instinct, I yanked it away. The chick didn't need to touch me. Over twenty types of bacteria lived on the human palm, and I didn't need to add hers to the ones that already resided on mine.

"Don't be offended." Emerson chuckled. "The dude's a total germophobe."

He might be the worst wingman in the history of wingmen. I didn't give a flying fuck about either of these women, but their friend? My gut tightened at just the idea of her. So I would appreciate it if he didn't make me look like a total douche canoe.

But the redhead's face lit up like my aversion to bacteria was the best news she'd heard all week. "What a coincidence, since our girl's a doctor."

"That's debatable, Jana." Wren tipped her head back and forth, as if weighing the idea, her dark hair dancing over her shoulders.

How was being a doctor debatable?

"But it seems Dragon is more of an acquired taste. Something you savor *once* rather than repeatedly like your go-to drink."

"Exactly." Emerson tipped his bottle at the dark-haired beauty. "You and me, we speak the same language."

She laughed, batting her long lashes, and my friend leaned in and whispered in her ear. The guy was a total man whore. He should have been wearing a sign that said *lock up your sisters and daughters*. I didn't do the bar thing often, and I rarely hooked up with random women. Hadn't in years. But Emerson? People loved the happy third baseman, so he had new women laughing in his ear practically every day.

"Hot but an asshole." Jana clapped her hands and held them in a prayer position in front of her chin. "Just what the doctor ordered."

The women turned to one another, wearing matching smirks, then looked at me once more.

"We're totally going to bail. Take care of our girl." Jana blew me an air kiss, grabbed her purse from the tabletop, and sauntered toward the exit without looking back.

"Come on." Wren yanked on Emerson's hand.

The guy shrugged and followed behind her like the puppy dog he was.

I shook my head. If he ended up back at our place with both of them and they kept me up all night, he'd be out on his ass and searching for a new apartment.

"They left?"

I spun at the sound of the soft voice behind me. She'd come back. Maybe this night wouldn't be a total disaster after all.

As she stepped up beside me, she had her lips pressed together and she was scanning the bar. While she assessed our surroundings, I drank her in, studying the path my lips wanted to take: The swell of her tits against the blue fabric. The flat stomach exposed by her crop top. And the belly button I wanted to sink my tongue into.

Before she thought I was a creeper, I forced myself to meet her eye. "Let me buy you a drink?"

The long pause that was her response left me in knots.

Avery
3

THEY LEFT?

Mr. Tall, Dark, and Broody had asked me a question, but I wasn't focused on his words. Jana and Wren were wild cards. I probably shouldn't have left the table, but I figured they'd pair off with the guys, and I could slip away. I'd head home, snuggle up on my comfy couch, and watch a cheesy Hallmark movie. That's how I typically ended nights out. So why was the better-looking of the guys still at this table when everyone else was gone?

I swallowed thickly and turned to the broody man beside me. "What did they say to you?"

Did they tell him he should fuck the bad boyfriend vibes out of me? I mean, how possible was that? Like if he hit the right angle, would they shoot out of my ear or something?

He cleared his throat and narrowed his eyes on me. "Just that they were leaving and I was supposed to make sure you got home."

I pressed my lips together and bit down on them. Neither Wren nor Jana would worry about me getting home. Not only did I live practically around the corner, but they weren't the type to have those thoughts. Neither would even pause before following a rank stranger down a dark alley alone, and I couldn't count how many times I'd yelled at them for leaving their drinks totally unattended.

"I highly doubt that." I cocked a brow at the big, hot liar.

His dark eyes tracked over my face, and he pulled a quick breath in through his nose. "They told me to take care of you." Ah. That made more sense. "I assumed that meant get you home safe."

I shrugged. "Normal people would assume that. But my friends are insane, so to them, that meant make sure I have multiple orgasms."

The man in front of me choked on a cough, like my statement had shocked him. We were at a bar on a Saturday night. What did he think people were doing here? Personally, I wasn't here for that, but if I took a poll, at least 87 percent of the people in this bar would tell me they were here to find a person to hook up with for the next few hours.

"Anyway." I toyed with the base of Jana's empty wineglass, spinning it a few times while I fought the nerves fluttering through me. My fingers trembled as I did, almost knocking the glass over.

It was saved when a large hand wrapped around the bowl of the glass, steadying it.

I forced my focus back onto the gorgeous guy who kinda made my stomach jump. He remained focused on my face, his scrutiny so intense it sent a shiver down my spine.

Might as well just get the truth out there, because if Wren and Jana came back, they'd tell him. If they hadn't already. "Their mission tonight was to find a guy who would fuck the bad relationship juju, or something like that, out of me. I'm surprised they didn't mention it."

Between the narrowed eyes and locked jaw, he looked ready to break something, but then again, the heat in those dark irises could be attraction. I could be wrong. No one had ever looked at me like they wanted to toss me against the first available surface and make me scream their name. I wondered if that was what he was thinking right then.

My core tightened at the idea of being shoved against the wall. What would his long fingers feel like biting into my skin?

Like he was on the same page, he dragged his tongue along his bottom lip.

That tiny movement alone made my knees wobble. Call me a puddle on the floor, because that's how I felt.

Jeez, I needed to get it together and remember that I had no intention of going home with anyone tonight.

"Is fucking emotional turmoil away your goal too?" He pressed his lips together and angled in a little closer, his scrutiny burning me up from the inside out. And the deep voice? It rocked through me, suddenly making me consider whether that should be my goal for the night.

But I shook my head, pushing away the lust clouding my judgment. "I just wanted a girls' night out. Relaxing, not stressful." I was supposed to avoid throwing myself into yet another bad relationship.

He rested his forearms on the tabletop and leaned in even closer. "But?"

He watched me like he was interested in what I had to say, so I kept going. Why the hell not? I wasn't trying to impress this guy.

"I broke up with my boyfriend of six months because it turned out he was using me to get a job with the—" I snapped my mouth shut to keep from spilling too many details. "Some people I know. Even though he was the jerk in the situation, I still felt like a loser. My friends are trying to help me move on."

He studied my face, his expression as intense as ever. Though he was young, probably my age, the hard lines etched into his skin and the rigid jaw made him look so much more jaded.

"Can I buy you a drink?" he asked for the second time.

Sounding like a hot mess made him want to hang out with me? Didn't know that was a thing, but who was I to complain? "Why not?"

He turned to the table and scanned the wineglasses and the bottles scattered about. Then he turned back to me. "What would you like?"

Interesting. Unlike most of the guys I'd dated, he didn't just assume one of the wineglasses belonged to me. Even after six months, Joe hadn't realized that I hated wine. But this guy had taken the time to ask.

"Bud Light."

He gave me a clipped nod and strode for the bar. While he waited, he glanced over his shoulder a few times, wearing a surly glower. The look confused me. He wanted to buy me a drink, yet he didn't seem too happy about it.

While I waited for him, I brushed a couple of guys off, gently informing them that Mr. Tall, Dark, and Angry at the bar was getting me a drink. When he returned, he was carrying two bottles. One was brown and had a blue label, and a second was a brand I'd never seen before.

Easy Out.

"I've never heard of that." I picked up his bottle and read the label. The logo was pretty—a ring of small flowers surrounding the words *Easy Out.* Craft brew from Long Island. Huh. And they serve it in Boston? Must be an up-and-coming brand.

His deep brown eyes shifted between me and the beer. "Did you want to try it?"

"Sure." I lifted the bottle to my lips and relished the cool, refreshing liquid. When I set it in front of him, I licked my lips, assessing the flavor. "It's almost citrusy."

He blinked twice and swallowed. "Did you want it?" As he pushed the bottle toward me, it scraped along the wooden tabletop.

As much as I enjoyed the flavor, it seemed rude to take both drinks. I shook my head. "I'll stick with Bud Light."

The corners of his mouth pulled down, almost like he was uncomfortable, and he stared at the drink. But then he shook his head and focused on me again. Finally, he wrapped his long fingers around the bottle, brought it to his own lips, and took a sip. The way his Adam's apple bobbed as he swallowed did funny things to my stomach and made my thighs clench. Wow. His neck was sexy. Long and smooth and tan. His hard jaw was peppered with more than a five-o'clock shadow, and his lips were full and pink.

My breath hitched. This guy exuded sex. But I wasn't here for that. I straightened and jumped back into the conversation.

"So how'd ya find this brand? I've never heard of it."

"It's my dad's favorite." The way his eyes twinkled when he spoke made me think he might actually smile. "This was the first beer he gave me at sixteen. Guess it stuck."

I couldn't help the gasp that escaped me. "Sixteen? My dad would have shot me if I'd had beer that young, and yours was the one handing it to you?"

"He was a single dad, just trying to do his best." Rubbing his palms together, he ducked his head and focused on the table, like maybe my comment had offended him.

"I didn't mean that in a bad way." I laid a hand on his forearm.

The already corded muscles tightened under my fingers, and he followed my movement.

I continued, not wanting him to think I was criticizing. "It's cool that your dad was chill."

He relaxed under my touch, but only slightly. It still felt like I was holding on to a rock. Whatever the guy did to strengthen the muscles in his arms was working for him. I grazed my thumb along the skin of his wrist, and again, he followed the movement, fixated on the contact.

He cleared his throat. "Dad's big on rites of passage. He wanted me to have my first beer with him." He was assessing me again, but he didn't push me off his arm. "It was never a taboo thing at my house, so I never cared about drinking myself stupid."

"My dad was strict about everything." I rolled my eyes. Strict was putting it mildly. "He can't find his chill even now." I chuckled.

I was twenty-seven, but more often than not, my dad acted like I was still a little girl.

"He and my mom divorced when I was too little to remember. I think he worried about being good enough." Raising a child while so involved in major league baseball couldn't have been easy. It was hard to keep me from hearing about all kinds of drama with players and in the industry overall. So he totally overcompensated and became a general. Although maybe it was just his personality. He was that way when it came to most things in life.

"My dad is awesome. Good at everything, especially being chill. I aim to be more like him." The broody hottie frowned.

My heart squeezed, and warmth unfurled in my chest. How swoony was it that this grump loved his family?

"Did your dad grow up on Long Island?" The Easy Out must have come from somewhere.

He nodded. "Me too."

Wow. I wouldn't have guessed it. He didn't have that strong New York accent. He pronounced his *H*s, and his *O*s didn't sound like *aw*.

And yet the traitor might be a bagel-loving Metros fan. I leaned back in my seat and crossed my arms.

He chuckled, and my heart skipped. Holy shit, he was hot when he was glaring, but that quick almost-smirk caused my body to ache in a way that it hadn't in entirely too long. My heart beat a bit faster, and I shifted in my seat. God help me. If he actually smiled, I might combust.

"My Long Island roots aren't a disease you can catch."

"Says you," I accused, but I failed to stop the smile that pulled at my lips. "When did you move to Boston?"

He scanned my face like he wasn't sure he wanted to answer the question. Finally, he sighed. "This week."

I sat up straight again and pressed a hand to my chest. "Really? I feel like I should draw you a map of all the good spots." I laughed.

His lips quirked and pulled up in one corner, and I swore my body clenched at the idea that this grump might smile. Even more, that he might smile at *me*. "I'd love that."

Apparently, his wish was my command. I grabbed a bar napkin and opened it wide before glancing around. "Maybe the bartender has a—"

The Sharpie hit the table next to my napkin and rolled.

I caught it quickly and cocked a brow at him. "Was that in your pocket?" Not to be judgy, but what kind of grown adult carried markers around like that?

In response to the question, my grump locked his jaw and scowled. Hmm. Inspiring an expression that *wasn't* a glare was almost a challenge.

"Do you have other colors? Because, really, I like rose gold," I joked.

He grunted, then a silver Sharpie dropped onto the table next to the black, followed by a royal blue. The way the colors appeared kinda felt like magic.

"No gold," he grumbled.

"Rose gold," I corrected.

He sighed. "You sound like my sister when she shows me the same gray five times and tells me they're different."

I chuckled but reached for the silver and got to work drawing lines. "No, rose gold is a color."

Once again, his mouth almost lifted up in corners. "Show me where it falls in the rainbow, and then I'll believe you."

"You know." I pointed the capless marker at him. "I think you pretend to be grumpier than you are. I keep seeing a smile trying to come out to play."

The chair scraped along the floor as he pushed closer to me and angled in. The air filled with the rugged scent of leather spun with a hint of something rich like bourbon, making me want to arch in and get a better whiff.

"Explain this masterpiece to me."

My quick sketch of the blocks around the bar and then down to the harbor wasn't impressive in any way. A ten-year-old probably could have done it better. But it was the information that mattered, not my artistic ability. "Are you teasing me, grumpy?"

He rested a hand on my chairback and dipped his chin. "Hell, yeah, I am, Blondie." Gently, he tugged on the end of my ponytail.

The move made my breath hitch. Every cell in my body tightened as I craved his touch. My skin tingled as he moved in so close I thought he might press his full lips against the exposed skin of my shoulder. I held my breath, willing him to do just that.

"Where are the best places?"

That question jarred me back to the moment. To my crappy picture. "Umm." I cleared my throat. "Let's start with the important stuff." I pointed out one location after another. "Best sandwiches, best gym, best dry cleaner, best vanilla latte, best pizza, best banana pancakes—"

"Banana what?"

"Pancakes. Tell me you've had them before." I whipped my head to the side to eye him, my ponytail draping over one shoulder.

He had shifted so close his breath danced against my cheek as I tilted my head. His gaze lowered from my eyes to my lips and hovered for one second before returning to the napkin. "I've never had them before." He traced the pancakes I'd drawn. "Can't say this curvy lump makes me wanna try them either."

I scoffed. "Okay, Mr. Artist. You draw something."

His hand was on my arm before I could blink, sending a shiver racing up my spine. Warm, strong fingers circled my wrist and pulled it toward him. He rolled my charm bracelet down to my hand and picked up a Sharpie. Then he studied my face once again as he brushed his thumb back and forth over the skin just above my wrist.

I forgot to breathe. My heart hammered, and my body thrummed along with each beat. It took me a second to realize he was asking for permission. Slowly, I nodded, and he pushed the blue cap off with his thumb.

The cool tip pressed against my forearm, and he drew a V-like shape. The pen moved back and forth quickly, in swoopy motions, like it took no effort on his part, though I couldn't tell what he was drawing. After a moment, he released my wrist, but he didn't step away. No, as I examined it, he stayed close, the heat of him soaking into me.

"Birds?" There on my wrist, he'd drawn two doves wrapped together in the shape of a heart. This man was an artist who carried markers with him. That alone was strange, but the fact that he'd drawn birds? What a thing to randomly draw on the arm of an avian veterinarian. Wide-eyed, I took him in.

His throat bobbed as he swallowed. "Lovebirds." He was so close his breath ghosted over my skin. I froze, wanting him to move just the inch closer. To close the gap and press his full lips against mine. But he hovered where he was, letting his hot breath dance against my mouth.

"You drank out of my beer. That means we've pretty much already kissed, except without any of the good part."

In a trance, I nodded and tipped my chin, moving a breath closer.

"And I love the good part." His voice was a whisper. And an instant later, his lips were pressed to mine.

The touch was electric. The shock that rushed through me sent my heart racing. Desire and need coursed through my system as his warm, full lips molded to my own. With a groan, he cupped my face with one hand and pulled me closer.

When the hard, flat plane of his chest pressed into me, I sighed, opening for him. He took the invitation and swept his tongue into my mouth, tangling it with mine, owning me. I pressed harder into him, needing more, but as I did, he pulled back slightly.

My stomach sank at what I worried was rejection, but when I got a good look at his face, all I saw was the same need that hit me the moment he touched me.

"I'm not going to fuck you to help you get over your ex." His pupils were so dilated they eclipsed his dark irises as he scanned my face. He leaned into my ear and whispered, "But if you come home with me, I guarantee you won't remember his name in the morning."

Christian
4

WHEN THE DOOR slammed shut behind us, my lips were already on hers. A small voice in my head told me to slow down, but it was drowned out by the pounding need to claim her. My place was around the corner from the bar, and yet keeping my hands to myself for the eight-minute walk had been the most difficult chore of my lifetime. She had said things—words—and I'd tried to listen. But all I could think about was the way her lips had felt on mine. So I was bad company. Worse than normal.

But now she was mine.

Mine. It was what I'd wanted from the second I'd locked eyes with her. Normally, I was more hesitant with people. I liked personal space, and even with women, sharing my drink would never fly. But all I wanted was my mouth on her. To touch her. To have her touch me.

I kissed her again, wishing I could get even closer. So I slid my hands under her ass and lifted. Without missing a beat, she wrapped her legs around my hips. The heat of her core consumed me, making my already hard cock weep. Though I told myself to be gentle, to go easy on her, I couldn't help the way my fingers bit into her as I massaged her inner thighs. With a step forward, I pressed her into the wall and deepened the kiss. Our tongues danced, and the taste of her flooded my mouth.

More. I wanted more. Of her. Of this.

I rocked into the apex of her thighs, forcing her flush with the sheetrock behind her. Her needy mewls echoed in her throat and vibrated through me as I continued exploring her mouth. *Jesus.*

I pulled back and rested my forehead against hers. Our ragged breath mingled, and the way her soft, sweet scent surrounded me made my cock throb.

"Bedroom?" I asked. If she didn't want this, now was the time for her to speak up.

She smiled, and damn, I loved it. My grumpy ass wasn't the type to believe in soul mates or love at first…kiss…but her smile whacked me hard in the chest, then settled deep, clinging to me and silently whispering *don't let her go.*

She glanced over my shoulder and gasped. "It's gorgeous."

I didn't bother to turn. Nothing could beat my current view. Full lips, pinker than before because of my teeth. Just a hint of beard burn across her cheek. The small marks were evidence of my presence, and I wanted to add more.

When she focused on me again, I slowly lifted my thumb to brush her bottom lip.

She let out another gasp, this one barely audible, when I pressed, causing her lips to part. Eyes locked on mine, she flicked her tongue along the pad of my thumb. The move sent a shot of lightning through me.

With a groan, I pushed my way into her mouth, and she sucked on the digit in response. My cock surged, and blinding need clouded my brain. Desperate for more, I rocked into her. She released me with a pop, and I dove back in to dominate her mouth with mine.

I grasped her hip and slid my fingers below the hem of her shirt, relishing the warmth of her skin. Still needing more, I moved higher, only stopping when I found the lace of her bra. I flicked a thumb back and forth over her nipple, and she arched into me. A deep moan escaped her and vibrated through me as I continued to toy with her and she thrust her hips against me.

I pulled back and took her in—heavy-lidded eyes, pink cheeks, heaving chest. "I can't decide if I want to eat your pussy so I can lick you through every one of your moans or if I want to feel you strangle my cock as you come."

She leaned in and brought her lips to my ear. "God, I want that."

The feel of her breath on my neck had me pulling her tight against my cock.

She groaned against me, her lips ghosting over my earlobe. "I want you so bad."

I sucked in a harsh breath as heat licked up my spine. That was all I needed to hear.

"Both. I'm fucking doing both," I panted. I gripped her ass cheek hard and shuffled toward my room.

She stumbled along with me, not letting go, through the apartment until we stepped into my bedroom and I kicked the door shut behind us.

Sitting on the edge of my mattress, I pulled her onto my lap so she straddled me and rocked my hard cock into her. Her lips found mine again, consuming me, drowning me in her kiss. She pressed into me with a desperation that rivaled mine, the heat of her soaking through the layers of material between us.

I broke the kiss, and she arched her back, pressing her perfect little tits to me. I needed to hear her whimper again, this time with her breast in my hand so I could feel the sound work its way out of her. Inching her shirt up her torso, I grazed the soft skin of her ribs and palmed her breast. Then, in a blink, I tore the shirt over her head.

I sucked in a hard breath at what I'd exposed. "Fuck me, Blondie. You look perfect in red." The contrast of the bright lace against her pale skin had my cock pulsing. "But I can't fucking wait any longer to see you in nothing."

"Then I guess I should get rid of these." She hopped off my lap and toyed with the waistband of her jeans. Then, with her lip caught between her teeth and her focus fixed on me, she slowly worked at the five buttons.

One, then two. She stopped there, showing just a hint of red lace.

My heart sped up and my hands twitched. But I was frozen to the spot, waiting with bated breath.

Three. The gap opened more.

My dick pressed hard against the zipper of my own pants, desperately trying to break free.

Four. Five. The jeans hadn't fallen yet, but I couldn't stop myself.

I ran a finger along the top of the lace, ghosting over her skin.

She shivered.

I dipped my thumb under the fabric and rubbed back and forth between her hip bones.

The jeans puddled at her feet, and she stepped out.

My cock pulsed at the sight. In all my life, I'd never seen anything more perfect than this woman in red lace.

Fixated on the apex of her thighs, I dipped my thumb lower, teasing, almost there but not quite.

"Oh, Blondie, I can already tell you're wet and ready for me." I pulled my hand back.

"Don't tease me." She whimpered.

I stood, towering over her, and yanked the shirt over my head.

"Oh, baby, I intend to spend the entire night teasing you over and over again until you can't say anything but my name." I locked my hand behind her head and pulled her to me again.

Our kiss was fire. And when her breasts pressed into my bare chest, we both groaned. Without letting our lips part, I spun and dipped her back until she was laid out on the bed beneath me. Hovering over her, I flicked my thumb over her nipple.

Her answering moan vibrated through my body, straight to my dick, increasing the pounding need to claim more than just her mouth.

I pulled back and simply stared at her. Lips swollen, cheeks and chest flushed pink, eyes dilated. I kissed down her jaw, over her neck, licked at her pulse. Goose bumps broke out across her ivory skin as I continued my examination. I pressed my lips to her collarbone, and she shivered. Her response sent an answering rush of desire zinging through me. Moving lower, I found the clasp of her bra, and with one flick, her breasts were free. I pushed the material back before gently nipping at one nipple.

Her hips surged into my chest as she desperately sought friction.

Smiling against her, I brushed my thumb along the bottom of her breast.

Her breath caught. "Please," she begged as she thrust again.

I dropped my shoulders and wedged her legs apart so I could slip between her thighs.

"Do you want my lips here?" I dipped my head and rubbed my nose against one thigh, then the other, inhaling deeply. Her arousal might be my new favorite scent. "Or here?" I pressed my mouth against the damp material covering her pussy, letting my hot breath wash over her.

Her legs quivered on either side of me, and the need to taste her pounded through me.

"I want your mouth on me." The words were so breathless they were barely audible.

I nipped at the red material and yanked back, pulling them away from her wet center. Then I tugged them down her legs with both hands so that she was bare in front of me. Pink and glistening.

I sucked in my bottom lip, tasting only a hint of her from her panties, and took her in.

"Every part of you is prettier than the last." I dipped down and gave her a long, slow lick. *Fuck.* I was in heaven. My body ached with the need to slam into her tight heat. But I wanted her coming on my tongue first. I lapped at her, enjoying her sweet, musky flavor like she was made for me.

"Oh God, please," she moaned.

"Chris." I lifted my head. "Say *my* name," I ordered.

Her blue eyes popped open and met mine, swirling with liquid desire. A smirk pulled at her lips. "Please, *Chris*, make me come."

The way she said my name sent a surge of pride through me. I zeroed in on her clit then, wrapping my lips around it and sucking. That simple move had her gushing and crying out. Fuck. I lapped and sucked, intent on not wasting a drop of her, until she writhed against me, using my mouth to give herself pleasure.

I matched her rhythm, learning what made her moan and what made her buck against me, until she was crying my name and spasming on my face.

I worked her through her release, and once she'd floated down again, I pushed up on my hands and knees, caging her against the mattress, and slowly pressed soft kisses up her body. Up her pelvis, her taut stomach, and that belly button, where I finally had the chance to dip my tongue in and swirl it. I pressed gentle kisses to one breast, then the other. Finally, I made my way to her mouth and captured her lips, letting her taste herself on me.

Like silk, her soft hands danced over my shoulders and down my chest until they hit the button on my jeans.

"In a hurry, Blondie?" I teased.

"More like so ready to feel you inside me." She flattened her palm against me.

On instinct, I thrust against her. Damn, I wanted that soft skin wrapped around me. But if she got those fingers locked around my dick, I wasn't sure I could hold on to my control and not come all over us both. So I pulled back. In one movement, I stood at the end of the bed. Quickly, I shucked off my pants and dug a condom out of the drawer of my nightstand.

From where she was sprawled out on my sheets, she watched me, her gaze getting caught on my dick. My heart rate picked up even faster, and my cock jumped at the sight of her undressed and spread out, looking at me like I was a sight worth savoring.

I rolled on the condom and gave myself a swift pump. As I did, she wet her lips.

"Like that?" I did it again.

"I'd like it better if I was the one doing it." She shifted to her knees and reached out.

I gritted my teeth at the featherlight brush of her fingers along my length. When her small hand wrapped around me, my eyes drifted closed, and when she squeezed, I nearly embarrassed myself.

"*Fuck*." My hips shot forward, pressing my cock deep into her fist.

"I need you inside me." She stood and pressed her body against mine, her hand still wrapped around me.

I dipped low to take her mouth again, but she spun and gently pushed my shoulder. I acquiesced, letting her guide me onto the bed. Our tongues tangled as she straddled me, pushing me flat on my back. In one swift motion, she lined herself up with me. I rested my hands on her hips, but she didn't need to be guided in the motion.

Kissing me hungrily, she sank onto my cock, pulling me into her tight pussy.

My vision blurred and swirled as she rocked against me, pulling me deeper into her tight heat. I thrust my hips, meeting her every move, enthralled at the way she threw her head back. Engaging my abs, I lifted and took one tight nipple into my mouth for a hard pull.

"Yes, Chris," she moaned, rocking faster.

My abs tightened further, and my legs locked. I thrust hard, on the brink of losing my control. Shit. I gritted my teeth, willing my need to release inside her to abate. She needed to be first. With one hand still firmly on her hip, I slid the other down her heated skin and found her tight bundle of nerves. With my thumb, I pressed against it and moved in a circular motion.

Two or three revolutions later, her orgasm hit, and she clenched against me. The way she pulsed around me launched me higher, pushed me farther. I snapped and flipped her onto her back so I could slam into her. Harder, faster, until the telltale tingle at the base of my spine ignited into sparks shooting through my extremities. Instinctually, I thrust, again and again, into the heaven that would forever leave me crying for more, until my world exploded. My vision tunneled until the world disappeared completely and euphoria filled my senses. I collapsed on top of her, burying my face in her neck, enjoying the feeling of her soft, warm skin against every part of me, and stayed like that for a long moment while I caught my breath.

When my vision had returned and I could feel my legs, I pushed up. "Give me one sec." I headed to the en suite bathroom, disposed of the condom, washed my hands, and brushed my teeth.

As I stepped back into the bedroom, Blondie sat upright, bringing the sheet with her, and scanned the space.

"I should probably—"

"Stay." I wanted more of her. Her time, her lips, her body, her mind. More of it all.

She paused with a small frown that I swore made my heart leave my chest. But finally, her lips pulled up slightly.

"Okay, I'll stay."

Avery
5

CHRIS'S dark lashes fluttered slightly in his sleep. I was tucked into his side, with my head resting in the crook of his neck. His long arm snaked around me, and even in sleep, he held me close. He'd nodded off moments after returning to bed, but I remained wide awake. Too many thoughts ran through my head to really settle down.

Don't spend the night.

That was Wren's rule.

But no part of me wanted to leave. Not just because he'd made me come so many times I'd be sore tomorrow, but because he looked at me like I mattered. Like he saw *me*, average Avery, and he liked what he saw. The thought was ridiculous. This was a one-night stand, and I was under no illusion that it would be anything else. Even if he had told me to stay.

In the dark of his bedroom, I brought my wrist close and studied what I could see of the lovebirds he'd drawn. Was he an artist? I winced, because I didn't have the first clue. I hadn't even known his name until I was naked and about to come on his tongue. Regardless of the personal details we'd shared, our connection was something I'd never felt before.

I studied the man beside me again. His lips moved, although the words he mumbled were too low to pick out. How cute was it that the grumpy guy talked in his sleep? Maybe he'd say something I could tease him about tomorrow.

Tomorrow.

The thought made me smile. So much for not getting attached. I shifted, settling again, and Chris's arm tightened around me.

"No, Blondie. Stay," he mumbled, rolling to his side and tossing a leg over mine. He didn't open his eyes as he nuzzled into my neck. A moment later, his breathing evened out, and he was sound asleep again.

From the look of things, this grump was attached to me too. That wouldn't be horrible, right?

I closed my eyes and soaked in his warmth, willing myself to doze off. Fifteen minutes later, when I was still wide awake, I carefully slipped out from under his heavy leg to search for a glass of water.

My jeans were next to the bed, but the thought of struggling into them in the middle of the night wasn't the least bit appealing. If I wore my shirt and nothing else, then I'd end up wandering around in his apartment half-naked, and that was more than the insecure girl who lived inside me could handle. So I tiptoed over to the dresser. Hopefully Chris wouldn't mind if I borrowed something. I cracked the second drawer and found exactly what I was looking for. I snagged a black T-shirt from the top of a stack, shook it out, and slipped it over my head. Then I snuck out of his room.

The hallway was as dark as the bedroom had been, but the lights of Boston lit up the open living area. Once again, I focused on the windows. The view of Boston Harbor was gorgeous. If he was an artist, he was clearly a successful one, because this apartment cost more than I could afford. And it wasn't like the Boston Zoo didn't pay me well.

I shuffled to the floor-to-ceiling windows and took in the city below. Man, what a view.

I could just make out the entrance to the zoo from up here. I'd been the avian veterinarian specialist there for two years. It had been a stroke of luck that the position opened up just as I was finishing my fellowship with the zoo. A position like mine wasn't typical for a recent college graduate, especially at a place like the Boston Zoo, where any job was highly sought after. But my boss, George, and I had worked well together, and he'd been impressed with my work ethic and drive.

The sound of keys in the lock had me spinning around and tugging on the hem of the T-shirt that fell halfway to my knees. Light flooded the room as the guy who'd been at the bar with Chris walked in.

"Oh." He shot me a toothy grin that made him look more like a ten-year-old than the twentysomething he had to be. "Your friends are going to be giddy. I told them there was no way you ended up back at our place."

My cheeks heated and my stomach twisted. "Uh." I scanned the apartment; Chris hadn't mentioned a roommate. "I wasn't snooping. I just came out for water, and the view distracted me."

"Cool." He dipped his chin. "I'm Emerson. I don't know if I said that earlier or not. But please don't call me Bambi." The laugh he let out only made me more confused.

I blinked at him. Why would I call him Bambi?

He headed toward me, a lightness in his step that made it seem like he wasn't fighting the same gravity that cursed the rest of us. Even when he crashed into the coffee table like it had suddenly jumped into his path, he wasn't fazed. "I'm not drunk. As unbelievable as it is to some people, considering what I do, I'm just clumsy." He stopped beside me, hands in his pockets, and surveyed the skyline. "God, this place is gorgeous." His eyes sparkled, like he couldn't quite believe that he lived here.

Although his word vomit was a little disconcerting, he was the opposite of intimidating. Still, it felt weird to be standing beside him, barely clothed, at almost two a.m.

"Chris is asleep, so I'm going to grab some water and…" I pointed lamely toward Chris's room.

"I got you." With a wink, he spun and wandered to the kitchen, bumping his hip into the marble island, then pulling the fridge open. "Think fast." The words registered only seconds before a plastic water bottle was flying at me.

If my father hadn't been doing the same thing to me for my entire life, I'd have been smacked in the face with it.

"Amazing reflexes, bebé." He cracked the lid of his own water bottle and, bouncing to a beat I didn't hear, he danced around the island and the leather sectional back toward me. "Did my boy whine about our big game tomorrow?"

I froze with one hand still on the cap and narrowed my eyes at Emerson. "Game?" Chris hadn't mentioned anything about tomorrow. But *game*? I scanned the well-built man in front of me. Everything about his physique screamed athlete. A lot like Chris...

"He's pitching his first major game, so he's got the jitters."

Ice ran through my veins, instantly freezing me to the spot. No way. I swallowed.

"You play baseball?" My voice was pitched too high. Entirely too high. The guy probably thought I was a screechy demon. I cleared my throat and tried again. "Like professionally?"

Okay, that was better. Almost normal. My face felt weird, though. My nose was scrunched, and so was my brow, like I smelled something bad. He didn't smell, so it would probably be in my best interest to act less disgusted by the idea of America's pastime. But these guys couldn't really play for the Revs.

Chris...*Chris*. Not Christian Damiano.

Not the new pitcher...

My heart and stomach plummeted in synchronicity, right out of my body. Hell, all the way to the bottom floor of this high-rise.

Emerson chuckled and rocked back on his heels. "He was serious about the whole being unemployed thing."

What the hell did that mean?

My grip on the bottle tightened, and apparently, I'd loosened the lid more than I thought, because a volcano of liquid erupted, shooting straight at the man in front of me.

He jumped back and waved his hand, laughing.

With a gasp, I dropped the bottle to the floor in front of me. "Shit. Sorry."

He shrugged and scooped it up with far more grace than he'd possessed so far tonight. "Eh, it's just water. This carpet thing'll dry. But I'm the Revs' third baseman, and he's their new pitcher."

My toes were damp, and the water was slowly seeping closer. I'd created a puddle. Yup, a puddle. But I couldn't focus on the mess. Because *new pitcher*? Christian Damiano...

Like a trailer for the worst movie of the year, my brain ran through what I'd heard about spring training, highlighting the key Damiano parts.

Total hothead. No idea why Langfield called Damiano up...

Do you know what Damiano did when he was pulled today? Flipped the bat rack and told me to go to purgatory. Said it would be a fitting fate for me to be stuck wondering if I'd been doomed to hell rather than rotting in the known...

Freaking Damiano told the reporters that he shouldn't have been pulled and that he couldn't be blamed for the lack of faith the coaches show their players...

Talent is one thing, but the kid can't control himself when he's angry. The sound bites are going to fuck this season...

Ya know what Damiano said today? He said the reason I wear a higher-profile hat isn't because I'm old. *It's because my demon horns need room to breathe.*

"You okay?" Emerson asked.

I blinked back to the moment. Back to the dark room. How long had I been standing here?

"Yeah. Yeah." I nodded too aggressively. "So cool. *Base*ball." That came out weird. I forced a smile and pumped my fist. "Go team."

For the first time, Emerson wasn't smiling. In fact, his brows were pinched like he was concerned, like it had finally occurred to him I might be insane.

I had to get out of here. "Well, good luck tomorrow." I turned and rushed back to *Christian Damiano's* room, snatched my jeans and shoes off the floor, and flew out the door, away from yet another bad decision.

As I walked home wearing my jeans and Chris's shirt, I made myself a promise. Something had to change.

Christian

6

AT THE SOUND of my alarm, I slapped at the device to shut off the awful buzz. Then I spun and reached out for the beautiful blond beside me. But I was met with cold sheets and nothing more.

I cracked my eyes open and scanned the room. She'd tried to get out of bed in the middle of the night, but when I'd pulled her close, she'd cuddled right into me. The sigh that left her lips had whispered through every cell in my body, even when I was half-awake. But now she was gone.

Her thong and shirt were still strewn on the floor next to my side of the bed. Had she really fled my house half-naked? What the fuck happened?

I snagged yesterday's boxers off the floor and tugged them on, then left my room.

Emerson stood in the kitchen, fully dressed, beaming at me far too brightly. "Morning, roomie. Need a good-luck hug?"

Jesus. Why did I decide it was a good idea to live with the unicorn of happiness?

I glared at my chipper roommate. "Where is…" Shit. I didn't even know her name. How was that possible? The connection I'd felt with her was like nothing else, and yet I'd been a shithead last night.

Because not only had I *not* gotten her number, I didn't even know her name.

"The blond?" Emerson raised a brow at me.

I had one second to decide how to play this with him. And I had no intention of wearing my heart on my sleeve. So I shrugged. "Yeah, where's Blondie?"

"She was here at two. She and I had the weirdest heart-to-heart. She sprayed me with water, and we both laughed."

I ground my teeth, trying to be cool, and asked, "Why'd she spray you with water, man?"

"Women." He shrugged. "Who the hell knows." Then he snapped a finger and pointed to a plate on the counter. "Made a burrito for you. Car service will be here in ten, so unless you want to be trending because of all that." He waved a hand up and down, gesturing to my lack of clothing. "Get clothes on."

How the hell was he so cheery at seven fifteen a.m.?

I supposed I should be appreciative of the guy. Emerson might be all sunshine and rainbows, but he didn't harp on shit. That, thankfully, meant there wasn't another mention of the blond on the ride to the stadium. And it was time for me to take a page out of his book and forget her. I needed to be in the zone.

> Pop: you focused? Let go of the shit that doesn't matter. Just focus on you, the ball, and the catcher's glove.

I smiled. After my morning workout and warm-ups, I'd made my way to the locker room to get ready. My AirPods had been in my ears for the last forty minutes, and my phone was set on Do Not Disturb, successfully allowing me to tune everyone out. It was just me, and I was in the zone. The only contact whose texts and calls appeared on my screen and chimed in my ears was Pop. My dad was the calming force in my life.

> Me: in the zone, pop

> Pop: good, Miami is tough but their two best hitters will swing at a slider for no damn reason.

That was my dad. The guy who thought he knew the batters better than my coaches. But I loved him for it.

> Me: I'll keep that in mind

> Pop: Did you relax last night like I said?

My thoughts instantly went back to Blondie. Her smile, her laugh. The feel of her skin under my lips. The way she looked writhing beneath me.

> Me: Yeah, it was a good night

"What's got you smiling like that, Dragon?" Mason Dumpty, our center fielder, called across the locker room loud enough to pierce through the noise-canceling setting of my AirPods.

I glowered at him, and in response, he chucked a sunflower seed at me. At least this one hadn't been in his mouth first. It wouldn't have been the first time he'd pulled shit like that.

Mason tipped his chin up and hit me with a shit-eating grin. "I think it's a chick."

"One hundred percent," Emerson agreed next to me.

I yanked an AirPod out and whipped in his direction. "Fucker."

He shrugged, his eyes dancing. "What? I may not know her name, but I know she exists and that you were pissed when she disappeared on you."

The man had no filter.

"Ooh." Dumpty, always the shit stirrer, rubbed his hands together. "Sounds like drama."

I crossed my arms, willing the annoyance surging in me to chill the fuck out.

"You don't really think Dragon wanted the chick to stay, do you?" Kyle Bosco, our right fielder, jumped in. "Honestly, with your issue with germs, I'm surprised you even let an *icky girl* get that close."

I flipped him off. "She does not have germs." The words were out of my mouth before I considered them.

"*Ooh!*" the guys all chanted again.

I hated them all.

"Why are we acting like assholes?" Coach walked in and crossed his arms over his chest, chin held high. "Are we focused on the game we're playing in a few hours, or are we fucking around?" Tom Wilson scanned the room, ripping into every one of us with his signature glare. The guy acted like this was the Marine Corps and that we should all fall in line and call him sir. Fuck that. Respect had to be earned.

"But Coach T." Mason smirked. "Dragon's got a girlfriend. Getting laid might improve his crappy moods."

Wilson homed in on me, and I stared back blankly. Neither of us blinked as we watched one another.

But I didn't want to get into another pissing contest with the man. So with a huff, I shut my eyes and slammed the AirPod back into my ear. It was time to focus on the game plan, so I tuned out the teasing and all thoughts of Blondie. And then I spent the final forty minutes before I walked onto the field playing the game in my mind.

Part of me wished I could be less intense. Be like my teammates and play cards or ping-pong to alleviate stress before games. But the smiles on the faces around me during the national anthem? The joy that emanated from my teammates when they ran onto the field? That wasn't me.

I held my hands out for the ump check. "Is that alcohol?" he asked, sniffing.

"Hand sanitizer." I pointed to the ledge. "League checked already."

"Oh, that's right." He smirked, obviously remembering that I was the weird germ guy.

"Resin bag?"

"Don't use it."

"And we don't toss the ball around the bases after an out." He shook his head, but I just walked away, not giving a shit what he thought. There were a lot of germs on the ball, and the fewer people that touched it, the better.

As I stepped onto the sand of the pitching mound for the first time as a major league player, my heart clenched. The bright light that shone down and the roar of the crowd sent goose bumps skittering along my arms. I'd worked my entire life to get here, and I was going to smash the hell out of this game.

I pulled in a deep breath and pushed aside all thoughts that didn't affect what was happening on this field. Then I exhaled and focused on the catcher just in time to see my favorite sign. Yes, I would come out with a bang. I gave him a nod, and with one more cleansing breath, I wound up and let the ball fly.

It roared past the batter and hit the glove with the *thwap* that I had no doubt made the guy's hand burn. A beautiful *104* flashed on the jumbo screens around the field, and the crowd went crazy. The running joke was that my nickname came from my surly attitude, but the people who really paid attention to the sport knew I went by Dragon because I threw the fire, and for seven innings I did. Which was why it was a kick in the balls to see Coach Wilson trotting across the grass to the mound one batter into the eighth inning.

"It's my second fucking walk of the game," I growled. Pulling me now would be utter bullshit.

"And it's the top of the eighth. There's no reason to kill your arm or our chance at winning because you want a higher pitch count." Coach Wilson held his hand out for the ball.

"I said I'm *not* done."

Coaching was about more than just commanding players. Listening was just as vital as every other aspect. My coach with the farm team understood that a pitcher knew his own arm. This asshole didn't get that.

Jaw locked tight, he narrowed his blue eyes on me. "I said you are. And who is the coach of this team?"

I glared straight back at him. "Apparently Satan." With that, I shoved the ball into his stomach hard and stormed across the grass and down the steps to the dugout, silently putting a curse on that man and all his future offspring.

Avery
7

"Oh, how I missed this view." Jana surveyed the field below us.

"I know." Wren lifted one brow and smirked.

The three of us were in my dad's box at Lang Field, watching the game. I'd successfully avoided the place all season, but the girls were dead set on coming today and wouldn't take no for an answer.

"Avery might hate the baseball boys, but man, do I love their pants." Wren tilted forward and tapped her plastic wine cup against Jana's.

"And damn, the new catcher's ass is perfection." She hummed and stared at Cortney Miller as he squatted behind the plate. "Even with your ban on all things male, you have to admit that."

"I didn't ban all things men." Dramatic much? I had just decided that the answer to my dating problem was to take a time out. "I'm taking a year off from dating. That's all."

"And a year off from orgasms," Wren scoffed, bringing her wine to her lips.

"Just the male-induced ones." Jana patted my knee and bumped her shoulder against mine. "Did you try that Starlight clit stimulator I sent you?"

"Yeah, and oh my God—"

The sound of a throat clearing had me snapping my mouth shut. I held my breath and peered over at the box next to us. When I caught sight of the team's owner, Beckett Langfield, my face flamed. He was standing at the railing not ten feet from us. Although his box was next to my dad's, he was usually inside, not in the open-air seats near where we typically sat.

Oh, good lord. Please don't let him have heard me.

Not only was he Dad's boss, but the guy was gorgeous. He was very Henry Cavill-esque and *very* happily married.

At least I hadn't finished my sentence. If I had, I'd never be able to look the man in the eye again. His younger and equally hot brother stepped up next to him in a matching Revs jersey.

"Ladies." Gavin smiled. "Love the throwback Wilson jersey, Avery."

"Gotta support Dad." I shrugged and glanced down at the jersey my dad had given me years ago. The blue jersey sporting the original logo with the drums and stars matched one of the three soldier mascots in the grass.

Gavin assessed each of us, his brown eyes warm as always. "We haven't had the pleasure of seeing you yet this season."

"Avery's avoiding baseball this year, but we forced her to come today so we could see the new catcher." Wren pointed to number eight.

"Yes, we want an introduction to that Thor-like god, Cortney Miller." Jana waggled her brows.

"Doesn't Tom have rules about you fraternizing with the players?" Beckett frowned at my friends, shoving his hands into his pockets.

Yes, my father did. He had all sorts of rules. And he had no idea that I'd broken a *big* one a few months ago. I hoped like hell I could keep it that way. Hence, why I'd been avoiding this place like it was the plague.

"Besides," Beckett said, turning back to the field, "Cortney's dating someone."

"Is he?" Gavin turned to his brother. "Who's he dating?"

Beckett grunted. "You don't know her."

"*I* don't know her." He pointed to himself, then poked his brother's shoulder. "But *you* do?"

"Duck you." Beckett stomped back inside, all storm clouds, with his brother on his heels.

"Did he just call his brother a duck?" Wren slapped a hand over her mouth and giggled.

With a shake of my head, I shrugged. The Langfields dominated Boston sports, owning both the hockey team and the baseball team. Every one of the four brothers was hot as fuck, but they were each their own brand of weird.

"So the Starlight?" Jana asked.

"No. We are not talking about my"—I glanced back at the box next door—"orgasms," I whispered. "Not here."

"I personally think we should talk about the guy who is becoming the most talked-about pitcher this season." Wren wiggled in the seat beside me. "I think someone here might *know* him in every sense of the word."

Ignoring my obnoxious friend, I focused on the pitcher's mound and the reason I'd avoided Revs games all season.

Christian Damiano. Gorgeous. Moody. A thorn in the Revs' side. Hands down the best sex of my life. And, according to *Sports Illustrated*, baseball's most popular bachelor. Wasn't that a kick in the teeth?

I sighed, still annoyed that the damn man hadn't mentioned his occupation. If I had known who he was, that night would never have happened. But it had. And, irrationally, the way he was being paraded around as a bachelor irked me. Even if he was. Even if I had no claim on him. We'd shared one hot night months ago, and I hadn't talked to him since.

And there he was, standing tall, all handsome and broody, on the mound, pitching another great game. For all the bad press, the temper, the comments about my dad being evil, he had a fastball like the league hadn't seen in decades. If only he could get his attitude under control.

That still stumped me. The man I met at the bar was grumpy, sure, but I never would have described him as explosive, which was the term the media threw around most when they talked about Boston's new favorite hothead.

"Earth to Avery," Jana called.

I blinked, and when I turned back to my friends, both were smirking. Dammit. They'd caught me staring at Mr. Tall, Dark, and Moody.

"You promised we wouldn't talk about him." I focused on the field again, doing my best to avoid direct eye contact with either of my friends.

On the field, the team's mascots stood along the wall by third base. Two of the three Revolutionary War soldiers rode fake horses. The costumes were one piece and made it look as though the soldiers wearing blue regimental coats were seated on the animals. Over their coats, each wore a different jersey. One matched mine, the original look. Another wore pinstripes. The third wore the royal blue city jersey and carried a drum that he beat constantly as they pumped up the crowd.

The two on horses stuck their horses' hooves out, attempting to trip the drummer. In retaliation, he bopped them on the head with his sticks. I shook my head at the idiocy, then went back to scanning the field.

My attention caught on a bird flittering in the air on the first base foul line. It was black and white, with orange legs, and its beak was bright orange and yellow, with just a hint of blue. Aw, the clown like bird was a *puffin*.

But how on earth had a puffin ended up in the stadium? Rock pigeons and sparrows were common, and of course a goose or two popped up from time to time, but I'd never seen a puffin.

A colony of them lived near the harbor about a quarter mile from here. I'd seen them venturing short distances from home periodically, especially the younger males, but puffins typically they didn't come into the city.

I tracked the bird as it landed in the dirt. When the ball boy moved, it flitted to the away team's dugout. It was definitely a puffin. I'd bet the cameras were on him now. They were the adorable Easter bunnies of the avian world. Absolute clickbait. A few fans leaned over the railing, trying to touch it. In the process, they startled it, and it took off across the field, flying straight toward third base and the mascots. And on the mound, Chris had just started his windup.

No.

My heart plummeted, and I swore the world around me slowed. All I could do was watch in horror, hand over my mouth, as the ball left Chris's hand and headed toward home plate. The trajectory aligned perfectly with the small black and white ball of fluff.

I winced as the ball smacked into the bird's right wing, and I jumped to my feet as the puffin tumbled through the air and crashed into the dirt.

"Shit." I pressed my palm to my forehead as a collective gasp echoed around the full stadium.

"Is it dead?" Wren clutched her chest.

The small creature twitched in the grass as a handful of players moved around it.

I swallowed past the lump that had lodged itself in my throat. "I don't think so."

But with the speed at which Chris could throw a ball, the best-case scenario would be a broken wing. I winced again at the thought of what that poor bird would have to go through to rehab that wing.

My phone buzzed in my pocket, making me jump. I pulled it out and found a new text from my dad.

"Should you do something?" Jana asked before I could even open the message.

"I—" I looked out at the field again; multiple players surrounded the now screeching bird.

Beckett appeared at the railing separating our box from his. "You." He pointed at me. "Go do your bird doctor stuff."

I blinked at him.

"There isn't anyone more qualified to deal with this than Boston Zoo's head of avian medicine." He was practically growling. "The Revs just got past hating kids and running over dogs. We can't hate birds now."

My phone buzzed in my hand, and I finally unlocked the screen.

Dad: Avy, this is a you thing

Dad: I'm sending security up to get you.

Just as I was opening my mouth to assure Beckett that I'd handle it, a knock sounded on the door. I glanced down at the field again, and my stomach twisted into a painful knot. I guess my days of avoiding Christian Damiano had come to an end.

Christian
8

"SHOULD WE TOUCH IT?" Cortney Miller was on his knees next to the small black and white bird I'd hit with my slider. He looked up at me, his catcher's mask resting on his head, like I was even remotely qualified to answer his question.

I didn't know the first thing about injured birds. The poor thing's wing was bent at a weird angle, and its screeching made me feel like a monster. I hadn't seen the little guy until I'd released the ball, and by then, it was too late. Thank fuck I hadn't thrown a fastball.

"Should we?" He held a huge hand out. The little thing was barely bigger than his palm.

But when he got close, it snapped its colorful beak at his fingers, and Cortney yanked his arm back and clutched it to his chest protector, almost falling on his ass in the process.

"Maybe you try, Dragon." He hopped up, towering over my six-foot-two frame, and pressed on my shoulder like he wanted me to bend down and fix it.

"I'm not touching it." The bird might look like a fluffy little clown, but with the number of germs birds carry? Hell would freeze over before I took even another step closer to that germ-infested creature. I felt bad for it, and I had no doubt I'd feel shitty about hurting him for weeks, but regardless of all that, I wasn't *touching* it.

"Something has to be done." The umpire crossed his arms over his padded chest and surveyed Cortney, then Vance Craig, the first baseman who had been at bat for the Braves when this fiasco happened. "We can't play the game this way."

Slowly, more of my teammates had moved our way, and we were surrounded by a small crowd, though they all stood a few feet back. Apparently, no one but Cortney, Vance, and I were willing to get too close.

"I've always been told not to touch a hurt animal. If you do, it's a good way to lose a finger." Vance shook his head and stepped back, leaving us to deal with the little guy.

"Vet's on the way," Coach called from the dugout.

The small bird squeaked and flopped around like it was trying to stand. It only succeeded in toppling over again, and as it did, it let out a heart-wrenching yelp of pain.

"Aw, the poor thing. Let me through."

My heart stuttered at the voice coming from behind the wall of onlookers. I'd recognize it anywhere. I snapped straight and scanned the people nearby until I found the source. A small blond wearing an out-of-date royal-blue Revs jersey was making her way through the crowd.

Blondie. My heart kept up its uneven rhythm as she moved closer. I had to fight the urge to smile at the sight of her. I refused to be the asshole who was caught smiling about a wounded animal. But I had spent two months visiting every place on her map over and over again in hopes of finding her. And now here she was, headed my way with a wet towel in her hands.

The moment our eyes locked, my skin tingled in anticipation. This time, I was getting her name, her number, her address, and all her social media handles. I wanted it all. Every possible way to contact this woman who I hadn't stopped thinking about, fantasizing about. The sheer number of times I'd jerked off to thoughts of her was embarrassing.

My heart started to race in my chest. I was beginning to worry that I might need to see a cardiologist. I wanted to touch her, take off that stupid jersey—the one emblazoned with the retired number that belonged to the man I couldn't stand—and replace it with my name on her back. Mark her as mine.

She held eye contact for only a moment, her expression impossible to read, before looking down at the bird.

In that moment, I realized *why* she was on the field. *She* was the vet. Typically, I was the type to curse the universe and the idea of destiny, yet I was ready to high-five the hands of fate. Because damn it if luck wasn't on my side. My Blondie happened to be here when we needed a vet? If that wasn't providence, then I didn't know what was.

"Hey, little man," she said softly as she bent next to it.

Without thinking, I moved right in and crouched beside her. She swallowed like she felt my presence next to her, but her focus stayed on the bird. She set the towel in the grass, then carefully steadied the animal with a hand on each side of it, minimizing its thrashing. But it let out a noise that sounded like a whimper. "Can you help me, Chris?"

A thrill raced down my spine. Although her tone was formal, she remembered me.

"Absolutely. What do you need?"

The bird jerked at the sound of my voice.

"Whisper, please. Don't startle him." She darted a quick look at me.

Pressing my lips together, I gave her a nod. Now that her eyes were locked with mine, I couldn't help but stare into their blue depths. God, I had missed her. For a moment, she watched me just as intently, but then she quietly cleared her throat and focused on the little guy between us. "Cup your hands."

I obeyed. I'd do anything she asked. Still in a daze, I hadn't processed what she was doing, and all of a sudden, the bird was in my hands, and she had the towel wrapped over the little creature's beak and head.

"W-what are you doing?" I stuttered. Fuck. I was holding a wild, germ-infested animal in my hands. My heart was racing for a completely different reason now. I had to fight the urge to leap away. I couldn't hurt the little guy more than I already had.

The corner of her mouth lifted. "Helping him. It's a sedative. I'll need to crate him and take him back to the office, but sedating him will make it less traumatizing."

The bird twitched, and then warm liquid oozed into my palm.

My stomach lurched, and I gasped. "It's leaking."

"Leaking?" Cocking one brow, she looked at me, then the bird. When she focused on it, her lips twitched almost imperceptibly. "Ah. Sometimes, when they're sedated, they release their bowels. It's normal."

Release their *what*?

"Oh shit." Mason Dumpty clapped his hands behind me.

"Literally." Bosco laughed.

Literally? Ice ran through my veins as I searched my Blondie, hoping to hell she was messing with me. But then the smell hit me. I dipped my head again and studied the thing in my hands.

Shit…as in, this thing shit in my hands.

My stomach flipped like I'd just crested the hill of the world's tallest roller coaster.

I did not have bird shit in my hands. No way.

Closing my eyes, I swallowed once and then again. When I cracked them again, sure enough, ugly green goo coated my palm. The substance wasn't quite liquid, but it wasn't quite solid either. My stomached heaved. I was not puking in front of this woman. No way. But damn, I wanted to.

"You okay, Dragon?" Emerson stepped up beside me.

Holding my breath so as not to breathe in the acrid smell of this bird's shit, I eyed my roommate, desperate for his help, but the jerk was silently laughing.

I glared at him, and the fucker only shrugged in response.

"Don't worry." Blondie patted my shoulder. "It's the perfect consistency. Just like applesauce."

A hoot of laughter came from behind me. I couldn't tell who had a death wish. I was too busy gagging to find out. Applesauce would forever be on my *do not eat* list.

"And the olive-green color means he's healthy."

That was great news, but *I* might die.

The. Bird. *Shit.* In. My. Hand.

"He can't get sick from touching bird shit, can he?" Miller asked.

"No, it's unlikely this little guy has any germs."

I couldn't feel my legs. *The bird shit in my hand.* I needed to get this thing off me. Now.

"Here." She held her hands out.

Thank fuck. I turned toward her and had to work not to toss the thing to her. Almost instantly, a towel was thrust at me. Hands shaking, I wiped them as best as I could, then dropped the towel to the ground and reached for another. I needed water and soap and hand sanitizer. Hell, I needed a full-body decontamination treatment.

"You okay?" Blondie asked.

It took me a moment to process her words. She sounded like she was in a fishbowl.

Her blue eyes were lit with concern. She cradled the little bird close, careful of his wing. She tilted her head and gave me a reassuring smile. The move made the ends of her ponytail brush along one shoulder. God, she was pretty. I really need to know her name.

A throat cleared loudly behind us. "Avery," Coach Wilson snapped.

My girl lifted her chin and looked past me.

"Get going. We have a game to play."

My spine snapped tight at the command. This asshole had no right to speak to her like that. I pushed up to my feet and whirled, glaring at him.

"Don't talk to her that way."

Tom Wilson crossed his arms and snorted a breath out of his nose. "Don't tell me how to talk to my daughter."

My heart stopped, and I swore the ground opened up beneath me.

No way.

Satan could *not* have produced Blondie.

Tom stood before me, eyes narrowed as if waiting for me to respond. But I had no words.

His daughter. She was his daughter. My attention shifted to the woman who'd spent a night in my bed. I lifted a brow in question. And in answer, she averted those blue eyes and focused on the grass at our feet.

"Wait," Coach Wilson said, taking a step closer. "Do you two know each other?"

"No." The words were out of her mouth before I could even blink.

"Good." Tom scowled at me. "Keep it that way." Then his attention shifted to his daughter. "You know my rules, Avy."

Suddenly, the pieces I'd been trying to fit together for months clicked into place. Emerson said she'd freaked out when he mentioned that we played for the Revs.

Slowly, she tilted her chin up again and looked at me. And in her gaze, I saw the truth. She was a daddy's girl, and the man utterly hated me.

"If you wash your hands, you'll be fine," she assured.

The words didn't compute in my brain, because I didn't feel at all fine.

Christian
9

IT WAS odd to see new faces in the team room. Although this one wasn't all that new. She was the owner's new wife's best friend. But we hadn't officially met.

The all-star break had just ended, and the team had played well. I hadn't pitched today, but I was up tomorrow. I'd only started once since hitting the bird, and just like then, I didn't feel on my game. It wasn't just about hurting the little guy—who, according to the news, was doing okay. No, I was distracted.

"Hey." I stepped up to Dylan, the fun redhead who was friends with Beckett Langfield's wife. She was smallish and spunky, like she could be friends with Tinkerbell. "Christian Damiano."

I preferred not to shake hands, but when she reached for mine, I forced myself to let her touch me. If I made the rules, people would nod in greeting and leave it at that rather than invading each other's personal space. I'd even tolerate fist bumps. Knuckles were way safer than palms.

She tilted her head and assessed me, like she was remembering things I didn't realize she knew about me. "Dragon?"

I cleared my throat, shaking off the unease of her perceptiveness. "'Cause I throw the fire."

"Is that the official reason for the nickname?" The sparkle in her eye called me a liar, but she went on, wearing a smile that reminded me too much of Emerson's. "My son, Liam..." Dylan pointed to the food table.

I followed her line of sight, and my heart stopped. This woman was talking, but I couldn't hear or see anything except the other woman half a room from me.

Avery Wilson.

All blond hair and blue eyes. God, I remembered all too well what it was like to get lost in them. The girl was stuck in my head in a confusing loop. I swung between annoyed as fuck and turned on every time I thought about her. If she'd told me who she was, if she hadn't run away the second she found out I played for her dad, maybe we'd be in a different spot right now.

It took a great deal of effort, but I finally forced my attention from Avery. I scanned the room, not really focusing on anything, until I hit Coach. The instant I did, he narrowed his eyes in accusation. The man was constantly waiting for me to fuck up so he could jump all over me. He'd fined me twice already this season for running my mouth. But if he acted like Satan, then he deserved to be called out.

I'd promised Pop I'd be better, so I was working on keeping my head down and shutting the fuck up. With that thought in mind, I turned back to my conversation with Dylan.

"Your son is a Miller fan, huh?"

The redheaded teenager was wearing our catcher's jersey. I thought Dylan might be sporting Cortney's number too, but I couldn't see her back to confirm.

She pressed her lips together, and for the first time, she didn't look all-knowing. "Well." She sighed. "He was. When Cortney played for the Metros. But since the trade, it's...complicated."

Complicated. That was the word of the day, wasn't it? Because that described the situation between Avery and me too. We hadn't spoken in two weeks. Not since I saw her on the field. Not that we'd really had a conversation that day either. She had pretty much left with the bird the second the dad bomb was dropped on me. After all, she'd had a bird to help, and I'd had a game to pitch.

Now Avery was scooping pasta salad onto a plate and chatting with Liam.

Since she was here, it was as good a time as any to clear the air.

"She's pretty." Dylan's comment jarred my attention back to her.

"Oh, no. She's just…" I cleared my throat, playing it off, even as my cheeks heated. The last thing I needed was to be caught obsessing over the coach's daughter. The daughter of the coach who hated me with a fiery passion. The woman I had spent *two months* looking for. The woman who knew exactly where I was the entire time.

And I was back to pissed off.

"Hi, Firefly." Cortney came up next to us, saving me from having to bumble my way out of a conversation about Avery. "Dragon."

Although he acknowledged me, he was solely focused on Dylan.

That was interesting. What would Langfield think about the Revs catcher he'd recently brought on falling for his wife's best friend? I half listened to a back-and-forth about food before Cortney leaned in way too close for there to not be something going on between him and the fun redhead.

Very interesting.

"So, are you two?" I waved my finger between them.

A smile lifted Cortney's lips, and I could practically see the *yes* on the tip of his tongue, but Dylan beat him to the punch.

"Friends." She shrugged.

A jolt went through my teammate's body, and he blinked like he'd been physically struck.

Damn. It sucked to be friend-zoned. Not that it had ever happened to me. I wasn't the nice guy women tended to befriend. But I could imagine.

"Oh." I shook my head.

In response, Cortney scowled, silently telling me to stay the fuck away from Dylan. Which was fine.

"That's cool."

Cortney bowed out of the conversation then, clearly upset, and headed for Liam. And with a single wave, Dylan wandered after him.

With a deep breath in, I garnered all my willpower and pushed down the anxiety that had once again flared inside me. Then I headed straight to my own potential dumpster fire. Avery, having already finished filling her plate of food, was now sitting at a table, surrounded by kids. Either she was attempting to be social with the coaches' wives, since they were the only adults close by, or she was avoiding me. I typically wouldn't go anywhere near the kids' table.

Why would I want to hang out with some guy's wife? And kids were pretty much petri dishes teeming with bacteria. *No, thank you.*

Yet here I was, striding through the crowd across the navy carpet of the team room.

Avery wasn't looking my way, but by the sudden tightness in her shoulders, she sensed me as I approached. Thankfully, she stayed seated rather than fleeing from the room.

"Hey, Blondie." I dropped into the empty chair beside her, nudging her shoulder as I went.

The hair at the back of my neck prickled, as if I was being watched, but I didn't turn and search for the culprit. Half the team was probably looking at me. It took some fucking balls to sit with Tom Wilson's daughter. And that was for any run-of-the-mill player. Me? I might be signing my own death warrant by talking to this woman. I was the guy coach Wilson wanted off his team because he thought I was more trouble than I was fucking worth.

It wasn't my fault the guy hadn't bothered to get to know me.

"Chris." She wasn't looking at me, but a flush crept up her neck as I watched her.

Holding back a grunt, I gave her a once-over, unable to look away from the swell of her breasts just visible above the scoop of her shirt as they turned the same pretty shade. Damn. She'd looked just like that right after she came.

My body tightened in response to the memory.

I swallowed hard and shifted in my seat, hoping to make my jeans more comfortable.

What was it about Avery that had this effect on me?

I didn't have the best track record with women. I wasn't the type to be another notch in a woman's bedpost, but I wasn't the nice guy a woman wanted to bring home to mom and dad. Normally, I left pretty quickly after a hookup, or I'd usher the woman out the door when we woke up. It wasn't a thing.

However, waking up without Avery that morning *was* a thing. And every time I'd seen her since, I'd gotten more addicted. And I needed another hit of this woman.

"Did you come over for a reason?" she gritted out, like she was clenching her jaw. "Because you know exactly why this can't be a thing."

Yes. Her dad hated me, and there were some vague rules about not fraternizing. Although could it even be considered fraternizing if Avery didn't work for the team?

Instead of getting tense, I sat back, rested my hands on my lap, and tapped my right pointer finger twice on my left wrist. "Did you just imply that you're too good to talk to simple baseball players like me, Dr. Wilson?"

Her blue eyes shot my way. "I did *not* say that." Her brows were pulled low like she was frustrated, but that only encouraged me. I really liked teasing her.

"I love how your baby blues spark when you're turned on."

"I'm annoyed." She set her fork down and rested her arm on the table.

It wasn't close enough to touch my own arm, but I could feel the heat radiating off her, and that did nothing to help me control the need that was clawing at me now that I was in her proximity.

She glared up at me, but her long lashes made it impossible for her to look menacing. They were the kind of lashes most woman strove for by caking them with mascara, yet Avery's face was completely makeup free.

"Hmm. So it happens when you're annoyed *too*?" I slid my hand a fraction of an inch closer so my pinkie barely brushed hers. I couldn't help but smirk at the goose bumps that rippled past the silver charm bracelet on her wrist and up her arm.

She might be annoyed, but that wasn't the only emotion she had for me.

This thing between us was a third person at the table.

Hell, I was annoyed too. Annoyed with her for disappearing on me.

Pissed off that her dad's unfair opinion of me carried more weight with her than what she'd learned about me herself. But maybe if we started over, slowed down so she could see who I was...

"How's Puff Daddy?" The bird seemed like a safe topic.

"Puff Daddy?" Her brow creased. "The puffin?"

I nodded. I might have named him in my head. "He's at the Boston Zoo with you, right?"

She lowered her chin and pressed her lips together. Skeptical, I guessed.

I shrugged. "I read a few news clips. Wanted to make sure he was okay."

Her gaze softened, and the girl I remembered from months ago finally smiled at me. "He's doing better. He'll never fly long distances again, but he's already starting to use the wing."

"Good." I bowed my head and clenched my fists on the tabletop. "I was feeling shitty about it."

She placed her hand on top of mine, and her warmth seeped into me, instantly soothing the guilt that had reared its ugly head once again. The charms on her bracelet clinked as she rubbed her soft palm over the back of my hand.

"Accidents happen, Chris."

My name from her lips, in that soft whisper, made my gut clench. Focused on the movement, I noticed the birds on her bracelet. I was just about to ask about them when a throat cleared behind me, and she yanked her hand from mine. I shifted in my seat, only to find Coach Wilson's blue eyes shooting daggers at me. Just when I'd gotten through Avery's prickly walls, he had to show up again.

"Sup C-Tommy?" I leaned back and draped an arm over the back of Avery's chair.

He zeroed in on the space between my arm and his daughter's back like he was debating whether he was offended by the way I was touching her chair.

Oh, buddy, I'd touched way more than her chair. And I intended to do it again.

I smirked.

He ran his tongue over his teeth. "This is the exact sort of trouble you're supposed to avoid, Avery."

Her answering smile made my throat feel thick. She was so fucking stunning.

"I'm well aware of all this guy's shortcomings." She patted my arm.

This time, it was my body doing the betraying. It took every ounce of strength I possessed to fight the shiver that raced up my spine as she pressed her palm into my forearm.

But then her words registered, and the irritation was back. "Shortcomings?" I sat straighter in my chair.

She chuckled but turned back to her father. "However, Dad, I won't come to games if you insist on babysitting me every second like I'm twelve. Either let me be an adult or stop asking about why I avoid Lang Field."

Tom and I snorted in surround sound. The Langfields had quite a bit of gall, naming their stadium Lang Field. The two of us eyed one another and shook our heads. As dumb as the name was, it was very Beckett Langfield.

"I think it's cute." She shrugged.

"You would," Tom and I said at the same time.

He frowned at me, the expression once again full of all the irritation he typically reserved for me.

I shrugged and pushed to my feet. "She looks like the type to get Langfield's humor."

Oddly, Avery stuck out her hand to me. "It was nice to officially meet you, Christian."

I scrutinized her for a heartbeat. What the fuck? We'd already fucking met. And until this moment, she'd called me Chris. But as I gave in and took her hand, her game became clear. She pulled away quickly, leaving a ball of paper behind.

And wasn't that a fun turn of events? Avery Wilson had just given me her number.

Christian
10

Me: Is giving me your number your way of saying that you missed me?

Blondie: Haha, no. I just wanted to make sure we're good before next Wednesday.

Me: What's next Wednesday?

Blondie: Did Hannah not tell you about the photo op?

Me: Who the hell is Hannah?

Blondie: You know Hannah. She works for Liv. In the PR department.

Me: Oh. I blocked her after that damn cover mess

Blondie: Blocked? You can't block your PR team.

Me: The hell I can't. Did you see what they did to me?

Blondie: umm...you mean when they made you baseball's most popular bachelor? Lol

Me: Do you have any idea what it's like?

Blondie: can't say I do.

Me: People want to talk to me, Blondie. And touch me

Blondie: Must be torture.

Me: You have no idea

Blondie: So you won't be there on Wednesday?

Me: ...Scroll up...

Blondie: Photo op at the zoo with the puffin.

Me: Puff Daddy?

Blondie: GIF of a woman shaking her head

Me: Trust me. He'll love it

Blondie: Oh, you know him now?

Me: When someone shits in your hands, it creates an instant soul-deep connection

Blondie: GIF of a woman spitting out her drink

Me: Will you be there on Wednesday?

Blondie: Yes

Me: Then I'll see you Wednesday

Avery
11

AUGUST

"Where is the star of the show?"

Startled, I sat up straight. And there, in my doorway, Chris was leaning against the frame, decked out in his Revs jersey and baseball pants.

Since last week, we'd been texting randomly. He'd been nothing but sweet and funny, and it was messing with me. Take now, for instance. The sight of this moody, broody man should not have me tamping down a smile. Yes, he was sexy, but I had a plan. And I wouldn't let him derail it.

"Puff's over there." I nodded to the small area I'd set up for him on the other side of my office. I couldn't quite bring myself to call him Puff Daddy, so after a back and forth, we agreed on Puff. And I had to admit that it seemed as though the bird liked the name.

Since the Boston Zoo didn't have a puffin exhibit, he didn't have a dedicated home while he was healing. Atlantic puffins were social birds and lived in groups. Since he spent most of his time with me, he and I had become our own little puffinry. At night and when I was busy tending to other residents of the zoo, Puff spent his time in quarantine in one of the large rooms that housed a pond. But when I was working in my office, he was happier near me.

Chris sauntered in and set a white cup on my desk. "For you." Without waiting for a response, he turned to the fenced-in area.

I had set up a few large fake rocks around a plastic kiddie pool with a built-in slide. It wasn't anything special, but the little guy chirped happily and splashed around.

"You're really living the life, huh, Puff?"

The comment was laced with so much sarcasm it made my stomach sink. "Hey, don't knock my pool."

"Who doesn't love bright neon blue swirls." He cocked a brow.

Here at the zoo, we tried to create environments that resembled homes to our animals, and the white and blue did look like the icy arctic seas. "It looks like water."

"To who?" He snorted.

With a roll of my eyes, I decided to ignore the snark. I picked up the cup and lifted the lid. "Is this a vanilla latte?"

"With almond milk."

I set the cup down and frowned at the man bent down by the bird's fence, studying him as he ran a hand over the scruff on his chiseled jaw.

"How'd you know?" I left the question at that. This was my drink. It was what I always ordered.

A lump formed in my throat as he turned and studied me. I could guarantee not one of my last three boyfriends would have remembered that I only drank almond milk. Yet this guy who barely knew me had somehow brought me my favorite latte?

"Lucky guess." He shrugged and turned back to the bird.

In return, Puff was watching him, his little black and white head tipped to the side as if he was sizing up the big man. He hopped across the rock, getting close to Chris.

Puff had made a great recovery over the last three weeks. Although his wing didn't lie completely flat like it should and his flight distance was more a long jump, in the water, he swam with ease, and his wing's range of motion was almost at 100 percent.

Chris cleared his throat and shifted back onto his heels. "He seems good."

I sipped my coffee and took him in: the suddenly rigid posture, what looked like a hint of a grimace on his face, and the distance he'd just put between himself and the bird. The unease that suddenly radiated off him had me wanting to show him that Puff was harmless. Especially since the two of them would have to get chummy really quickly when the photo shoot started in about twenty minutes.

"Here, watch this." I stood and headed for Chris. Crouching beside him, I set my coffee cup on the floor. "Puff," I called.

The little sweetie chirped in response.

"Hmm, seems like someone likes his name." The sexy smirk that flitted across Chris's face was impossibly smug.

"Don't be cocky." With an eye roll, I turned back to the habitat. "Puff," I called again.

This time, the little bird jumped straight over to us.

Chris tensed beside me, but he didn't back up.

"It's okay. He won't jump the fence unless I show him that he's allowed."

He pressed his lips together so tightly they almost turned white. Like maybe he was about to call me a liar. But I intended to show him exactly how well Puff's husbandry behavior training was going. Once the little guy was directly across the fence from me, I waved my hand back and forth and turned my head along with it.

Almost instantly, Puff copied the motion, tipping his head left and then right.

I froze with my hands in the stop position, and when Puff stopped too, I dropped them at a right angle, then lifted them again. Puff followed, nodding his head up and down. Then I spun my pointer finger in a circle, and Puff jumped into the pool and swam in quick circles.

"You're teaching the bird party tricks?" Chris snorted.

"We don't call them that. They aren't for entrainment. It's cute, but it's really so we can see how he moves his wings and his neck and back muscles. It's referred to as husbandry behaviors. But he loves to show off." With a laugh, I stood, reached over the fence, and rubbed Puff's head. Then I tossed him a small fish from the little cooler next to the enclosure.

Puff barked his happiness and then took off into the water with his treasure.

"Should you feed him like that?"

I tilted my head and focused on Chris, who was frowning at me. "What do you mean?"

"Shouldn't you wear gloves?"

I shrugged. "He's not sick. He's healthy as a horse. Right, little man?"

The puffin ignored me completely, happily distracted by his treat. So I headed over to wash the fish off my hands.

"He doesn't carry disease or germs that'll make you sick?" Chris picked up my cup and set it on my desk, then wandered over to the bookshelves and scanned them.

"Nah, he's a pretty clean bird." I picked up my coffee and took a sip, propping my hip against my desk.

Chris lifted a photo. "This has to be your mother; you look just like her. Is this Italy?" His attention bounced from the photo to me and back again.

"Yeah, we were in Italy. My stepdad, Dave, is a pilot. He mostly flies international, so when I was a kid, we traveled with him a lot. I was four when he married my mom." Once I got to high school, I spent more time with Dad, since they were always off on some new adventure, and I had school and homework. As much as I griped about Dad's rules, even with his baseball schedule, he provided a lot of the consistency in my life.

Chris studied another photo, his eyes narrowing. Ah. That was one of me with my dad.

Nothing I'd seen or heard in the last few months had made it seem like Dad and Chris would ever get along, but I was starting to wonder if it was because they were more alike than either wanted to admit. It was probably best if I just avoided any notion that it was possible.

I took another slow sip of my latte and watched him study more photos. "Did you show up early just to hang out?"

He set a photo on the shelf and turned to me again. "No, I wanted to check on Puff, see how he was, before we take pictures. And you said you missed your afternoon coffee, so I figured I should grab one so you wouldn't rage."

When we texted earlier, he'd said he'd see me later, and I had joked that he might not want to because I hadn't had time for coffee.

"I don't rage."

"Not what I hear." He raised a single bow.

That small move alone made my entire body tighten. What was it about this guy that was so damn attractive? It was almost like every cell in my body came alive when he was near.

He sauntered over and leaned against the desk next to me. Our arms almost brushed and my heart skipped.

"So." He shifted and crossed his legs at the ankles. He took in the entirety of the room and perused my shelves of avian books and the framed photos of a dozen varieties of birds hanging on the walls. Finally, he focused on Puff again. He cleared his throat and rubbed a large hand over his jaw, almost like he was nervous. "You go back to the shitty boyfriend?"

Oh. My chest pinched. Because, although he hadn't asked me about it, I had run out on him. We probably needed to talk about it. I bowed my head and shook it, searching for a way to start this conversation. When I looked up, I found him watching me. "No."

He pursed his lips, like he was waiting for an explanation.

"But…"

He let out a heavy sigh and nodded. "Ah. New guy."

My heart lurched. "No."

His dark brown eyes narrowed, and his brows lowered.

"I'm taking a sabbatical."

Now his brows shot up. "From work? Are you going away?" He tipped his head, swatting at the lock of hair that fell over his forehead.

Still watching me with an intensity that had me squirming, he gripped the edge of my desk, wrapping his long fingers under it tight.

The move brought with it a memory, a feeling, of the way those same fingers bit into my skin. Like an idiot, I was practically gawking at his hands, which then made me notice his strong thighs. My core heated as the phantom sensation of them tangled with mine washed over me.

He shifted, the muscles there pulling on the tight pants. I had to swallow so I didn't drool. I had to stop this. I wasn't dating or hooking up with anyone. Even Chris. I needed a reset.

"Avery?"

Right. He'd asked a question. "No, I'm not traveling."

Clearing his throat again, he searched my face like he was looking for an answer.

But it was one he wouldn't find without my words. I needed to spit it out. Maybe if I did that, things could be normal with us.

"Now that you know who my father is, this will make so much more sense." I dropped my shoulders and studied the carpet in front of me. "My last two boyfriends? It turned out they were more interested in getting jobs with the Revs than dating me."

His jaw locked, and he turned to face me fully. "What happened?"

I gave him a half shrug, still keeping my focus averted. "Noah broke up with me after my dad told him he couldn't get an internship in the team's front office. Joe used my email account to send my dad his résumé." I glared at the gray carpet beneath me. "With a note begging Dad to do *me* a favor."

A weird sound left Chris's throat. It sounded like a mix between a growl and a squeak, if that was even possible.

"They aren't the only people I've had issues with. When I was little, the kids at school were only interested in being friends with me because I was the baseball player's daughter. In high school, after Dad was hired as the pitching coach for the Revs, guys would ask me out and take me on a few dates, all so they could get pointers or lessons."

The ache in my chest that never completely went away flared as I continued. "In college, it was to meet the players or get tickets to the games. And like a dumbass, I kept thinking it was okay. Even when it came to things that weren't baseball related, I always let the men I dated take control. If they wanted to go out, then I'd get dressed up and go, even if I'd rather have a quiet night in."

I sighed, sinking lower, wishing I'd kept my mouth shut instead of rehashing it all, but it was too late to change that now, so I might as well lay it all out.

"If they wanted to watch only stupid action movies, I'd sit beside them on the couch without complaint. And I didn't argue when they refused to watch rom-coms or serious dramas. Because if I didn't like all the things they did, then they might not like me enough to stick around."

As painful as it was, thinking back on it was the reminder I needed. It reinforced my decision to spend time figuring out what I wanted in a relationship and to build a firm idea of how I wanted and deserved to be treated. Maybe I'd learn to give myself more credit so I'd stop letting guys use me for what I could give them.

"Anyway, I recently decided to take a year off from dating, and from men, so I can figure myself out. Hopefully, I'll come out of this with the ability to stop picking shitty guys."

"Right." With a clipped nod, he rubbed roughly at his jaw.

Was he about to tell me how dumb that was? Try to talk me out of my plan?

He swallowed hard and met my eyes. His swam with a darkness I couldn't place. Whatever the emotion, his expression didn't look anything like the ones Wren and Jana had given me when they told me my plan was stupid.

"I'm sorry if I forced you into anything you didn't want to do that night."

Whoa. My stomach sank. That wasn't at all what I meant. "Wait, no." I clutched his forearm, and the muscles there went rigid. "You didn't pressure or force me into anything."

Silently, he searched my face, wearing a pained expression.

"Chris," I pleaded, my heart squeezing tight in my chest. "I *wanted* you that night. I wasn't saying I didn't."

His only response was a small frown.

"I planned to spend the night. I wanted to get to know you. But when I found out you played for the Revs, it hit me. I was jumping into something too fast again. There are rules against me dating players. And—"

"Whose?" he demanded, his brows pulled low.

"My dad's." My father had rules for everything, but dating his players had been a hard no from the second I turned eighteen.

He didn't say anything for a minute, just tapped his finger against his wrist two times before looking back at me. "Does he have rules against you being friends with his players?"

I had never asked. Not that I'd give my dad the power to make that kind of rule. Dating his players could become an issue. I could see that. A problematic breakup had the potential to cause drama for my dad, and he hated drama. But he couldn't make that argument about friendships.

I pressed my lips together and shook my head. "He doesn't."

"Good. Then we'll start there." With that comment, the grump beside me smiled a real smile. The first I'd ever seen from him. I wasn't prepared. The sight made my stomach flip and sent goose bumps shooting up my arms. God, he had a gorgeous smile.

I shook my head and took a deep breath to center myself. "I still firmly believe you only pretend to be grumpy."

He laughed and bumped my shoulder with his. "Pretty sure no one would agree with you. Now that we cleared the air, should we get the show on the road?"

"Sure." I took another large swig of my coffee. Then I stood and grabbed Puff's harness off the desk.

"Are you going to walk him like a dog?"

I chuckled as I swatted at him. "No. Normally, we'd crate the birds to move them, but we're just going outside, so although I can't let him run free, I don't want him crated. Between the people we'll pass and the other animals, he might get twitchy, so I'll keep him harnessed for this."

"Does he *like* that thing?"

Aw, the grumpy Gus was worried about Puff being comfortable. How cute was that?

"If he shows any signs of distress, I'll stop. But so far? Watch." I walked slowly to the bird's enclosure and whistled.

Without hesitation, Puff headed my way. After I'd clipped the tiny harness around his right leg, he jumped onto my arm and rushed up to my shoulder, his favorite place to chill.

Though this time, the second he made it all the way up, he took a flying leap at Chris and landed on the top of his head.

Wide-eyed, Chris threw his arms out and stumbled back. "I...uh." He was frozen, focused on me, twitching like he was forcing himself not to swat at the bird or make a run for it.

I tapped just above my collarbone, and in response, Puff hopped down and positioned himself on Chris's left shoulder.

"He likes you."

Chris swallowed, his face going pale. "Is he going to shit again?"

I giggled, and Puff chipped out happily. "Maybe, but it's good luck."

"For who?"

"You."

He scowled. "That's insane."

I shuffled closer to them and held out my arms. "I don't make the rules, but I'll get him down."

"No, it's okay." With another thick swallow, Chris brought his arm up and across his chest and tapped lightly on Puff's foot. "He's okay."

"This should make getting photos easy. They'll be happy that he's already perched on you."

"This shit is the exact reason I blocked Hannah," he mumbled, heading to the door.

"So why are you almost smiling?" I asked as I followed him.

"I'm asking myself *the same damn thing*."

I skirted around Chris and Puff and guided him to where the photographer had set up. It took almost no time to get a shot of the two. Both man and bird looked perfectly happy in every image. Much to Chris's chagrin, the photo trended for the entire week, and a video clip of Puff rubbing his beak in Chris's hair went viral with over one hundred million views. Even I watched it a few times.

Avery
12

Me: There's a package on my desk addressed to Puff Daddy.

Chris: Did you open it?

Me: I'm worried about what kind of a crazy person sends mail to a bird.

Chris: Uncalled for

Me: GIF of a person laughing

Chris: Just open it. It will start to smell if you let it sit too long

Me: You ordered sand eels for him?

Chris: They are his favorite, right?

Me: How did you know?

Chris: I read, Blondie...

Me: Aw, you're reading about puffins? How cute.

Chris: I have a lot of time to kill while I'm stuck on the planes with the team

Me: Wait. OMG. What is this?

Me: photo of a teeny-tiny bracelet that hadn't been tied

Me: Did you make a friendship bracelet for Puff?

Chris: One of the girls Miller lives with loves making them. After all those damn pictures, she thought Puff and I should match

Chris: Photo of his wrist resting on an airplane tray table sporting a blue and white beaded bracelet

Me: Adorable

Me: Photo of Puff with a blue and white bracelet on his right leg.

Christian

13

"USUAL TABLE, BOYS?" Pam, dressed in her usual pink shirt, smiled at us as we stepped inside our favorite breakfast joint. Before we could even respond, she grabbed two menus from behind the podium and was moving across the black and white checkered floor, past the booths and tables and red stools along the counter, at a pace that said she didn't have time for us to fuck around. The almost seventy-year-old woman with blue-gray hair had the energy of six people in their prime.

While she waited for us to catch up, she dropped the menus on the glossy white tabletop and stepped back.

Emerson and I gave her appreciative nods and slid into the red padded bench seats on either side of the booth.

This place was on the map Avery had drawn for me months ago, and we'd been coming here every Tuesday since. At least when we were in town. It was clear this wasn't a regular breakfast stop for her like I originally thought, since I'd yet to run into her here. Even so, we continued to come. The truth was, I enjoyed the mom-and-pop atmosphere, even if I'd never ordered the banana pancakes she'd drawn.

Pam pulled a pencil from behind her ear and slid the pad from her black apron. "Coffee and OJ for you, right, handsome?"

"Absolutely, beautiful." Emerson, always the flirt, smiled. The woman was old enough to be his grandmother, but that didn't stop him.

"Water?" she asked me.

After I'd given her a quick nod, she hustled off, slipping around the counter and hurrying along the polished silver wall to the drink station.

Neither of us opened our menus. After four months, we knew what we liked.

"Chris?"

At the sound of my name in such a musical tone, shock rocked down my spine.

Emerson looked past me and smirked. "Fucking finally."

No freaking way she was finally here. I spun and looked over my shoulder. Sure enough, she stood not far from us, wearing a pair of ripped jeans. Her hair was pulled into a ponytail, and her face was makeup free. Utter perfection. Though smiles didn't come to me easily, when in this woman's presence, I had to fight the urge.

I scooted out of the booth and strode for Avery, who was eyeing one of the backless red stools at the counter like she planned to sit there. The redhead from the bar was next to her.

"You stalking me, Blondie?" I asked, even though I was the one who had been coming here for months hoping to see her.

She rolled her eyes, but the smile she gave me was bright. "Stalking requires a pattern, not just a random accident. Who are you here with?"

"Emerson." I half turned and lifted my chin. "Want to join us? We haven't ordered yet."

With a shrug, she turned to her friend. "You good with that, Jana?"

"Ooh, my clumsy little ball of joy is here? Maybe he'll spill another drink on someone." Jana rubbed her hands together and wandered toward Emerson. "Long time no see." She scooted in beside him.

He leaned over to peck her cheek, then he rested his arm along the back of the red leather bench behind her. "My morning just got immensely more enjoyable, bebé."

"Are we ready to order?" Pam reappeared just as Avery and I had slid onto the opposite bench.

Not one of us had opened a menu, but we each nodded. Jana ordered first, choosing a breakfast sandwich that I had tried a few times. Avery got the banana pancakes, and Emerson and I opted for omelets.

Avery rested her forearms on the white tabletop, her bracelet clinking against the surface. I'd noticed the charms on her wrist before but had never had the opportunity to really study them until now. About seven charms hung from the woven links around the bracelet, each a different species of bird, from what I could tell. I ran a finger along the pelican charm, then the eagle.

"Do they have significance? The different types of birds?"

She assessed the bracelet with a melancholy smile. "It's weird letting go of animals you love. But it's *necessary*." She hit that last word hard, then swallowed audibly. "They deserve to live the best lives we can offer them. But sometimes that life is in the wild. Sometimes it's with their flock at another zoo. But to me, it's a loss." She spun the silver links on her wrist, her chin tucked and her head bowed low. "I buy myself a charm to remember them. So I can keep a piece of them with me."

I set my hand on her forearm, and she turned, giving me a watery smile.

"Does that happen a lot?" Emerson asked, sitting a little taller across from me.

"Yes, she's cried over the loss of many birds in the last two years," Jana said.

With a shrug, Avery cleared her throat and picked up my glass of water. Without asking, she brought it to her lips and took a slow sip. The woman sure had a thing for stealing people's drinks. I wanted to be annoyed, but she was so damn cute. And she went on before I could express my irritation with her liquid thievery anyway.

"No matter how much I tell myself not to bond with them, I can't help it. Like with Puff."

My whole body went rigid at the sadness in her voice when she spoke about the bird. What did she mean *with Puff*? With the party tricks alone, anyone could tell the bird was happy as a pig in shit when he was with her. Who wouldn't be? If I spent my days being doted on by Avery, I'd be the happiest man alive. He had that pool in her office too. Plus, he had the run of the entire tank in the hospital area when Avery couldn't keep him with her. What more did he need?

"What about Puff?" I demanded, turning to face Avery fully.

I was the reason he didn't have a normal existence anymore, so I'd gladly do whatever it took to make sure he was happy.

She sighed. "Puffins are social birds, but we don't have a puffin exhibit. Although he's adapted to me, he won't be happy without a true puffinry."

"A what?" I frowned, pulling out my phone to see if I could order one, whatever it was.

"Like a colony, friends, another bird to bond with."

I deflated. Dammit. That was not something I could order on Amazon.

"Like a mate?" Emerson chuckled.

I rolled my eyes at the idiot. It was always about sex with him.

"Well, yeah." She shrugged a shoulder, and the gray scoop of her shirt slipped down, revealing creamy white skin.

Of their own volition, my eyes zeroed in on the indent of her neck, the slope of her collarbone, the curve of her shoulder. My fingers had run along that same skin, had elicited a shiver as I'd done it. She'd been so responsive to my touch that night.

I shifted on the bench and forced myself to focus on her words, not her skin.

"He's the right age for a mate. That's probably why he was at the stadium in the first place. Looking for a female. The males tend to wander farther from their puffinry when they're searching for a mate."

"My kind of bird." Emerson smirked.

"You're such a man whore." Jana giggled. It was high pitched and annoying.

He smiled that stupid innocent smile he always wore. It totally belied his next words. "I won't lie about that."

Avery laughed beside me. The sound made my heart clench. Damn, I loved hearing her laugh. Noises were one of those things that irked me. Most fell into one of three categories—too loud, too grating, or shudder-inducing—but Avery's laugh lit me from the inside out.

"Anyway." Avery shrugged. "We'll eventually have to move him to another zoo. One that has an exhibit. If I could keep him, I would, but we don't have the money to pay to construct a puffin habitat right now. I've done a little preliminary research. There aren't many zoos in the US that have one. St. Louis is probably the closest. Maybe they'll want him."

I scowled. How much could an exhibit cost?

I was new to the majors, so it was probably more than I could afford. I rubbed my jaw and racked my brain. Maybe I could start a GoFundMe to cover the cost and keep the bird in Boston. I might have to unblock Hannah and ask her about it, since she handled stuff like that for the Revs.

"Your omelet."

A white plate with a checkerboard rim appeared in front of me, snapping me back to the present. Next was Avery's short stack of pancakes. She must have given Emerson and Jana theirs first, because he was already scooping up a forkful of breakfast potatoes.

"That smells so good." Avery tipped closer to me, her shoulder brushing mine, and sniffed my plate.

Normally, I liked to keep more space between people and my food, but I didn't want to sound like a dick and tell her to back up, so I inhaled deeply, grasped for patience, and waited.

"I've never had the omelet here. Can I try it?"

Splitting meals was *not* my thing. In fact, I never let anyone eat off my plate. Not even my dad or my sister.

Emerson chuckled across from me. "Dragon doesn't share well."

I glared at him. Did he *have* to make me sound like a total asshole?

"Oh." Her face fell, and she sat up straight again, taking her warmth with her.

My heart sank. Now I didn't only sound like an asshole. I *felt* like one too.

"You can try it." I used my knife to cut a small piece, figuring I could slide it onto her plate.

But suddenly, she was clutching my fork, stabbing the omelet with it, and stealing the bite. She wrapped her lips around the metal in what felt like slow motion. For some, that might be a turn-on or whatever, but for me, the slow-mo move had my mind instantly racing with the knowledge that the human mouth was home to over seven hundred species of germs.

It was irrational, yes, because if she leaned over and kissed me right now, I wouldn't hesitate to explore every inch of her mouth. But this anxiety had latched on to me years ago, and there was no escaping it in this moment.

She hummed as she chewed, and once she'd swallowed, she said, "Wow, yum." Then she went in for another bite.

Now the germs were on my fork, my plate, and my food.

After she swallowed the second bite, she laughed and set the fork back on my plate. "I might need to order that next time." She looked at her short stack of pancakes with the bananas and whipped cream and tiny chocolate chips and grinned. "Probably not. I love these pancakes."

Heart racing, I stared at my plate.

"Need me to get you a new fork?" Emerson rested his forearms on the table and leaned in, smirking. Over the years, he'd made it very clear that he thought my germ thing was too much.

Was it? Maybe. But after my mother died of a staph infection that went septic, my father made sure we were conscious of germs. Naturally, I took it to the extreme, because I did nothing halfway.

I glared at my teammate, who was now grinning and seconds away from giving me shit.

"Why would he need a new one?" Avery frowned at Emerson, then turned her attention to me.

Before my roommate could make me sound ridiculous. I picked up my fork and scooped another piece from my omelet. "I don't." I popped the bite into my mouth and decided right then that Avery was like Puff. Neither of them had germs, and I wouldn't stress over it.

Emerson sat back, smirking once again, watching me eat. He had his chin lifted and his chest puffed out, as if he was proud of his status as the keeper of my secrets.

"Just finish your damn eggs." I glared at him.

"You two have such an unusual vibe." Jana pointed her egg and cheese bagel at us.

Avery scooped a bite of nothing but whipped cream. In fact, other than my eggs, she'd only eaten the whipped cream and chocolate chips so far. She licked the white fluff off her fork in a move that was far sexier than she intended, eyeing me. "Yeah, I swear you don't like that you like each other."

Emerson laughed silently, his shoulders shaking. "Spot on. It drives him insane that I'm his best friend."

"Puff's gonna be jealous. He thought the bracelet meant he was your best friend." Avery tapped the blue beads on my wrist.

Now the asshole across from me snorted. Karma intervened, and he choked on his eggs. Thank fuck he clamped a hand over his mouth while he pulled himself together.

When Emerson had found his composure, I dropped my fork and sat back, crossing my arms. "To think I was going to buy breakfast for all of you."

Avery giggled but went back to her plate.

"Are you going to eat anything but the whipped cream?"

She froze with her fork in midair. "I have a system," she said, absolutely serious. Like I was ridiculous for not knowing her method. "Whipped cream first. Because it's my favorite." She licked another dollop of it off the fork. "Bananas next, because they usually have the most whipped cream remnants." She pointed her fork at the cream-covered slices. "Then if I have room, I might eat a few bites of the pancakes."

Frowning, I scrutinized her. "So…" I cocked my head. "Why don't you just order bananas and whipped cream?"

"Who eats just bananas and whipped cream for breakfast?" She shook her head like I was the crazy one in this conversation.

"You." That was my entire point.

"No." She scooted the plate a little closer to me and pointed at it again. "Clearly, there are pancakes here."

I looked at Emerson, because that shit didn't make sense. But he just smiled and shrugged, then went back to chatting with Jana.

"Want one? I'll never finish them all." Without waiting for a response, she hooked the lower pancake with her fork and pulled it out from under the top one. With a plop, she dropped it onto my plate next to my half-eaten omelet.

I frowned at the damn thing. No, I didn't want it, but I hated to waste food, and Avery didn't seem to have that issue.

Pam came by with a drink refill and finally brought Avery her own water. Maybe now she'd stop drinking mine.

"You guys are off on Friday, right?" Jana set her bagel on her plate. "You should come out with us."

"Like a double date?" Emerson asked, his eyes dancing.

"We can't label it that way," Jana huffed, hitting Avery with a frown.

"I'm doing a dating cleanse." Avery had finally finished the whipped cream and was now working on the bananas.

I was working on the pancake she'd dropped onto my plate.

"The fuck?" Emerson looked from her to me, wearing a scowl that was so unlike him.

"Right?" Jana shook her head.

"Jana thinks it's dumb. Wren does too. But I'm taking a year off from dating to rid myself of all my bad habits. It's a good thing." Avery was more confident about it today than she had been when she explained it to me last week.

Hot anger flared up inside me at the idea that men had treated her so badly in the past. In this moment, I wanted nothing more than to track them down and teach them a lesson in how to treat women.

"So it's a just friends thing. Want to come?"

Emerson met my eyes. The question there wasn't whether I was in. He was silently asking me what the hell I was doing with her if she wasn't dating.

I ignored him and focused on Avery again. Beneath the table, I tapped my wrist twice. "We'd love to."

Fucker always wanted to go out, so he wouldn't complain.

Maybe Emerson didn't get it, but I knew what I was doing.

Did I love that she wasn't dating? No. I hated it. But she deserved time to figure out what she wanted. And as much as I'd love to pull her into my arms and kiss her, just sitting beside her, eating her pancakes so she could have just whipped cream, listening to her laugh, was enough. For now. And I'd take this time to show her that we could have something great. Whether she knew it or not, she was giving me a chance to earn the spot of boyfriend when she was ready for it.

So I'd take friendship for now. Being just her friend might not be easy, because I wanted more. But when something was worth it, I was willing to do all the heavy lifting. Because if there was one thing I was sure of, it was that Avery Wilson was worth it.

Christian
14

Cortney tapped the back of his hand against his inner thigh twice and flashed four fingers. But I shook off the signal for the third time.

The sixty-plus feet between us didn't hide the way the catcher's shoulders tightened in response.

He stood and leaned into the umpire like he was speaking to him. Then he lifted his mask and trotted out to me. Even standing lower on the mound, the man towered over me. But he wasn't glaring. A lot of catchers I'd played with would have come out here yelling. They'd tell me to get my shit together and follow the game plan. But that wasn't Miller.

He lifted his mitt to one side of his face to prevent prying eyes from reading his lips. "This guy." Cortney tilted his man bun toward home plate. "Can't hit a slider. A fastball, though?" He cocked a brow. "He has no trouble sending those over the fence."

My stomach twisted. I hadn't thrown that pitch well in months. "There are other options. My slider's shit."

"I get it. Hitting the bird has fucked with the pitch, but you can't avoid it. Especially when it's this guy's Achilles' heel."

"No." I shook my head. "We'll walk him."

Cortney cut a look at the dugout, where Tom was scowling at us. "He won't like that. He was clear with you during pregame that he expected to see this pitch today."

I didn't need to be reminded. I'd heard him loud and clear. The only reason I hadn't told him to fuck off was because he was Avery's dad.

Although my night out with her last week had been nothing more than a few beers before we all went home—separately—it had been more fun than I'd had since the night I met Avery. So I wasn't purposely going to pick fights with her father. However, I hadn't specifically agreed to throw the pitch either.

"We'll walk him," I repeated.

My teammate toed the dirt and let out a frustrated sigh. "If we lose this game, then we have no chance at the wild card. You know that, right? And you won't get to pitch a playoff game."

His argument wasn't all that convincing. We'd have to win every one of the twelve games left in the regular season to make that happen. And with our schedule, especially since we had two games against the Metros, who were sitting at the top of the national league, our chances were almost nonexistent. The Revs hadn't made the playoffs in years. And although the Langfields had made a lot of moves to improve the team recently, we were in a building year. We weren't a playoff contender.

But it irked me that the guy who'd won three world series in his long career was pointing out how I wouldn't be setting foot on the field for a playoff game. I might have bitten his head off, but I got it. This was Miller's last chance to get there. He'd recently announced that he was retiring at the end of the season.

He must have talked Dylan out of the friend zone sometime after the day I met her, because they were having a baby girl in the spring. And their story gave me hope. If he could work his way to more with Dylan, then I could do the same with Avery. It would take time, but I could be patient.

"So?" Miller cocked a brow.

"Me throwing a shit pitch won't help anything. We walk him."

He shook his head and stalked back to the home plate. Instead of squatting, he held his arm straight out, and I tossed an easy ball his way.

He hadn't even tossed it back before Wilson was jogging across the grass.

"Who coaches this team?" he snapped the second he hit the mound.

A snappy comeback was on the tip of my tongue, but I bit it back. Instead, I pressed my lips together to hold in my frustration and shook my head. Cortney stepped up beside us, and Tom lifted his hand over his mouth to ensure the opposing team couldn't read his lips.

"We don't win games by walking batters when we don't fucking need to."

"We don't win by throwing shitty-ass pitches either." The man should know that by now.

"So don't." He looked at Miller and then back at me, then held his hand out. "Throw the slider or give me the ball."

Motherfucker.

I pulled my shoulders back, and although ten thousand angry words were fighting to escape me, I responded with a clipped nod. Wilson didn't bother to respond before he jogged back to the dugout.

When Miller was behind the plate again, he gave me two taps and four fingers.

Anger burned through me, and I clenched my jaw, but I pushed it all away and focused on the game. I took a breath and wound up. As I released the ball, an echo of a high-pitched screech of pain hit me, and I flinched. The ball floated rather than dropping like it should, staying level as it made its way to the plate. Fuck. It was easy pickings.

Based on the crack of wood, I didn't need to look to know the ball was gone. I closed my eyes and kept them shut as the crowd booed the batter, who was taking his lap around the bases.

At the sound of a throat clearing, I forced my eyes open. *No fucking way*.

Wilson stood in front of me with his hand out.

My stomach sank as my blood pressure skyrocketed.

"You made me throw a pitch that I told you was shit, and now you're fucking pulling me?"

He kept his palm out flat and blinked at me without speaking.

"No fucking way."

His jaw went rigid and his eyes narrowed to slits. "You just gave up a two-run homer. I'll ask you the same question I asked when I was out here before. Who coaches this team?"

That fucking question made my head explode. "Who coaches this team?" I took a step closer. "A fucking moron who will never lead us to the playoffs if he doesn't open his ears and listen when his players talk. An idiot who'd rather run his fucking mouth than give his players the respect of hearing them out. No, he's too much of a dumbass to bother with that shit." As I dropped the ball in the grass halfway to the dugout, I already regretted my words and the fine that was sure to come.

As my cleats hit the bottom step of the dugout, I didn't slow. I brushed the trainer away and continued down the cinderblock halls. I didn't want to talk. I needed to cool off before I took out my anger on anyone else. I yanked my jersey off and threw it on the floor. Next came my cleats and pants. A minute later, I was headed for the shower, dreading the texts that would be waiting for me when I was done.

With a towel around my waist, I pulled in a long breath and pushed down the dread and disquiet threatening to consume me. Then I snagged my phone off the shelf in my locker.

> Pop: Four fucks, one shit, and name calling. Not your best.

> Pop: Didn't even need a lip reader for this one. The announcers could even tell what you said. And throwing the ball? Kids are watching you. You're setting an example, and it's your responsibility to be a good one.

I rubbed the back of my neck. I knew I'd acted like an ass, but I wasn't wrong.

Avery
15

I PUSHED through the door of my Thursday afternoon happy place. Arti's Subs was, in my opinion, the best sandwich place on Boston Harbor. And the Thursday special? It's what foodgasms were made of.

"Hey, Avery." Arti smiled at me as he leaned his beefy arms on the glass case that displayed the variety of sandwich meats he offered. Arti cooked 90 percent of it in-house, and he purchased the bread from a local bakery that had perfected the onion roll. All thrown together, it made for the best North Shore roast beef in all of Massachusetts.

"How's wedding planning?"

His daughter was getting married in a few weeks. For months, every time I stopped in, he'd been going on about the torture she was putting him through.

He heaved a sigh the size of Texas and shook his bald head. "Don't start with that shit."

The bell on the door behind me jingled, and Arti looked past me.

"Hey, Dragon. Give me one second, and I'll grab your order."

My heart skipped at that name—*Dragon*—and I spun. The second I laid eyes on him, my heart took off at a furious speed. Holy heck, the man was gorgeous. He'd been photographed wearing glasses, but I'd never seen him wear them in person. And damn if he didn't have the Clark Kent vibe going. He looked *good* in Rev's blue, but like this? I was having a hard time taking in a full breath. He was in a pair of gray practice pants and a white T-shirt, with his Rev's hat on backward. The scruff that normally brushed his jaw was thicker, as if he hadn't shaved in a couple of days. Add in the black-rimmed glasses, and it made it hard to breathe.

"Hey, Blondie." The corner of his mouth lifted in that *I'm not going to smile* look he'd perfected.

"Hi." I shifted on my feet.

I hadn't heard from him since he'd called my dad a dumbass on national television. He'd apologized to the press after the game, saying he'd let his frustration get to him in the moment and that he shouldn't have lashed out. As far as I knew, it was the first time he'd ever apologized for an outburst.

From there, most of the questions the media had for him revolved around the problems with his slider. And although he said it wasn't because of hitting Puff, I knew better. He was still harboring guilt about it.

"You stalking me?" he asked. It was his favorite line when we ran into each other in the wild like this. It had only happened four or five times in the last few months, but in a city the size of Boston, maybe it was a lot.

I shook my head. "Stalking requires a pattern, not an accidental meetup."

A deep chuckle rumbled from his chest and sent a shiver through me. "Yeah, you'd have to know where I go on certain days and be on the lookout for me in order for it to be considered stalking, right?"

"Exactly." The old me might have done that. Thrown myself in his path over and over, all but screaming *pick me, pick me*. God, I felt pathetic just thinking about it. But we were friends. There was no reason to vie for his attention or affection. And more than that, I wouldn't be that person again. "You're very casual today."

He rocked back on his heels and tucked his hands into the back pockets of his baseball pants. "Since I ended the season with a two-week suspension and don't get to travel with the team, I don't have much reason to dress up."

I winced. Because not only had the league fined him twenty-five thousand dollars, but my dad had suspended him for the last twelve games.

"It's okay." He shrugged. "I deserved it."

"Got your order here." Arti appeared behind the counter again and slid a large brown bag toward Chris. "And I grabbed you your usual." He nodded at me and set the small white bag next to the brown one.

Chris pulled out his phone. "Put it all on my bill."

"You don't have to." He'd paid for my beer when we'd gone out a few weeks ago, and he'd bought my breakfast both times we'd bumped into each other. Not to mention the coffees he'd brought with him each time he'd come to see Puff.

"I don't mind."

"I know you don't, but you keep paying for things, and now this friendship is unbalanced. Let me get it." I pushed my card across the counter.

He swallowed and furrowed his brows. "Uh. Okay, but that's not just my salad."

"Oh." My stomach sank, though I couldn't explain why. The man was baseball's most eligible bachelor. Of course he dated. I didn't know why I got the impression he didn't. "I guess you should probably pay for your date's food. I'll pick up the tab next time."

"No." He shook his head. "It's Hannah's lunch."

I tipped my head. "Hannah? As in the woman you blocked?" Wow, that had taken a sharp turn. Although enemies to lovers *was* a thing. It could explain the reason he'd had fewer outbursts over the last month or so. Maybe he was trying to impress her.

He smirked and tapped his phone against the reader to pay for all the food. "I can see your mind working. It's not a date. I'm meeting with Hannah to talk about a project." He took a breath and blew it out as he scrutinized me with what I swore looked like a little nervousness. "Actually, if you're not busy, I'd love it if you came too."

"You want me to come to your meeting with Hannah? Did you unblock her?"

He ran his tongue over his front teeth. "Out of necessity."

I tilted my head and studied him. "What's so important?"

"If you come, you'll find out." That almost smile was back, and it made my stomach flip.

"Well, now I'm curious, so I can't say no."

With our bags in hand, we walked the three blocks to the Langfield compound. Since they owned both the baseball and the hockey teams, they'd built the stadiums side by side, and the corporate offices were housed across the street. There was a rumor that a players-only bar existed in the tunnels under the space between the two stadiums, but I'd never seen it. Supposedly, it was invite-only. Had Chris ever brought anyone down there?

I glanced at him. The veins in his arms were prominent as he gripped the bags of food in front of him and glared straight ahead. He clearly had something on his mind, even though he didn't say much. That mysterious and broody vibe only added to his sex appeal. He may not have had a date today, but he was a gorgeous guy in his twenties. He definitely dated.

The idea took some of the pep out of my step. But I couldn't harp on it. He had a right to do what made him happy.

"Do you not want to come?"

I jumped at the sound of his voice. He hadn't spoken a word since we left the deli, and I was still fighting with myself to release all thoughts of Chris and his dating life.

"No, I do, but..." I nibbled on my bottom lip as a new wave of anxiety washed through me. "Is she going to mind that I'm here?"

My dad's retired number sat in the middle of the large blue outfield wall, and he'd gone down in history as one of the Revs' best pitchers. Plus, he'd worked with the team for years. But apart from the random game here and there, I didn't come by the stadium anymore. And I never intruded on meetings.

"I don't give a shit if she does. I want you there." He pulled the huge glass door open with his free hand and waved me in with the bags he was still clutching. "If you want to come and I want you here, why does anyone else's opinion matter?"

When he put it that way, he was right. So, with a smile, I stepped inside the building and headed to the elevator.

We stepped off on the floor that housed the PR department and the owners' offices, and he guided me to Hannah's office. When he knocked on the door, Hannah looked up. She was wearing a smile, but when her focus landed on me, it dropped. "Avery?"

My stomach sank right along with it. That was *not* the warmest welcome.

I shifted on my feet. For a minute, I'd been confident it was okay, but now? "Uh, Chris invited me." I peered up at him for backup, only to find him scowling at Hannah. "I hope that's okay?" The question was meant for her, but I was fixated on the vein pulsing in Chris's temple.

He huffed out a breath and stomped toward her desk. "*I* said it was okay. I don't give a shit what anyone else thinks."

Hannah snorted. "It's always such a pleasure doing favors for you."

This was a favor for him?

"It's going to create good press for the Revs, so don't pretend your help is selfless." He pulled a white paper–wrapped sandwich from the brown bag and dropped it onto Hannah's desk. "And I bought you Arti's."

She rolled her blue eyes. "Food and a piss-poor attitude. Doesn't get much better than that. But it's great that you're here, Avery. I have to go over this stuff with you at some point anyway." She sat back down at her desk and nodded to the chairs.

Chris slumped into one and ran a hand through his hair. "Langfield and Miller said they would do this without the fanfare, so remember this is for your social media shit," he grumbled, then turned to me. "You should sit. Hannah is never short for words, so we'll be here forever."

"They don't pay me enough to deal with the amount of grump I get around here."

I could imagine. Between my dad, Beckett Langfield, and a team full of athletes, she had her work cut out for her. And unlike Liv, her boss, whose efficiency and mom-like control had everyone quickly jumping in line, Hannah was young and looked sweet. So despite the backbone I knew she had, she tended to get the brunt of most of the guys' attitude.

She tapped a few keys, then turned her computer monitor our way so we could see the screen.

Project Puffinry

Tingles shot through me at the project title. I looked over at Chris as I finally lowered myself into the chair next to him, waiting for an explanation.

"Puff needs a habitat and a colony or whatever, so we're working on it." Chris waved a hand at the screen. "Langfield, Miller, the Revs, and I are setting up a fund that'll allow the zoo to expand the penguin exhibit to house a colony of puffins."

One million dollars? According to the data I was still processing, it looked as though the fund would be enough to double the size of the penguin palace.

Someone had obviously done their research, because they'd set aside two hundred thousand for additional birds. Though I never could have imagined the possibility, I'd dreamed of acquiring a colony for Puff and had done my own research on what it would cost to make it happen. Yes, I was a foolish optimist, but I was attached to the little guy. How could I not be? With that amount of money, I could easily get nine more puffins to join him in Boston. And the fund would more than pay for their care for the next few years.

Blinking back tears, I studied the frowning man beside me. Although I had joked about Chris being Puff's best friend, I had it all wrong. He acted a lot more like his parent. His initiative and the need to make sure he was cared for went far beyond him having a soft spot for the bird. Christian Damiano got so much shit for being a hothead asshole, but he was really a good guy.

Christian
16

Blondie: What do you mean did I show Puff the picture?

Me: Well, it doesn't matter if I like these damn birds. He's the one that needs them. So show him the pictures and let him pick. Or better yet, take him to meet the actual birds

Blondie: I'm not flying the poor bird all over the country.

Me: Fine. Then at least show him the photos

Blondie: Okay. Never mind, the avian department at the zoo will pick the nine birds.

Blondie: You're still coming to the party this weekend, right?

Me: I can't believe you talked me into this

Blondie: You can't be a stick-in-the-mud on Halloween. I won't allow it. Don't forget: you need to wear a red shirt. Emerson is green, Bosco is wearing a blue vest, and Dumpty is shirtless with a red tie.

Christian
17

HALLOWEEN

"I can't believe you're doing this." Mason Dumpty, our center fielder, threw his head back and cackled as I climbed out of the Uber behind him.

"Me?" Pushing past my teammates, I headed for the glass door of Wren's lobby. "You're the one who looks like women should be shoving money into your pants."

"From your mouth to God's ears." Mason jogged to my side, lifting both bare arms and flexing his biceps. The man was an attention whore, so naturally, he was ecstatic to learn he'd been asked to wear nothing but a pair of pants and a red tie. "But Dragon dressing up for Halloween? And actually letting another person pick the costume? That shit is so out of your wheelhouse."

I stopped and glared at my teammate, wondering if maybe I should have stayed home rather than deal with this shit. "She told me to wear a red T-shirt. Why wouldn't I go along with it?" With a huff, I spun and addressed the doorman. "We're here for Wren Cass's party. She's in 2203."

With a friendly smile, he waved us to the elevator.

Instead of dropping the subject, my teammates continued their annoying commentary all the way through the lobby and on the ride up to Wren's floor.

"Plus it's Aaavery." Kyle Bosco nudged me. "That girl has no idea that you'd do anything she commanded, and neither does her dad."

I was not talking about Tom Wilson. The man had been nothing but a thorn in my side all season. It was hard to imagine how he could have had anything to do with creating Avery. They were like night and day. The season had ended, so I *should* be enjoying a break from the man, but the dick couldn't leave me to my off-season workouts in peace. No, he was constantly riding my ass. And he'd forced me into taking press classes this fall.

So I had the pleasure of spending a couple of hours a week with fucking Hannah while she yap-yap-yapped in my ear.

"I wouldn't be caught dead dressed like fucking Aladdin, no matter who asked, Streaks." I scanned his blue vest and white pants. The guy looked like a tool, especially with the highlighted hair he claimed was natural.

"Avery knows you. She wouldn't tell you to." Emerson shook his head and grinned. "But I still don't get how you can be all buddy-buddy with a chick you fucked."

And it started again. I tamped down on the annoyance that sparked to life when he talked about her like that.

"Yeah. I mean, if the sex wasn't great, then fine. Maybe." Bosco frowned. "Except if the sex was bad, I'm not sure I'd want to hang around. In case, you know, she hinted at wanting it to happen again. So yeah, I'd avoid her." He nodded, as if making up his mind. "If it was good, I'd definitely try to hit that again. One or the other. Not this friendship limbo shit you've got going on."

My jaw ticked, and my heart rate sped up, but not in a good way. I'd been hearing this for months. "I'm not explaining this shit again," I gritted out. "We're friends. Stop trying to make it weird."

"That's what makes it fucking weird, man." Emerson laughed. "That you think you can be just friends."

I glared at him and squeezed my hands into fists at my sides. "I should have left you at home."

"If Avery hadn't personally invited all of us, you'd have left us all at home." He snorted.

"Truth. But I have a question." Mason rubbed his hands together, grinning at me.

Fuck. With an expression like that, I braced myself for the bullshit he was about to spew.

"What if she starts hooking up with someone? How does that play into this friends thing?"

Shit stirring. The man always did this.

"She's not dating." I bit the words out. Because there was no doubt in my mind that I'd react poorly to her hooking up with anyone.

"Yeah." Bosco nodded as the elevator opened onto Wren's floor. "But dude..." He stepped out and glanced down the hall. "Dating and fucking don't always go hand in hand. I don't date, but..."

He didn't need to finish the thought, and I didn't want to hear about that shit anyway. I had no doubt that out of the four of us, I'd gone the longest without sex. I was okay with that. I didn't want just anyone. So it was whatever. And Avery...

"She's not hooking up with anybody," I snapped, stepping out of the elevator behind Streaks. From the sound of the music bumping down the hall, it was easy to determine which way to go. "And drop it now, please."

By the way the bass vibrated through the floor as we approached the apartment door, I knew this wouldn't be my thing. But I'd made a promise, so I was here.

Though I doubted anyone inside could hear it, I pounded on the door. After several seconds, it swung open, and the sight that met me had me locking my jaw to fight the smile that wanted to take over my face.

"Blondie."

Her short-sleeve bubble gum–pink dress highlighted her gorgeous legs. Even though we'd known each other for months, I'd never seen her hair down like this before. It was done in some kind of beach curls. My sister would know what to call them, but when she started talking about shit like that, I tuned out.

"You came!" She blasted us with a smile that matched the sparkly crown on her head. "And you followed my direction perfectly."

As if I'd let any of the guys come along if they hadn't followed her instructions to a T.

"Of course we came." I angled in and gave her a quick hug. Instantly, I was engulfed in the cupcake scent that always lingered, even though she spent most of her day with birds and dead fish.

She pulled back before I was ready, but I stepped away quickly when she did so I didn't get more shit from my teammates.

As I did, every one of them was watching me with a shit-eating grin that said *you're screwed.*

"Hey, hotties." Jana rounded the corner toward us. "Boston Revs in the house." With her hands in the air, she danced toward us. She was dressed in a white bikini with a pink vest and some kind of...bubble hat? She snagged a red blob off the counter and sauntered to Kyle. "Your hat, sir."

It looked like half a red kickball with white paper circles taped to it.

"Damn, girl, looking good." Smirking, he flipped the stupid-ass hat onto his head.

Wren materialized from a mass of people crowding her living room. She was dressed in hot-pink shorts and a matching sports bra, as well as a hat. Hers had half a monkey head on it. "Mason Dumpty, I knew you'd crush Kong." She swiped another monkey head from the counter and strode toward him.

"Oh! I get it!" Kyle pumped his fist and chuckled. "Damn, you all are awesome. Come on, Toadette, let's go get a drink." He pulled Jana away.

"I'm lost." I assessed Avery, hoping she'd give me a clue.

Emerson pushed through to the front of our group and popped up on his toes, scanning the crowd of people. "Tell me Daisy's here."

"Oh, she is. C'mon, Luigi. We'll show you."

"Lead the way, bebé."

Wren turned on her heel and sashayed off, with Emerson and Mason in tow.

"Luigi..." I dipped my chin and took in my red shirt again. Then gave Avery another once-over. "Oh, Princess Peach."

She snatched a red ball cap from the counter and stepped up close so she could place it on my head. "Thatsa righta, Mario."

Fuck, she was cute. And she'd asked me to dress as Mario, and she'd chosen Peach. I liked that a little too much. Once she'd adjusted the hat, she rested her hands on my shoulders.

My body tensed at her proximity. But unlike the tension that usually raced through me when a person got too close, the need to step away wasn't what hit me. No, I was fighting the desire to latch on to her and pull her tighter to me.

With a step back, she tilted her head, making her crown tip just a little, and scanned me. "You make a perfect Mario, even without the full mustache."

"Good." I adjusted her crown carefully. "Because you're damn cute as Peach."

"I know, right?" She spun in a circle, showing off her full outfit. The move made her dress rise just a little, giving me an incredible glimpse of her thighs. "This was my best costume idea yet."

Forcing my focus away from her legs, I surveyed the apartment. In the corner of the living area, there was an enormous black tree with orange and white lights growing out of a pumpkin. It was decorated with all kinds of spiders and ghosts. And there had to have been at least ten jack-o'-lanterns lit up around the room. Along the kitchen bar were several black candelabras with white candles, and plastic cauldrons filled with what looked like a variety of punches. Everything fit with the spooky theme she'd mentioned when she told me she was helping Wren decorate for tonight.

I stuffed my hands into my pockets and rocked back on my heels. "Place looks good."

"It turned out great." She clutched her hands in front of her and beamed. "Want to get a drink? I had Wren get a case of that All Out stuff you like."

I shook my head and pressed my lips together, schooling my

expression. "Don't even start with that," I teased. "The last time we were out, I ordered you a Bud Light, but you drank my Easy Out, and I was stuck with the Bud."

She giggled and shrugged. "It's good."

"But Wren got it for *me* tonight?" I cocked a brow. She might be cute as fuck, but she was also full of shit.

Wearing an innocent smile, she pointed to the huge plastic pumpkin full of bottles and ice on the other side of the room. I grabbed a beer for each of us, popped the caps, then wandered back to her. I settled in on one side of the counter while she stayed on the other. She was so easy to talk to—had been since that first night—that I almost forgot we were surrounded by people.

"Damn girl, you got sticks for days." A half-drunk idiot wearing a goofy smile cozied up to Avery and blatantly checked out her ass. With an appreciative hum, he continued the perusal, scanning her legs.

I cleared my throat, tempering the annoyance already bubbling inside me. Avery and I were standing on opposite sides of the counter, but it seemed pretty obvious that we were talking. Not to mention we were wearing coordinating costumes. What the fuck?

I set my bottle on the marble island a little too aggressively, causing it to clank loud enough to be heard over the music.

That finally got the guy's attention. When he focused on me, his eyes went wide. "*Holy shit.* Are you Christian Damiano?"

What I wanted from the guy was a *sorry, man. I didn't mean to bother your girl,* but I couldn't have that, because Avery wasn't mine. So I'd play the *I'm a famous baseball player* card if it meant diverting his attention from Avery.

"Yup."

"Tonight, he's just Mario." Avery giggled next to the dude.

I rolled my eyes and tried my best to give her a look of irritation, but as always, when it came to Avery, it was impossible. Regardless, the guy was giving me his full attention now, just like I hoped.

"Will you sign my shirt?" he asked, his smile a little too wide and his eyes glassy.

This was exactly why I always kept a rose-gold Sharpie or two in my pocket. With a nod, I pulled one out and signed the fabric at the shoulder of his white T-shirt.

The guy spun around and picked up his beer. "Your fastball is fucking amazing, but when you called Wilson a dumbass, the world was with you, man." He lifted a fist for a bump at the same moment Avery's smile fell.

Truthfully, I still believed I was right that day. Tom Wilson needed to learn to listen to his players. But there was no way in hell I'd bump fists with the guy who was bashing Avery's father right in front of her. Hell, I wouldn't put up with people talking shit about him when she wasn't standing there, and I didn't like the guy.

With a step around the idiot, I approached the girl in the pink dress whose shoulders were slumped.

"Have you met Avery *Wilson*?" I asked.

The dude stumbled back, blinking, but he recovered relatively quickly and shot finger guns at us. "Your dad's the shit." With that, he scurried away.

I fought the urge to roll my eyes. Instead, I calmly took a pull off my beer.

Avery tilted her chin up and assessed me, expression guarded. Fuck. Her dad would hang between us if I didn't change the subject immediately. So I went for the first thing that came to mind.

"Can you believe he hit on you when I was standing right here?"

"Why wouldn't he?" She tilted her head. "We're not together."

That statement was like a punch to the gut. Fuck, did she have to sound like she didn't mind the attention from the douche?

"How does he know that?" I was the fucking Mario to her Peach. And I hadn't left her side in the twenty minutes I'd been here. Those seemed like pretty big clues to anyone who was wondering. Even if we really weren't together, like she said.

"Because you aren't giving off the signals." With her lower lip caught between her teeth, she perused the people around us. "See him?" She pointed to a shirtless idiot in a cowboy hat. Her eyes softened as she studied the guy and the woman beside him. "How he hovers?" She tucked a lock of hair behind her ear. "How he's always touching her, even if it's just a brush of his hand?"

No, I didn't see it. I wasn't looking at the cowboy or the girl he was with. No, I was entranced by the woman beside me. The longing in her eyes told me exactly what she wished for.

"And that guy."

I had no idea who she was talking about. There was no way I'd look away from her now. The guy didn't matter. Her words were all I cared about.

"The way he watches her. He's in a room full of people, but by the way he's zoned in on her, it's like he doesn't realize they're not alone."

I brushed my thumb along the soft skin under her chin and tilted it up, forcing those blue eyes to mine.

"Someday, someone will look at you that way," I promised.

It was the truth. She was the type of girl who inspired that kind of devotion. For months, I'd been working hard to *not* look at her that way. Because as enchanting as I found her, she wasn't mine. And I respected her choice to remain single.

She gave me a ghost of a smile. "I hope so." With a sigh, she twisted out of my grasp and brought her beer to her lips. As she did, her lips turned down.

"For someone who helped plan this party, you don't seem like you're having fun."

She dipped her chin and shook her head subtly. "Actually, I'd much rather be home."

Then why the fuck were we here? I would rather be home too.

I set my beer on the island again and gaped at her. "What?"

"I love setting up, planning the costumes. Decorating the ghost tree and making the spooky punch and the pumpkin mule. Even carving the pumpkins and making the food." She eyed all the snacks set out along the counter. "But now that we have to practically yell over the music and people keep bumping into me, I'd rather be handing out candy to trick-or-treaters and watching a movie."

I couldn't agree more. About handing out candy and lounging in front of a movie. I had no interest in all the work it surely took to set all this shit up.

"My building is full of families. We left a bowl out for the kids."

She might shoot me down. Hell, she probably would. But I'd take the shot anyway.

She turned to me and tilted her head back. A lock of hair fell into her eye, and there was no way I could talk myself out of tucking it behind her ear.

"Want to bounce? We could watch a stupid Halloween movie and hand out candy."

Slowly, she took me in, her lips pursed and her expression thoughtful. The delayed response had my heart clenching. I was holding my breath and preparing for disappointment when she finally said, "I'd love that."

I exhaled, instantly hit with a wave of relief. "Then let's go, Blondie."

Me: Photo of Puff and Avery with a plate full of turkey.

Chris: that's messed up

Me: What?

Chris: He's a bird. You can't feed him turkey

Me: Why?

Chris: Because it's like being a cannibal. It's like holding a plate of human meat

Me: ...

Chris: Not quite, but almost

Me: Okay, weirdo. How is Long Island?

Chris: It's okay. Gianna's boyfriend is here. There is something off with him. He's jittery and keeps looking at the clock

Me: maybe he's double-booked like me. I stopped in to see Puff after I left Dad's Thanksgiving dinner. Now I have to eat again at Mom and Dave's.

Chris: Don't feed my puffin any more bird meat. I'm taking the moral high ground here and saying it's not okay to force him into cannibalism

Me: Fine. Puff will stick to fish. Are we still on for movie night on Sunday?

Chris: Wouldn't miss it

Avery
19

DECEMBER

"Come on, Daddy Wilson. Us walking home is not an issue, I promise."

"I have told you repeatedly that you may *not* call me that, Wren." My father leaned back against the counter and crossed his arms over his chest.

"That's right, I switched to Papi Wilson." She pressed her lips together and lifted her dark eyes to the ceiling for a heartbeat. "Doesn't have the same ring to it, though."

My father's response was a glare that made athletes and reporters alike cower.

Wren only chuckled as she dried the last pot that I had washed.

It was Saturday evening during the offseason, and that meant dinner with Dad. Often Wren or Jana came with me, because they got a kick out of torturing him. I was especially thankful for Wren's presence tonight. It made it easier to avoid the topic I was sure my dad was itching to lecture me about. I'd been hanging out with Chris more than he might like. Though he wasn't privy to every detail of my life, he'd heard about the guys' appearance at Wren's party. And other than the night I met Chris, I hadn't hidden any of my run-ins with him from anyone. We still occasionally bumped into each other out and about, where anyone could see us. What Dad didn't know was that we got together for weekly movie nights, or that we texted every day. Or that we'd been having lunch together a couple of times a week when Chris came by to see Puff.

"I don't like the idea of you two wandering around the harbor at night." Dad's frown moved into full-blown scowl territory. "And I know my Avy is going to insist on checking on that damn bird on the way home."

Wren threw her head back and laughed.

With a huff, I pinned my dad with a sharp look I'd been told I inherited from him. "Eventually you'll understand and love that Puff is your first grandson."

"I'm too young to be a grandfather." He pointed at me." "You remember that." He probably was. He was only twenty-one when I was born. And even with all the stress that came along with coaching, his brown hair showed almost no signs of turning gray. He could easily pass for a guy in his late thirties rather than heading toward fifty. "Plus, you told me you weren't dating until you turned thirty."

"No, I didn't." I huffed.

Dad loved my dating hiatus a bit too much.

He shrugged and responded with a smirk. "I definitely remember that conversation."

"Selective hearing, Papi Wilson."

A shudder worked its way through me. "I have to veto that one." I shook my head at Wren. "You sound like you belong on the farm in the 1800s."

"I could get on board with that." Wren leaned on the peninsula of the counter and clasped her hands in front of her. "Especially if it means I get a hot farmer to keep me warm at night. Although with the number of orgasms I'd expect and lack of birth control back then, I'd end up popping out babies like they were breath mints." She snapped her fingers in rapid succession.

"Jesus." Dad dropped his head between his shoulders and shook it.

"Stop torturing Dad." I turned from my bestie to my father. "One thing before we go. Mom and Dave are going to Paris for Christmas."

His blue eyes narrowed, but he kept his mouth closed tight. He was likely holding back a comment for my sake. He didn't love Mom and Dave's free-spirit approach to life. Mostly because, for years, it made co-parenting hard. He'd often had to cancel his plans because they decided to travel at the last minute leaving me with him on his off weekends.

"And I know you have plans for Christmas."

He was taking a trip with his friends to an island somewhere in the Caribbean. Antigua, maybe?

"You can come," he rushed out. "A few of the guys are bringing their families. I'd love to have you. You know that."

I did. He'd invited me four times already.

I sighed. "I *do* know that. But *you* know that I have to work that week. And before you offer to stay home, I will be perfectly fine."

"I don't want you to be alone for the holidays."

"She won't be." Wren scooted around the peninsula and wrapped an arm around my shoulder. "You know I'll have her with me and my parents, Big Papi."

He huffed and crossed his arms over his chest. "That's David Ortiz."

"Oh. Hmm." She shrugged. "Well, I'll find something to call you."

"Mr. Wilson," he suggested for the millionth time.

I bit back a laugh. I knew better than to think that would stop their back-and-forth. My dad wasn't dumb, so he had to realize that too.

"That's what I called you when I was twelve."

"And yet my name hasn't changed."

"But I have." She battered her lashes at him.

I groaned, suddenly feeling like I might throw up. "Please don't flirt with Dad. That's gross."

She slapped the granite countertop with both hands and cackled. Dad just pinched the bridge of his nose and sighed.

"And with that, we're leaving." After I kissed Dad's cheek, I grasped Wren's wrist and pulled her to the foyer.

As we headed out, she called, "Bye, *Mr. Wilson*." With a grin, she pulled the door shut behind us.

I grasped her shoulders over her thick coat and forced her to look at me. "Please don't try to date my dad."

She snorted and mimicked my stance, now cupping my shoulders. "He's entirely too uptight to date me."

I wasn't 100 percent sure of that. "All the same, please don't."

She rolled her eyes along with most of her head, making her bangs dance across her face. "I like messing with him, but my parents would literally send me back to Minnesota and force me to live with family there if I came home and said I was fucking your dad."

I tried not to gag at the idea.

"But I hear what you're saying, and I'll stop if it bugs you."

Then she went right, but I stopped just outside the building and turned toward the harbor.

When she realized I wasn't beside her, she halted and spun to face me. "Aren't you coming?"

I pulled on one glove, then the other. "I'm meeting Chris at the zoo."

She smirked. "Right. Date night."

I tucked my chin into my blue scarf, hiding from wind, and shoved my hands into the pockets of my black pea coat. "We aren't dating. You know that. It's just movie night."

"You can't be friends with a guy who made you come repeatedly. That's not a thing." Batting the hair out of her eyes, she shot me a glare. It had been months, but she was still annoyed with me and my year of solitude.

I pulled my shoulders back. "I can and I am."

"That's insane." She shook her head.

"Then I'm insane." I shrugged. "But I gotta go. Love ya." I gave her an air kiss and took off left as she went right.

I walked quickly the rest of the way to the zoo. Winter had truly set in, and as I pushed through the door into the zoo's quarantine areas, I couldn't have been happier to escape the icy wind coming in from the harbor. I waved to the guy at the security desk and said a quick hi to

Dean, the vet tech on shift for the night, before I headed into the puffin's temporary home.

Chris was crouched behind the large indoor pond, with one of his denim clad knees pressed into a large rock for balance.

"No one thinks it's weird, Pop. For fuck sake, I don't break in. She gave me a set of keys. And they all know me by now. I've signed six hundred autographs for the staff here."

I chuckled. As much as he griped about it, I'd never seen him turn down a request for an autograph. And he never left home without at least two Sharpies in his pocket. Last time, he even had rose gold.

"Hey, guys." I shuffled up behind Chris.

He tipped his head up and frowned in that way he always did. "Tell Pop no one thinks I'm stalking you."

"If anything, they think he's stalking Puff, Mr. Damiano." I crouched beside Chris and was immediately hit with the bourbon and leather scent that never failed to make my stomach flip. I teetered a bit, and Chris wrapped an arm around me to steady me. On the screen of Chris's phone, his father gave me a warm smile.

"I keep telling you to call me Bo."

Chris looked so much like his dad. The only differences were the wrinkles around his dark eyes and the hair that was so peppered with gray it was more white than black.

His dark eyes sparkled behind the thin-rimmed glasses he wore. "I'll let you two enjoy your night. Just wanted to see my grandson. It's been a while."

"Don't call him that. He's a bird," Chris grumbled.

I couldn't help but chuckle at how closely his argument mirrored my dad's.

"It's not funny, Blondie."

"That's where you're wrong, Chris." Bo chuckled. "And if you'd provide me with an actual grandchild, maybe I'd stop referring to your bird as your child."

Chris sighed and shook his head. "Bye, Pop."

His dad just grinned and waved at us both.

When the call had ended, I grinned. "He makes me laugh."

"Me too. Most of the time." Chris helped me to my feet. "Just not when he starts in on the grandkid shit. I'm nowhere near there."

"Don't be too hard on him. You'll be a great dad someday, and I know he sees it."

Chris shrugged. "He always says my sister and I are the best part of his life and he wants me to get to experience the joys and stress of having my own kids."

"My dad says he's too young to be a grandfather."

Chris shook his head. Although he never made negative comments about my dad in my presence, nor did he let anyone around us, I knew that relationship was still strained.

"Puff seems to like the new birds," he said.

So far, we had added six of the nine we'd budgeted for. Two mating pairs and two females.

"Especially the one with the pink band." Chris tipped his chin, gesturing to one of the females.

I assessed the bird in question, then scanned the whole group of them. "We'll see in the spring."

"Still don't love how sad he looks now that all the color has gone from his face." Chris shook his head.

During the winter, puffins didn't look like the cute clowns they were most of the year. The white and orange faded, and their faces were dull shades of gray and black.

"Give it a couple months, and he'll be back to the Puff you know and love."

Chris smirked. "Love is a strong word, Blondie."

"We all know you love him." I bumped his shoulder. "That's how you got a key to this place."

Chris ducked his head and shook it, like I was ridiculous. If asked, he'd no doubt claim that he was given a key only because he was paying for the upkeep of the puffins until they got the foundation set up.

"C'mon." I wandered to where we kept snacks for the birds. We fed them all a few fish, and I had Puff do his new jumping trick for Chris before we headed out.

Once we stepped outside, he grasped my hand and pulled me toward him, away from the main road. "I'm in the parking lot."

"You have a car?"

The heat from his big, warm hand radiated through me, warming me instantly despite the bitter cold. When he loosened his hold, ready to release me, I tightened my grip. I wasn't ready to let go just yet.

He side-eyed me, his lips turning down in the hint of a frown. Was holding hands with a friend weird? Maybe, but he didn't pull away, so I went with it.

"We aren't hoofing it around Boston in the dark and in the dead of winter. Of course I have a car."

Dressed in jeans and Uggs and a thick coat, I was perfectly content. It was cold, sure, and the wind coming off the harbor this time of year was harsh, but I was used to winter. "I walked here from Dad's."

He side-eyed me again, this time working his jaw from side to side. "Next time, text me. I'll pick you up. I hate when you wander around the harbor at night."

I pressed my lips together, fighting a smile. Once again, I was having déjà vu.

He loosened his grip as we approached a black Mercedes that was already running, and this time I let him go. Ducking his head, he opened the passenger door.

I gave him a grateful smile and slid in, relishing the soothing comfort of the already warm leather seat. And I couldn't help but study him as he rounded the hood. His body was hidden beneath a heavy winter coat, but even so, his strength and grace were blatant. He really was gorgeous. And so, so misunderstood.

"Bambi?" Chris called as we stepped inside the apartment fifteen minutes later. He guided me in ahead of him and tossed his keys onto the small table by the door. It hadn't been here the first time I was at Chris's place. I wasn't sure if it was Emerson or Chris, but one of them liked decorating. Every time I came by, there were new pieces of furniture or décor or gorgeous artwork.

The new painting that hung over the table stole all the breath from my lungs. The point of view made it seem as though the artist had painted it while sitting on a boat in the middle of Boston Harbor at sunset. The colors of the city and its buildings were portrayed in a tranquil watercolor. The stadium was there, and so was the zoo, but the details blended together rather than standing out individually.

"This is gorgeous." I gently traced the bronzy frame with a finger.

"My sister," he grunted. "She's talented." Then he shook his head. "But she won't leave her crappy job at a marketing agency because her boyfriend works there."

I'd heard enough about Gianna's boyfriend to know that Chris didn't like the guy, but before I could ask him to elaborate on Gianna's job and her talent, Emerson peeked out from the kitchen wearing his standard big smile.

"I'm so glad we framed that painting."

Chris glowered at him.

Who was I kidding? There was no world in which Chris was the one decorating this apartment.

"What's your plan?" Chris grunted.

"I'm hanging out with you two if that's cool. And I made tripletas." He disappeared through the archway that led to the kitchen.

"Trip-a-what?" I asked as Chris helped me with my coat.

He pulled the closet door open and hung it along with his own. "It's kinda like a Cuban sandwich, but better."

"Sounds delicious, but I ate at Dad's."

"Okay." He tipped his head toward the TV mounted above the gas fireplace. "Go put on a movie, and I'll grab a couple of beers."

I shuffled into the huge living room and dropped onto the cozy leather sectional. "What do you want to watch?" I called out.

"Whatever you want" was Chris's hollered response.

A wooden bin on one of the end tables was labeled *Remotes*. The way the guys kept the place ultra-organized always made me chuckle.

I swiped the TV remote out of the bin and settled back onto the large sofa, tucking my legs under me and covering myself with a fuzzy blanket. With the remote pointed at the TV, I navigated through a selection of movies, waffling over what to choose. We'd done the Halloween-type horror movies during our first movie night, then I'd picked a couple of new releases through November, but it was Christmas, and during this time of year, I usually went for Hallmark rom-coms.

Chris wandered in and set the beers on the table with a *thunk*. One Bud Light and one Easy Out. He always let me choose and never batted an eye at my decision. If I wanted some of each, he was fine with that too. In fact, that was usually the way it went. We'd share them both.

He balanced his plate on his leg briefly and picked up his sandwich, but as the sauce oozed from between the slices of bread, he glowered at it. Huffing, he set it down again and dropped the plate onto the table in front of him.

"Grab some napkins, Bambi," he called over his shoulder.

"Should we go with an action? Or maybe a thriller?" I'd made him watch a holiday romance last time, and I didn't want to bore him to death by choosing another.

Emerson tossed a few napkins over Chris's head, and they floated from the sky like snowflakes and landed in his lap.

"It's like being glittered." The third baseman laughed as he headed back for his food.

Chris huffed a hard breath and shut his eyes. As much as Emerson made me laugh, he made Chris nuts. But he still loved the guy.

"Are there any new action movies out you've been wanting to see?" I asked again, watching Chris as he wiped his hands on a napkin.

"What?" Emerson dropped into the plush chair, his plate and beer in hand, and scooted the coffee table closer to him.

Chris snagged the beers before they tipped. "Careful."

Emerson frowned at the table, then at Chris, clearly not seeing the problem. "Dude, you promised me a small-town romance. That's why I stayed home. For the snow and Christmas magic that'll give me all the tingles."

Chris, who had his sandwich in both hands an inch from his mouth, gaped at his friend. "*Tingles?*"

"Yeah, you know, when the happily ever after is so good you almost cry. The kind that makes your heart tingle." Emerson's smile lit up the dim room as he shimmied in his chair, almost knocking his plate to the floor in the process.

I couldn't help but smile back at him. It was fitting that the man loved a good romance.

Chris, however, glowered and shook his head. "I didn't promise shit. I said you could stay to watch whatever Avery chose. If you don't get your *tingles*, you'll have to deal."

"Aren't you sick of Hallmark movies?" I asked him.

He dropped his sandwich onto his plate and frowned at me as he wiped his hands on the single napkin he had placed over his thigh.

"I don't care what you put on. I don't do this to watch the movie. I do this to be with you. So pick whatever you want."

He dipped his chin, signaling for me to proceed, but I was frozen in place. The words had been gruff, as was Chris's typical demeanor, but the sentiment behind them wrapped tight around my heart and squeezed. With a thick swallow, I reminded myself that we were just friends. Although his comment had been incredibly sweet, he hadn't meant it the way my brain had tried to take it.

Chris, apparently tired of waiting for me to snap back to reality, sighed and took the remote out of my hand. With quick efficiency, he scrolled to the icon of the movie I'd talked about after we had finished *Christmas Wish* last week and clicked it on.

"Yes!" Emerson pumped a fist. "This one is supposed to be the best of the year."

Chris rolled his eyes and dropped the remote to the table.

I, on the other hand, was frozen once again. Because this man had cued up the movie I wanted to watch without a reminder or any prompting.

"What?" he asked, pausing with the sandwich in midair once again.

"Nothing." I swiped the Easy Out off the coffee table, took a sip, and passed it over to him. "I just love movie night."

Christian
20

THE PLACE WAS LIT up with thousands of white lights. And there were almost that many people bustling past me. Small huts had been set up throughout the market, and every fifty yards or so, there were comfy couches and fire pits where patrons could rest or snuggle up with one another. I was trying not to be impressed, but some of the ice sculptures that littered the place made that hard. My sister would love this.

I snapped a couple of pictures and texted them to her.

> Gianna: Someone left their room.

I let out a grunt.

> Me: Wow Chris, that's so cool. Thanks for sending me pictures.

> Gianna: No way you expected me to say that.

Not really. People accused me of being the grouchy one until they met her.

But she was an artist, so although she didn't act impressed, I could almost guarantee that next week, she'd send me a painting of the harbor in all its Christmas market glory. It was her way of saying thanks without the words.

My breath floated in white plumes in front of me as I turned away from an incredible frozen rendering of Rudolph and took in the view of the harbor. It was frigid out here, but the stars were out, glittering in the sky and reflecting on the water, even if they were muted by the city lights.

I'd worn my glasses and had added a beanie to ensure that I didn't have to deal with fans yelling out "Dragon" all night long. That man, the Revs pitcher, was larger than life in Boston, and it sometimes got exhausting having to play the part.

So far today, I had spent a few hours at the stadium for off-season conditioning and had met with Hannah for my mandatory press training, which had thankfully been scaled back to once a week. My cheeks hurt after all the happy faces she forced me to hold while she asked me about my still sucky slider. It was slow going, but I was getting better at being chill. And right now, I felt totally relaxed, even though I wasn't home. That was almost unheard of.

Small town in the big city. That was the way I'd describe my night. This was Boston's biggest Christmas market, so why was I here? Because Avery had asked me to meet her here. That was all it took to get me to leave my apartment. The promise of seeing her tempted me in a way nothing else could. I'd told her I'd pick her up at the zoo, but she'd brushed me off, saying it was unnecessary and that she wanted to walk the block and a half. So here I stood, as close as I could to the zoo while still being in the Christmas market.

I turned away from the harbor and scanned the crowd, catching on a blond ponytail in the sea of people. Resting my elbows on the wrought-iron railing that separated the brick pavers from the harbor, I watched Avery weave her way to me.

When she locked eyes with me, she broke into a smile that warmed me from the inside out.

"Hey, Blondie." Going for unaffected, I gave the curl of her ponytail a small tug.

She stepped up close and patted my chest. "You beat me."

Of course I did. I'd been here for twenty minutes. No way would I make her wait on me. Avery deserved better than standing in the cold, waiting for some guy to show up for her. One of the many things I wanted her to understand implicitly was that a guy worth her time would be the one doing the waiting.

"So." I pushed off the railing and rubbed my gloved hands together. "Where are we going?"

"I'm starving. Let's get vegan grilled cheese from Roxy's and a cup of Chowda's clam chowder to dip them in." She scanned the vendors, her blue eyes bright, and pointed out two food trucks across the market.

I could tease her about the ridiculousness of ordering *vegan* grilled cheese with *seafood* soup, but I'd learned not to question Avery's food choices.

Internally, I was cringing at the idea of eating food made in the back of a vehicle that drove around the city, escaping health department inspections. But I pushed those thoughts aside. I'd been working to overcome my irrational fears, and this was one of them. So instead of complaining, I let her drag me through both lines. I even managed to swallow my objections when she paid for the spiked hot chocolate for us since I'd paid for the meal.

We found an empty table not too far from one of the many fireplaces peppered throughout the market, and once we were settled, I rested an elbow on the whiskey barrel table and watched her.

"Yum." Avery smiled around a bite of sandwich she'd dunked into the soup. "This is the best." She dipped it again, her eyes sparkling like the insane amount of twinkle lights overhead. "Eat quick," she said, pointing at my wrapped sandwich, "before it gets cold."

It was barely twenty degrees. Of course it would get cold. If we were sane, we'd be eating inside. Yet here we were. Instead of the vegan grilled cheese Avery raved about, I'd gone for the Southerner, a pulled pork sandwich with pickles. I had to admit that, questionable food safety procedure aside, it was good.

"You have to try this." She dunked the thick bread into the creamy clam chowder and held it out to me.

It had taken months, but I'd gotten used to Avery and her affinity for sharing food. But when it came to the clam chowder and grilled cheese, an entire host of doubts and concerns jumbled in my mind.

She angled over the table, holding the sandwich out, the puff ball on her blue hat bobbing. As she got closer, I was hit with her sweet scent. As always, that was all it took for my doubt to fade away. So as she held the sandwich closer, I took a quick bite. As I did, my bottom lip brushed against her thumb, sending a tingling sensation through me. I couldn't describe what that damn sandwich tasted like, because all I could think about was her soft skin against my mouth. The feel of her against me. The taste of her on my lips.

In a heartbeat, the past nine months faded into nothing, as if I'd had my hands on her, skimming down the curve of her waist and hooking her leg over my hip, only yesterday.

"See." She beamed, pulling the sandwich back and plopping into her seat again.

Though I wasn't ready to leave the memory behind, I blinked back to the moment.

"It's amazing, right?"

"Truth," I agreed, because the sandwich didn't matter.

She dipped it into the chowder again.

I picked up my own sandwich and rested my elbows on the table. "How did this start?"

"This?" she asked, cocking her head to one side.

"The market. The sandwich and soup dunking. All of it." I expected her to launch into a story about her mother. I'd heard many at this point, and they all included some kind of adventure. New places, new food, new experiences.

But instead of bouncing in her seat and diving into an animated story the way she always did when she talked about her mom, Avery cleared her throat, ducked her head, and swirled her black plastic spoon in her chowder.

The sudden shift in her mood made my heart lurch. What was with the hesitation?

"Dad and I come here every year." Her words were barely a whisper.

Oh.

I'd made a conscious effort to avoid the topic of her father so I wouldn't accidentally hurt her feelings. And it was probably good that I had, because in this moment, my first instinct was to scowl and tell her that I couldn't imagine the man spending even one second in a place that was meant for fun. But I bit my tongue. I wouldn't speak negatively about him in front of her. I'd decided that long ago. So instead, I separated the idea of the asshole I knew from the man *she* loved.

"Does he like grilled cheese and chowder too?"

She snapped her head up and focused her wide eyes on me, searching my face.

I schooled my expression into one that would hopefully convey interest rather than judgment.

She shook her head. "No, but this time of year is when Dad has the most free time." Her attention shifted back to her dinner, and she once again spun the black spoon in her cup of soup. "He always packed as much quality time into November and December as he could. He played for the Revs until I was fifteen and got hired on as an assistant pitching coach that next year. So February through October were controlled by baseball and necessities, like homework and chores. But," she said with a shrug, "November and December?" She scanned the water, wearing a bright smile. "Those were my months. We saw all the sights in Boston and did everything we could. Bolts Hockey games, Isabella Stewart Gardner Museum, the symphony." With her lip caught between her teeth, she focused on me again. "Dad loves the cannoli wars, so he and I wander the city finding the best ones."

Man, the guy sounded like a good dad. Or maybe Avery just brought out the best in people.

"Christmas market has always been one of our things. He likes it and hockey the most, I think. He and I were here on Wednesday night." She met my eyes again, waiting, like she was worried I'd have something negative to say.

I could respond a dozen ways, but only a few of those would be acceptable if I didn't want to wreck what I'd been working so hard to build.

I held her gaze and tilted a little closer, my elbows on the table once more. "So Christmas Markets and hockey, huh?"

"Yeah. They couldn't be more different, but we love them both." That brilliant smile was back, making the twinkle lights dance in her eyes.

"My dad and I bonded over hockey too. He took me to Islanders games all the time."

She let out a scoff, her smile turning into a wicked grin. "You can't be an Islanders fan."

"Nah. I've been a Bolts fan since the Langfield brothers took the ice."

"Nice. Boston sports are the best of the best." Avery took another bite. "We should go to a game."

"That would be fun." Since the Langfields owned both the Revs and the Bolts, getting tickets was as simple as putting in a call to Hannah or anyone else who worked in the Revs' offices.

"Did you play hockey?"

I sighed. "No, I needed to play sports that required less contact. Football, hockey, lacrosse?" I shook my head. "I couldn't handle them. Baseball allows me that bubble of space I need."

She tilted her head and assessed me, but she didn't frown and question me like I kept expecting her to. Avery didn't seem to notice that I was weird. But it was probably time to admit it.

My heart beat a little more forcefully while I wiped my hands on my napkin. Fuck, I hated bringing this up, but my end goal here was a future with her, and that meant opening up. "I don't know if you noticed, but I have a thing about personal space and germs."

A small crease formed between her brows, and she pressed her lips together for a moment, scrutinizing me. "What do you mean?"

I blew out a breath and made the admission. "My mom died of an infection when I was five."

I didn't remember her so much as vague moments with her. But I still remember how afraid I was that I'd catch what she had, or worse, that I'd bring germs home to my dad or my sister. To five-year-old me, the idea that I might be left alone if something happened to them was terrifying.

"Since then, personal space, illnesses, germs, all of it, have been a thing for me. I don't typically like when people touch me. So hockey was out. Players have to be in one another's personal space far too much for me to be comfortable."

She set her spoon down on a napkin and reached out for the hand I rested on the wooden barrel between us. Before she could make contact, though, she pulled back and curled her fingers into a fist. Wearing a frown now, she watched me, her eyes bouncing from my face to my hand and back again. "Do you mind when I touch you?"

I went rigid at the sadness in her tone. The thought that she might not be herself around me anymore because of my confession sat like lead in my stomach. I covered her hand with mine and squeezed.

"No." That single word left me with an intensity that might have been a bit much for the moment, but I had to make sure she believed me.

She flipped her hand so her palm pressed against mine, and I linked our fingers together.

That was all it took for my body to relax again. Fuck. To say I didn't mind her touch was a gross understatement.

"Not at all, Avery."

When this woman touched me, there was no ounce of concern or panic. No, her touch did nothing but settle my soul and fill me with peace, and I had no idea what to do about that.

Christian
21

Me: What do you mean you're alone?

Blondie: I went over to Wren's last night, but today I'm just relaxing at home by myself.

Me: That's dumb. Come over to my place

Blondie: I'm not going to crash your family day.

Me: There's no way I'll let you spend Christmas alone. That's unacceptable. I'll come get you

Blondie: No way. You can't leave your family. They drove all the way from Long Island to see you.

Me: The hell I can't. Either you come over or I'm coming to you

Blondie: Okay. Fine. I'll come.

Christian
22

CHRISTMAS DAY

Once I'd gotten her to agree, I set my phone on the counter. I should have asked her what her plans were the second I found out I'd be in Boston for Christmas, but I assumed she'd spend the day with her family. Friends didn't skip family things to hang out on Christmas. And unfortunately, that's what we still were. But I was counting down the days to March, when her year of not dating would be up.

She was on my doorman's list of send straight up, so I didn't need to let anyone know. Well, that wasn't exactly true. Emerson had gone to his mother's for Christmas, but I did have my father and sister here.

"Avery's coming over," I announced to the open room, where my dad and my sister were playing ping-pong.

Gianna gaped at me, completely missing the plastic ball my dad sent her way. "On Christmas?"

My response was a grunt. I wasn't getting into it with her again. These two had asked about her at least a dozen times since they'd arrived. Maybe because I talked about her too much. Regardless, I'd been clear that she and I were just friends.

"Good. I've been waiting months to meet the girl." My dad smiled. "That's nine points for me. Gi, you've only got three."

Gianna slumped and set the paddle down on the navy-blue ping-pong table.

Emerson and I had picked it up last summer, and for months, he'd made me play almost constantly. Because if there was one thing my roommate wasn't great at, it was relaxing. It came as no surprise to anyone that the bundle of energy I shared the apartment with couldn't sit still to save his life. If he didn't need my help, I'd happily be living on my own. But for as much shit as I gave him, Emerson had grown on me over the years. And I begrudgingly loved the guy.

"Seems unfair that I don't get a handicap, since you and Chris are both the athletes and I'm not."

Dad chuckled and spun his racket. "You asked to play."

"It's better than sitting around and staring at the walls." Leave it to my sister to always have a reason to complain. "And Chris made us come here."

I'd had to make an appearance at Boston General's pediatric ward yesterday, thanks to Hannah, so I couldn't get to New York for the holiday.

My mind-reading father eyed me and cocked a brow. "Don't."

I put both hands in the air. "I didn't say anything, Pop."

"I see it in your eyes." He shook his head as he served and sent the little white ball across the net. "You're blaming the Revs for the hospital trip yesterday."

My sister missed again. She was almost as bad at table tennis as Emerson was.

"Well—"

"No." He pointed his racket at me and frowned. "Had you not acted like the backside of a mule all season, you wouldn't be doing positive publicity in the offseason. Remember that next year."

I sighed and forced my shoulders to relax. He had a point. Since I was still attending her weekly course on not acting like a dick to the media, it made sense that she'd insist I was the one to go. Fun stuff. "Okay, Pop."

My sister dropped the ball onto the table and swung but missed.

"Thank goodness Jake isn't here. He'd have a field day with this. God, I suck."

"You don't." I crossed my arms and reined in the anger that was bubbling up inside me. Her boyfriend needed to go. My sister had amazing talent. Maybe not at ping-pong, but at other things. But her piss-poor attitude and her affinity for guys who made her think she wasn't good enough constantly kept her down.

Her current boyfriend was one of the worst in a long line of douchebags. And I wasn't saying that because I was her brother and no one would be good enough. Honestly probably seventy-five percent of the world would be good enough. Gianna just chose the bottom ten percent every damn time. "Who cares if you're not good at ping-pong? You're designing a logo for the Boston Zoo, for Christ's sake. Be proud of that."

She scoffed. "Yeah, I'm designing it because my brother told them to offer the job to me." It was a dare to admit it.

I met my father's eyes in a plea for help. Anything I said now would upset her. Because yes, of course I suggested Gianna. But not because she was my sister. I threw her name in the hat for the zoo's logo because she was an incredible graphic designer. All I'd done was make a suggestion. The people in charge had chosen her based on talent, not on her connection to me. However, she wouldn't hear that. Not from me.

"So you invited a girl over to meet the family on Christmas, huh?" My dad was saving me from this train wreck while simultaneously throwing me to the wolves.

"Her parents are away." Though I wanted to rage over the notion that her entire family had left her during the holidays, I realized that it wasn't as simple as blaming Tom Wilson for being a jerk.

Since the day at the Christmas market, she'd begun talking about her dad more. I wanted her to feel comfortable telling me anything, and if that meant gushing about her dad, then so be it. And honestly, from the stories she told, Tom seemed a lot like my own dad. Just treading water as a single parent who figured things out as he went. And it was clear he'd done a damn good job. Avery was amazing, and knowing that he'd been her primary parent more often than not, I had to give him some credit for that.

Both my sister and my father were waiting for me to say more, but I just shrugged.

"What did you get her for Christmas?" My sister's question was pure challenge, but I wasn't taking the bait. I'd put a lot of time and effort into picking out the right gift for Avery. But if I told Gianna what I'd done, she'd make too much of it. Even if she'd unwittingly helped with it.

The sound of the doorbell was music to my ears. Thank fuck Avery had saved me from talking my way out of answering my sister's question. A little too eagerly, I spun and hurried to the door.

Avery stood on the other side, dressed in UGG boots, leggings, and her black puffy coat. She took me in from head to toe. "Am I underdressed?"

I gave her the same kind of perusal, my heart practically beating out of my chest. She looked perfect to me.

"We're in sweats, Avery. Chris dressed up to impress you," my dad called.

Pinching the bridge of my nose, I sighed. My dad and Gianna were sure to spend the rest of the day embarrassing the hell out of me.

"I've been dressed like this for hours," I muttered.

And since when did wearing a pair of jeans and a three-quarter zip on Christmas qualify as overdressed?

Shaking off the urge to snap back at my dad, I pulled Avery in for a hug. And I may have buried my nose in her soft blond hair and inhaled deeply as I did. Her sweet scent was quickly becoming my favorite.

She melted into my hold.

"Merry Christmas," I whispered and pressed my lips to the side of her head.

"Merry Christmas." She pulled back and beamed up at me.

Fuck, I was glad she was here.

As she unzipped her coat, I circled her so I could help her out of it. Once it was hung up in the closet, we headed to the living area to join my family.

"You got a tree!"

For weeks, she'd been giving me a hard time for not having one, but until four days ago, when Hannah insisted I visit the hospital, my plan had been to go home to Long Island for Christmas. So I didn't need one. Once I'd made plans with my family to come here instead, I'd gone on the hunt for a tree and ornaments.

"Can't not have one." I smirked.

She put her hands on her hips and huffed. "I've been telling you that for a month."

"Turns out you were right."

Not that mine could compare to hers. The tree in her apartment was full of history. It was loaded with ornaments she'd been collecting her whole life. It told a story. Mine? Three days ago, I picked up the last pathetic fake tree Walmart had and a couple of boxes of bulbs and threw it up.

"Come on." I shuffled deeper into the living room and waved at her to follow.

"Pop, Gi, this is Avery."

"You're adorable." My sister's ability to make those two words sound like criticism was impeccable.

Though I hated being too hard on her. She had her own issues. I couldn't count how many times I'd told Gi that she didn't have to be tiny and blond for guys to like her. And then I introduced her to Avery, who was the human embodiment of everything Gi envied. It had to hurt.

But my interest in Avery went so much deeper than her looks.

"Ha! Thanks. I spend most of my time covered in stray feathers and bird droppings, so I don't get that a lot," Avery chirped, holding a hand out to my dad. Her eyes went comically wide as he stepped up and slid his palm against hers. "Just at work. Not today. No poop today, so no worries." The moment the word vomit ceased, she winced, and a flush crept up her neck and spread across her cheeks.

I could watch this woman all day and never get bored. Her smiles and her frowns. Every one of her expressions was intriguing to me.

My dad chuckled. "I wasn't worried. And I appreciate the dedication. You're taking such good care of my grandson."

"Oh man." Avery laughed, slapping a hand to her chest. "Has he finally stopped complaining when you refer to Puff as his son?" she teased, elbowing me in the ribs. "He still gives me crap when I call him Puff Daddy's daddy."

"Who names a bird Puff Daddy?" Gianna scowled.

"I said the same thing." Avery giggled. "But it grew on me."

My sister tilted her head and cocked a brow in challenge. "Kinda like my brother?"

Avery assessed me, her eyes as soft as her expression. "Chris doesn't get enough credit. He wants most people to leave him alone, but he's a *really* good guy."

I clenched my hands at my sides to keep from rubbing my chest, because as she gave me a sweet smile, my heart, which normally didn't give much of a shit, exploded in my chest.

Avery
23

I FANNED my cards out and surveyed them again. Supposedly, aces were definite tricks, but I wasn't sure I understood any other aspect of the game. It all seemed like a gray area.

"Um, one?"

Chris rolled his lips between his teeth, fighting a smile. That no doubt meant I was underbidding *again*.

"Spades is confusing, isn't it?" Gianna said from where she sat beside me on the sofa.

I was glad I wasn't the only one who thought so. Both men at the table obviously didn't agree. They acted like the rules were as simple as Go Fish.

"Nah. And you're getting better, Avery," Bo encouraged.

It baffled me that this man had raised Chris and Gianna. From what I'd gleaned through the phone calls I'd overheard between him and his son over the months and our time today, he was a cheerleader through and through. His kids, on the other hand, sure knew how to make the glass seem half-empty.

"Yeah, last time was awful." She shook her head at her father.

"It's my favorite game. Don't knock it," Chris huffed from where he was positioned on the floor across from me. "Thanksgiving was only bad because we split the teams wrong."

Gianna nodded and tucked her long, gorgeous hair over her shoulder. She was the epitome of everything high school Avery had wanted to be. Her thick, shiny hair had been blown out and hung in loose curls. Every time I tried to style my hair in a similar way, I got the curling iron stuck. Her dark eyes were big and depthless, and her lashes were impossibly long. When she smiled, which I'd only witnessed twice so far, it practically knocked me over. She was just so *pretty*. And though I was hesitant to admit it even to myself, there was a time when I would have paid money for the kind of cleavage she sported. Chris said she was never without a boyfriend, and now I could see why. I had no doubt there was a line of guys just waiting for her to give them the time of day.

"The two of you ganged up on Jake and me at Thanksgiving. You should have known you'd crush us."

"Your boyfriend insisted on that." Chris scowled at her.

She glared right back with just as much intensity. I tried not to smirk, but it was nearly impossible. This grumpy dynamic was wildly entertaining. Honestly, it was shocking, but Gianna might have Chris beat in the cranky department.

"It helps that since you've teamed up with Avery, you've miraculously developed the patience of Job."

"Children." Bo chuckled, setting his cards on the coffee table. "I'm supposed to be working on keeping my blood pressure down. Why don't you help me out and quit all the fighting?"

Gianna rolled her eyes. "Sure. Just as soon as you quit smoking."

"What?" Chris tossed his cards down and straightened, suddenly rigid. "Pop, you said you quit."

"I did. Mostly. I just sneak one now and again. My blood pressure is fine since I switched meds. Forget I mentioned it." He angled to one side and patted Chris's forearm.

Chris had pushed the sleeves of his gray quarter zip up to his elbows, so as he scrutinized his dad, all tense and broody, the corded muscles in his forearms went taut. Between that and the tan skin on display, I felt a little overheated. One of the downsides of being friends with Chris—and honestly, it was probably the only downside—was that he was so freaking hot. It almost wasn't fair.

With a long breath out, I forced the thought from my head and averted my gaze. This time, I focused on Chris's face.

The worry there was evident as he watched his dad. "It better be. We need you around for another fifty years, at least."

Bo scoffed. "Yup, we all live to 115 nowadays, right?"

"Exactly." Gianna almost smiled.

Bo shook his head, but he couldn't hide the smile overtaking him. It was clear how much he adored his kids, and though they were both a bit prickly, the feeling was obviously more than mutual.

"You bid two." Behind his thin glasses, his eyes shifted to his daughter. "And you said one." He nodded at me. "I'll go four—"

"Seven," Chris said before his dad could finish.

Gianna dropped her cards onto the sofa next to her with a growl. "There is no way you have seven."

Chris smirked. "Nope. But there is no way in hell Avery has one either."

I winced. I was worried I would overbid, so I'd developed a bad habit of underbidding.

Bo patted my knee. "It's teamwork."

"Yeah." Chris sent me a grin. "You and me, Blondie, we make a good team."

And apparently, we did, because after two more hands, we won the game.

"That, my friends, is our trick." Chris dropped a spade onto the table, officially putting us over the one hundred mark. Popping up from his spot on the floor, he bounced to a beat only he could hear.

God, he was cute. I never would have expected my broody friend to get up and do an adorable victory dance after winning a card game.

"Nothing like gloating to show how much your sportsmanship has improved lately." Gianna rolled her eyes.

Chris stopped his celebration and mussed her hair.

"Stop it." She swatted at his arm, and with a huff, sank back into the couch, smoothing out her locks.

"You two are going to make Avery think you were raised by wolves." Bo chuckled, raising a brow at his son. "Don't gloat."

"I'm not playing again." Gianna stuck her tongue out at Chris, who chuckled darkly.

Bo turned to her. "Or pout."

"I should probably go anyway. It's getting late." We'd spent the evening eating incredible food and playing ping-pong and cards. I'd had no intention of infringing on so much of their family time, but the hours had flown, and suddenly, it was almost nine.

"I'll walk you home." Chris stepped around the table and held a hand out to me. With a smile, I slid my palm against his. I had to fight the shiver that raced up my arm as his warm fingers enveloped mine. He pulled me to my feet gently, but I stumbled anyway and brushed against him before righting myself. Even after a full day, he still smelled like warm bourbon, and God, did I have to fight a groan when he was this close.

I swallowed and shook my head, grasping for clarity. "No, you shouldn't leave your family. I'll be fine on my own."

"Please." Gianna snorted. "We could use a break from him."

Chris frowned at his sister, but he didn't give up. After a round of goodbyes, he pulled me toward the door. Instead of pulling my coat from the closet, he turned and propped himself up against the closed door, watching me. "I have something for you."

My heart skipped. "I have something for you too." I felt silly buying him a gift. He made enough money to purchase anything he wanted, and we were only friends, but I couldn't let Christmas go by without giving him something.

"Oh yeah?" He cocked one brow and hit me with a smirk that made my stomach tumble. His smiles were small and infrequent, but they almost knocked me over every time.

"It's still under the tree at home. I didn't want you to feel weird, so I didn't bring it." Ducking my head, I scuffed my UGG on the tile floor. "I figured I'd give it to you at our next movie night or when you came in to see Puff."

"Why don't we go back to your place, then?" He stood up straight again and hovered over me until I finally looked up and met his eye. Then he pulled out my coat. While I slipped it on, he disappeared, and when he returned, he was carrying what looked like a clothing box wrapped by a five-year-old. He'd thrown on a gray beanie and his coat too.

"Ready?" He pulled the door open and held out his hand. I stepped out first, and then we headed down the street. Snow was piled up along the sidewalks, but the sky was clear. And although it was freezing, the wind wasn't bad.

Halfway to my place, he came to an abrupt stop and tipped his chin toward the bar where we met back in March. "I can't believe it's been almost ten months already."

Standing beside him with my hands stuffed into my pockets, I took the place in. The big windows that faced the street were dark tonight, but from here, I could still see the high-top table where we stood that night.

My chest squeezed tight at the memory. It didn't seem like it had been that long since I met this man. And yet it seemed like it had been forever. Most days, the time before I met Chris felt like a lifetime ago. When I'd made the pact with myself not to date for a year, I secretly thought I'd give up quickly. But I'd stuck with it, and the months had honestly gone so fast. In the beginning, I wondered if I'd feel like I was missing out on life, but my life felt full and perfect. And in just over two months, my dating hiatus would be over, and hopefully, I'd make better choices now that I didn't feel so desperate to be in a relationship.

I turned and took Chris in. What would that mean for us?

He was watching me too, his teeth pressed into his full lip, his expression warm and cautious. That tumble my stomach had been taking more and more often happened again.

A gust of wind blew my hair into my face, and before I could get it under control, he used a finger to push it aside. He brushed my cheek, and I forgot to breathe. His brown eyes met mine and held. He radiated warmth, not only physically, but in his gaze. Cupping my cheek with that same hand, he stepped closer.

For one second, I thought maybe he'd lean down and press his lips into mine. And in that moment, it hit me—I wanted it. Badly. I angled closer, silently begging him to do the same.

"You're freezing," he whispered, tucking my gift under his arm.

I stumbled back a little, my heart sinking, but he steadied me. Once

THE FALL OUT 129

I had both feet flat on the ground again, he pulled the gray hat off his head and settled it on mine.

"Come on." He draped an arm over my shoulder and dragged me to his side. Then he pulled me down the sidewalk toward my apartment building.

I was warm and wrapped in the deep woodsy spice of his cologne, but disappointment lingered. As much as I enjoyed this, and him, I wondered if maybe I wanted more. Did I?

It had been good to focus on me and not some guy for the last few months. I'd wanted this time. Right?

"Hey, Tim."

Startled, I practically jumped out of my skin. We'd been walking in silence, but as we approached my building, Chris tipped his chin to the man bundled up in a thick coat and a hat who stood at the glass doors to the lobby.

"Dragon." My doorman, who'd quickly gotten used to Revs players dropping by, pulled the door open for us.

Chris put his hand on my lower back and guided me inside and into the elevator. My apartment was half the size of Chris's, and though I didn't have a view of the harbor, I loved it.

In the corner of the living room, my lit Christmas tree greeted us. While Chris's tree was neatly decorated with gold balls and white lights, mine was a chaotic mix of ornaments from places I'd been and ornaments my parents had given me throughout the years. The lights changed color every few seconds because it was impossible to choose just one.

Our trees were surprisingly representative of the differences between us. But I liked the contrast. Did he?

As always, he helped me with my coat. I hadn't thought much of the gesture before now, but as he slid my puffy jacket onto a hanger, then draped his much bigger black coat over it, warmth spread through me, and a pleasant buzz started, like I'd had a beer or two and was feeling relaxed.

"You okay?" He frowned at me in concern.

Probably because I was standing in the middle of my small entryway, staring at him like I was shocked he was here.

Good golly, we were friends, and he was here all the time. Why was I acting weird?

"I'm good." With a shake of my head, I moved to the tree and picked up the bag I'd put under it for him.

When I turned around, he was already settled on the couch with one arm slung over the back and my gift on the cushion beside him.

He chuckled. "How did you find a Christmas bag with Puff on it?"

"Oh, I'll never give away my secrets," I joked, dropping onto the couch and holding it out to him. But Amazon made it stupidly easy. One search for a puffin gift bag, and I had my pick of twelve.

With a roll of his eyes, he snagged it from my hands. Then he was pulling the red tissue out of the bag like he was a kid again. When he peered inside, his brows pulled low. "What...?" He lifted the white tablet out and looked at me, wearing a confused frown.

"Turn it on," I prompted with a nod.

Chris set the bag on the floor by his feet. Then he pushed the button. It lit up, and there on the screen was a live feed of the habitat in quarantine that currently housed Boston Zoo's ten puffins. It would be their home until next month, when the addition to the penguin area would be complete.

His lips parted, and a harsh breath escaped him. "So I can watch him from wherever."

"Maybe it's dumb." I picked at an invisible speck on my leggings, suddenly rethinking my gift idea.

I had a couple of these devices so I could check on the animals remotely when I had concerns. And Chris had been complaining about not seeing Puff as much as he'd like. Once the season started, it would only get harder for him.

Chris was still staring at the screen as Puff walked along the rock and half jumped, half fell into the water.

He broke out into a smile bigger than I thought he was capable of, and my heart almost leaped right out of my chest.

"It's not dumb at all. I love it." He squeezed my leg, and a zap of electricity coursed through me. "Look. He's doing that swim flip thing he loves."

Finally, he tore his attention from the screen and propped it on the coffee table in front of us.

Sliding his gift off the couch, he let out a low hum. "I didn't even think about finding a cool bag like yours. And honestly, it looked better when I first wrapped it." Frowning, he took in the uneven side, the crinkled red and white paper, and the weird corner, like he was noticing it for the first time. Then he held it out to me. "Hopefully it's the thought that counts."

I took it from him, immediately noticing that it was too heavy to be clothes, even though the box was the right size. For a minute, I thought it might be his jersey. He'd teased me endlessly about wearing a jersey that was older than most people's cars. But it was Dad's, so I wasn't getting rid of it.

Inside the box sat two small bundles wrapped in white tissue, along with a larger one.

"Do this one first." He pointed to one of the smaller gifts and hit me with a grin that made my core flare with heat and throb in a way I'd never experienced before.

Was it the red lights of the Christmas tree, or had the man always been this freaking hot? He ran his hand over his chiseled jaw as he studied me, which I'd discovered months ago meant he was nervous. Did he feel the electricity humming between us tonight too?

When I still hadn't moved, he lifted the squarish gift, and when he placed it in my palm and our fingers brushed, the tingling throb quickened. Our eyes met, and for a split second, I swore desire burned in those deep brown irises. Before I could confirm it, though, he dropped his focus to the bundle in my hand and cleared his throat.

"Are you afraid to open it, Blondie?" he asked, his tone teasing and his expression once again full of tempered contentment like it had been all day. Maybe I was reading too much into this.

Swallowing down the butterflies still swarming, I pulled the tissue back. Inside was a white porcelain oval. Chris flipped it over and set it in my hands again. And when he pulled back, I was looking at a scene from the Christmas market. The ornament had been painted with renderings of Roxy's food truck and the Chowda stand. The hut where we'd ordered spiked cocoa was there too, and so was the fireplace we'd sat near to stay warm.

"How?" When I looked up, he was fixated on my face and wearing the smallest smile.

"I sent my sister a picture that night, and she painted this." He swallowed thickly, the move drawing my attention to the column of his throat.

Memories of the way he shuddered when my lips pressed on his pulse washed over me, making my core heat once again. He was still watching me, his focus intense and full of what I swore was interest. My heart sped up as I studied him.

"I had it put on an ornament, because as much as you love the market, it should be on your tree." He turned to the tree then, breaking our connection.

"Thank you." I pushed away the nervousness that had taken over tonight and took a deep breath to center myself. Then I opened the next present. This bundle was the smallest of the three, and it was featherlight. I unrolled the tissue carefully, and a small silver charm landed in my palm.

When the details came into focus, my throat closed up, and all I could do was stare.

After a long moment, he cleared his throat. "I won't let Puff leave Boston, but he deserves a spot on your bracelet anyway." His tone was light, like he was joking, but that didn't take away from his thought-fulness.

I lowered my head and blinked several times to stop my eyes from welling with tears.

He gently plucked the small silver bird out of my hand. "The guy at the store said it would be easy to get on." He studied the small clasp, then eyed my wrist. "He left it open enough. Can I try?"

When he brushed his callused fingers over my arm, a shiver worked its way through me. With my arm held aloft, he attached the puffin charm, then examined his work, his breath dancing over my skin and causing another round of shivers. He tightened the ring clamp locking the silver bird on, and pulled back, but he didn't let go of me.

"That should work, but if it doesn't stay tight, he said I could bring it in to have it soldered on."

By the time he released me, my heart was running a marathon in my chest, and I was at risk of passing out from a lack of oxygen.

"The last gift," he said, "is more for a laugh, but it comes with a second part. Hannah's been holding on to it all day, and she might lose her mind if I don't let her post it to the Revs' account before the night is over."

That statement piqued my curiosity. Chris rarely had positive things to say about Hannah unless Puff was involved. Most of their interactions had to deal with press etiquette, and in that respect, she still drove him crazy. The rectangle left in the box looked like it could be a picture frame. Maybe it was a mockup of the logo for the new puffin exhibit.

He pulled out his phone and sent off a message.

Hit with another wave of anticipation, I tore through the tissue quickly, and at the sight that greeted me, I coughed out a laugh.

It was a framed photo of Chris and Puff. Puff stood on a tabletop, and Chris, dressed in his Revs jersey, rested one arm next to the small bird and one behind him. The Santa hats they were both sporting were what made the photo. Puff's was embroidered with his name, while Chris's said *Daddy*.

Clutching the photo to my chest, I threw my head back and laughed far too loudly for almost ten p.m.

"Yeah, yeah. I knew you'd love that." Chris shook his head. "But here." He held out his phone.

I took it, trying to ignore the tingles that once again shot through me when our fingers brushed. On the screen was an Instagram post from the Boston Revs. The photo was identical to the one now on my lap, and it was accompanied by a caption.

Merry Christmas from all of us at Lang Field, especially Puff and Dragon. The two of them together are some kind of magic. To honor Boston's new favorite bird and the avian community around the world, we've set up Blondie's Birds, an organization dedicated to supporting the Boston Zoo's bird exhibits. Check out our website or Christian Damiano's bio for more information.

By the time I'd finished reading, I could barely see the words past the tears that had welled in my eyes. Swallowing the lump in my throat, I looked up at Chris.

He was wearing the softest smile. "I hate how sad it makes you when you can't keep your birds. This way, although you may not get to add many more charms to your bracelet, the zoo will have plenty of room to house them."

The tears finally crested my lashes as my heart exploded in my chest. "Thank you," I choked out.

"Smile," he whispered, gathering me up in a hug. "I like it better." As if he really couldn't stand it, he tickled my side lightly, causing me to giggle.

"You're just so damn sweet." I pulled back and whacked his chest. "My video feed seems totally lame now."

"Hey." He grabbed his tablet and clutched it to his chest. "Don't knock my favorite gift."

I rolled my eyes, then focused on the photo he'd given me again. My smile was back. It was impossible not to feel happy when looking at Chris and Puff in matching Santa hats.

Chris shifted on the couch beside me. "I should probably get going."

It was late, and there was no reason for him to stay, but my heart plummeted anyway. As much as I wanted him to stay, I had no good reason to ask him to. Plus, his family was in town, and they were probably waiting for him. After a long moment where we watched one another but neither of us spoke, he stood and went for his coat. I was frozen to the spot, unable to tear my eyes off the picture of Puff and his daddy.

Then he was beside me again. "Merry Christmas, Avery." He leaned down and kissed my cheek before stepping back.

I forced myself to my feet and walked him out. Once he was headed down the hall, I shut the door and wandered back to where I'd left my gifts. The white of the ornament contrasted with the brown tweed of my sofa, drawing my attention again. Gingerly, I lifted it by the loop through the top and inspected it again.

I took in the food trucks and the fireplace and even the wooden barrel table like the one we'd sat at. This time, my focus snagged on a new detail. One of the ice sculptures Gianna had painted was familiar. It was a pair of birds off to the side. They were woven together like the image Chris had drawn on my wrist months ago. My heart skipped as I realized I might be in trouble.

Because I might be falling hard for the guy who was supposed to just be my friend.

Avery

24

NEW YEAR'S *Eve*

"How do we get in?" Jana asked as we made our way down the tunnel under the stadium to an area that connected the hockey arena to the baseball field.

Even with Wren in bright red, it was Jana who stood out. Just the way she liked it. The dullness of the half-lit space did nothing to stop the sparkle of her gold sequined dress.

"Yeah, do we need a password or a special knock?" Wren's eyes lit up at the idea, like we were entering the CIA's headquarters or something.

"It's not a secret society. It's a bar where the Bolts and Revs players can chill without being hounded by crazy fans and media."

They'd be disappointed when they found out all we had to do was give them our names, since Chris had already told them we were coming.

"If we see Brooks Langfield, I can't promise I won't fangirl all over that gorgeous man." Jana shimmied her deep auburn curls as she spun in a circle, practically dancing down the corridor.

"Saint" Brooks Langfield was the Bolts' goalie and considered the good boy of hockey. He also appeared on billboards all over Boston in nothing but his underwear. And yeah, he was gorgeous. There was no denying it.

"Don't make me regret asking you two to come with me."

According to Chris, the teams had planned a New Year's Eve event down here in the hopes that the players could remain under the radar after yet another PR disaster last month. Between rumors of the team owner hating kids, Chris's blowups, and the scene with Puff, it had been a rough year. And there had been drama with a trainer and Bolts player not long ago as well. The PR team was probably in dire need of a peaceful spell.

Wren looped an arm around my waist and rested her head against mine. The heels I'd slipped into tonight made me almost as tall as her.

"No way you weren't bringing your besties to the players' New Year's Eve party. What would you do without us?"

"Not wear this." I glanced down at my impossibly tight silvery-purple dress, still sure it was too much.

"Why? Because you're afraid this dress will prove us right?" Jana spun to face us and walked backward down the concrete hall, her four-inch sparkling heels clicking with every step.

"The man started a charity for your birds and named it after you." Wren sent me a side-eye. "He stays in on Saturday nights to watch movies with you. And he pretty much adopted a bird you adore. He is so far gone, and you don't even see it."

I shook my head, causing my ponytail to slip over my shoulder. "Please stop pushing this." I hadn't mentioned my mixed emotions about Chris to them. If I did, they'd be relentless. Getting them to shut up about him was hard enough already.

"Personally, I think this dress will resolve any issues. When you walk in, Chris will fall out of his chair. He'll spend hours growling at anyone who comes near you. And then, finally, at midnight, he'll kiss you, and you two can live happily ever after." She threw her arms out and twirled.

"Sounds like a fairy tale."

If that were the case, then they were the Cinderellas tonight, with perfect hair and big smokey eyes. But I was just me, only in a tight dress. In reality, I'd done more work on Halloween to play the part of Princess Peach than I had done getting ready tonight. But I kept my mouth shut. I had no interest in bringing my friends down.

"And if we're shooting for fairy tales," I said, "then we need to find princes for the both of you."

"I don't know about a prince, but I'll take a hockey star." Jana laughed.

As we turned another corner, two men appeared out of nowhere, and the three of us stumbled to a stop. The taller one scanned us, then zeroed in on me. "Avery?"

I nodded, wondering if I really was supposed to give some kind of code word.

But then the other guy turned to the wall and pulled open a hidden door.

"And you said it wasn't the bat cave." Wren smirked at me, clutching my arm.

Okay, the wall thing was cool. Now that I knew where it was, it was clearly a door made to blend in with the cinderblock wall, but if these guys hadn't been standing here, I totally would have walked by. Which was probably the point.

The three of us stepped inside, only to find another hall, though this one was much smaller. After only a few feet, thought, the space opened up, and we stepped into a bar that looked like a sports hall of fame. The place was covered with black-and-white photos of the Revs and Bolts over the years. Towels and flags and bobbleheads in the likeness of dozens of athletes decorated the space. A dozen signed jerseys hung on the walls. The place definitely bled Boston blue.

"Wow," Jana said, her mouth ajar as she surveyed the many athletes that dotted the room.

"Jerseys are nothing compared to dress pants on these guys," Wren whispered.

"Ladies." Kyle Bosco slung an arm over Jana's shoulder, his silver button-down almost clashing with her gold dress. "Dragon said you were coming." He pecked Jana's cheek, then Wren's. Then he took a step back and tipped his chin at me. "You all look stunning, as always."

"Damn, bebé," Emerson called, heading our way. His attention was 100 percent homed in on Wren. His green eyes popped against his black-on-black suit. "You and the red." He splayed a hand over his heart. "Gonna kill a man."

"That's the idea." She laughed.

"Drinks?" Kyle nodded and herded my friends closer to the bar.

I took two steps away, moving farther into the somewhat crowded space, but I didn't see Chris. Every guy in here was bigger than the next, and though I was in heels, it was hard to see around them.

The younger Langfield brothers, Brooks and Aiden, sat in a corner booth with glasses of what looked like whiskey on the table in front of them. Brooks was wearing a frown and staring at something on the far side of the room.

I followed his line of sight, only to discover a blond tucked into a corner with Chris. Before I could get it under control, my heart lurched in my chest. They were both angled in and deep in conversation. After a moment where my body seemed to deflate, I realized I was watching them like Brooks had been, and I was probably wearing a similar expression, so I forced myself to look away.

Chris's friend Mason caught my eye and tipped his glass my way, but a heartbeat later, he turned his attention back to the brunette standing in front of him.

I stood where I was, feeling awkward and unsure of where to go. I didn't know the hockey guys, and my friends were already deep in conversation with Kyle and Emerson at the bar, no doubt assuming Chris had already appeared to keep me company.

Wringing my hands, I shifted on my black heels and forced myself not to look at Chris and the blond again.

"I'm *aboot* to tell you something no one should ever see." The voice that broke through my mildly panicked thoughts was deep and tinted with a mild Canadian accent.

Pressing my lips together, I turned toward it. I had to tip my head back to make eye contact with Tyler "War" Warren, the biggest right winger in the NHL. He was also the fiercest and most popular with the females of North America.

"What?" I frowned at him.

War's dark hair and blue eyes were a striking contrast to his white button down. "A beautiful woman standing by herself without a drink." He hit me with a wolfish smile. "How about we fix that situation?" He pressed one huge hand to my lower back and applied light pressure.

I allowed him to guide me to the bar, torn between thrilled and disappointed when his hulking frame completely blocked my view of Chris and the blond.

He rested his tattoo-covered forearms on the wooden bar top and lowered his head. "What would you like?"

With those four simple words, I was smacked in the face with memory after memory of the turmoil and uncertainty that came along with the dating game I'd walked away from so many months ago. The pit that had always formed in my stomach as I tried to ascertain what the person I was chatting with was looking for. Whether there was a spark of chemistry or hints of compatibility.

I pushed the doubt aside. Tonight wasn't about impressing a man or acting in a way that was expected of me. Most of the women here were probably drinking wine or champagne. A quick scan of the room proved that to be true. But I was determined to continue being true to myself. I was done with trying to force myself into the mold of what a good-looking man might want.

"Light beer?"

War gave me a nod, then turned to flag down the bartender. While he waited, he roughed a hand along his smooth jaw and surveyed the other people nearby. While he was focused on them, I studied him. Objectively, he was good-looking, and his accent was hot. But there wasn't a single spark of attraction between us.

"Can I get a Coors Light and Tanqueray and tonic?"

When the bartender set our drinks in front of him, he slid the bottle of beer to me and dropped one elbow to the bar.

"It's rare to see a woman here by herself." He cocked a dark brow.

That was probably true, since this place was invite-only. I shrugged and pointed to Jana and Wren. "A friend invited a few of us."

War leaned back and regarded my friends. As he shifted, I got another glimpse of Chris. When the woman grasped his arm. I averted my gaze and picked at the silver label on my bottle. My chest burned, and so did my eyes, but I blinked back the sensation. The warnings I'd been given about maintaining a friendship with a man I'd slept with raced through my head. For months, my friends had claimed that jealousy would get one of us eventually. It hadn't been an issue before. I had to stop making it one now.

"He seems busy, though, so I don't think I'll stay long." That was probably the best solution. As long as I didn't have to watch him flirt with someone else, it would be fine.

War took a sip of his drink, eyeing me the whole time, then set it next to mine. "Why go?"

"As much as my friends love hanging out with all of you guys and that excitement." I waved a hand around. "I'm taking some time off from this kind of thing."

"Hmm." He lifted his chin, all confidence, like he had my number. "Because you like playing hard to get?"

I spun my bottle of beer on the bar top, frowning. "Very much the opposite. I was way too eager for way too long."

He chuckled. "You're kind of adorable."

"You're kind of big and intimidating."

Christian
25

"ARE WE DONE?" I asked the woman standing in front of me for what felt like the fourteenth time.

Sara Case was the Hannah of the Boston Bolts. There were a few differences between the two, though. For starters, Sara was blond. And unlike Hannah, she didn't let go until she got her way. And apparently, today, she'd set her sights on convincing me to appear on a morning show to talk about the bird project. And she would *not* take no for an answer.

"You started this project, and now you have to market it." Sara held a hand out. "And don't try to tell me it's Avery's project. You didn't even ask her before you set it up."

She was right. But I'd done it because I wanted her to keep her birds. And I wanted to make her smile. That was it. I figured we'd get donations, though I never expected the success we'd had. And I figured the PR team could handle the nitty-gritty details and leave me out of it. But now I'd been forced into dealing with the intricacies that came along with the foundation, as well as the publicity.

"I get that," I growled.

"So can I tell them yes?" She angled in closer and cocked a brow.

Movement in my periphery caught my attention. Wren, wearing a bright red dress, was slipping into a booth with Emerson and a few of the other guys. That meant Avery was finally here. I tapped my wrist twice, reminding myself of what was important.

"Fine," I huffed. At this point, I'd say just about anything to end this conversation so I could find Avery.

With a grin, she clutched my arm, only pushing me closer to the edge.

I glared at her, then glared at where her hand rested against my skin, fighting the urge to shudder.

"Sorry." She yanked her hand back. "I forget you don't like that."

I looked over her head. That wasn't the only reason I didn't want her hands on me. There was a very large Langfield in a corner booth who was about ready to break my nose. And there was no way in hell that her patting my arm was worth that kind of pain.

"Are we done?" Because I was itching to find Avery. Just being in her proximity would settle me. The only reason I came out tonight was because I thought she and her friends would like it here. They could hang out with the guys and have a few drinks, and I'd get to spend the evening with her.

"Yes." She nodded. "I'll email you the details. And again, *please* unblock Hannah. I don't have the time to be the middleman between you two."

With my jaw clenched tight, I stared at her.

"Well?" she asked, her brows lifted high.

"What? I'm not going to apologize. I'm not sorry for ignoring her. I don't want you people talking to me, and I have to deal with her enough as it is."

Sara's response was to throw her head back and laugh.

Whatever. Finished with the conversation, I stomped across the room to Eddie Martinez, our shortstop, and his wife, who were sitting with Emerson and Wren. I stood over the table, arms crossed, and waited.

Emerson smiled up at me, looking too young to even be allowed in the place. "You okay?"

I ignored him and turned to Wren. "Where is she?"

She leaned forward and peered around me, then lifted her hand and pointed a red nail at the bar.

I spun and scanned the space. When I found her, my shoulders bunched and my hands clenched of their own accord. Because Avery was standing at the bar, chatting with War and Daniel Hall. Hall's nickname, Playboy, fit him perfectly, and War wasn't any better. Both men were known for the time they spent with puck bunnies.

The shiny purple fabric of Avery's dress clung to her every curve. And the way she was leaning on the bar? Fuck. I couldn't decide which I wanted to do more: toss a blanket over her so no one could see her ass looking that incredible or run my hand up her thigh and give one perfect cheek a nice swat. I could almost feel the sting in my palm and envision the way her creamy skin would turn red.

But I wasn't the one she was focused on.

No, she was focused on War, who was smiling down at her as she spoke. And Hall was propped against the bar, checking out her ass.

I squeezed my fists even tighter at my sides and took a step toward them, only to come to a halt when Mason stepped in front of me.

"Hey," he said, leaning to one side, then the other, blocking my view of Avery as I tried to look around him. "Let's not hulk out, okay?"

I gritted my teeth and fought the urge to ram him out of my way with one shoulder and continue my path to the bar.

"You were busy, and they're just talking." Emerson appeared behind me and squeezed my shoulder. "I've been keeping an eye on her. And she's not dating, remember?"

The tight knot in my chest loosened and I unclenched my fists. Fuck. Avery deserved so much more than an idiot who lost his temper all the damn time. I had to be better than that.

I took a breath and let it out slowly, forcing my brain and my heart to calm. "I'm fine."

With a nod, Mason stepped to the side. Emerson gave me another pat on the shoulder, and then they were gone.

I pushed down the last embers of anger and slowly headed toward the bar.

"Nope, my dating sabbatical will last until March. No matter how many times any of you ask." Avery's laugh floated on the air and engulfed me. "I'm 100 percent committed to my timeline."

My shoulders slumped. That admission shouldn't surprise me, but I swore there had been signs at Christmas that hinted at her being interested in more. At the time, I was sure she was feeling the buzz that I felt every time we were together. But I had promised myself that I'd give her the time she needed, so I'd do that.

"Hey, Blondie," I said, finally approaching.

She spun, and her face lit up. "Chris."

Fuck. My heart lurched at the happiness that radiated from her. Maybe it was wishful thinking, but I swore the smile she reserved for me was different from the one she gave the rest of the world.

War eyed me over her head, his expression unreadable. He and I weren't that different. Hotheads who were the bane of the PR team's existence. We typically joked about it when we bumped into one another. But we wouldn't be laughing much more if he didn't walk away now.

As if reading my mind, he dipped his head. "Nice meeting you, Avery. Have fun with Dragon." He lifted his glass to me, then turned to Hall. "Come on, Playboy, let's go."

"Can I have two Easy Outs, please?" I asked the bartender as he passed.

A moment later, he popped the caps and slid them across the bar.

"They stock Easy Out?" she asked, holding her bottle up and examining it like she hadn't seen the label fifty times or more in the past nine or ten months.

"Requested them for you." I pushed the mostly full Coors away, knowing she wasn't really a fan.

She hit me with another knee-weakening smile. "You're always so good to me."

"Come on." I slid an arm around her back and led her back to a booth.

And that's where I stayed for the next three hours, content to listen to her talk to me or any of the dozen people who stopped by throughout the night.

We watched the ball drop on the TV over the bar, and at midnight, I pulled her in for a hug. When I pressed my lips to her forehead, I silently promised that this year would be the year I'd get to call Avery Wilson mine.

Christian
26

"Damiano," Tom Wilson called across the cages where I was working my shoulder. The slider from hell was still haunting me. And although I wouldn't pitch full games for a few more weeks, I wanted it worked out before we left for spring training in Clearwater.

I walked to the fence and raised my chin, but Wilson didn't leave the doorway.

"My office before you leave." Without giving me a chance to answer, he spun and strode away.

I shook my head. For Avery, I was putting all my efforts into getting along with Coach, but the man made himself hard to like.

"Dragon?" In the cage next to me, Mason was working on his swing. Now that Miller had retired, Mason would need to carry the team bats. "Do you ever worry that he'll ask you about Avery?"

Worry was probably the wrong word. I assumed that he'd eventually ask me about her. But it wasn't a worry now, because there was nothing to tell at this point. I thought his daughter was amazing, and she thought I was a great friend.

"Don't stir up shit, Dumpty. I'm not worried about him." With a frown, I shook my head, then got back to work. I threw a couple more sliders, feeling a little better each time. I'd finally gotten to the point where I could pitch without flinching. When it was time to clear out for the day, I headed upstairs to Coach's office.

I knocked on his door and was instantly met with a pair of blue eyes that were more familiar than one would expect. Avery may have inherited her eye color from her father, but not an ounce of the joy and warmth that shone in his daughter's was reflected in his. He was pure intensity.

"Shut the door."

The clipped tone didn't bode well for how this conversation would go. But I closed the glass door gently, then stood in front of the desk, waiting for him to get on with it.

He scowled up at me and barked out a "sit."

I locked my jaw and swallowed back my annoyance. For Avery, I could keep it together. So without a word, I followed his command. He scanned me from head to toe, his expression as hard as ever, but he didn't say anything.

He'd called me in here, so I waited silently, refusing to fidget or break eye contact as I did.

Finally, he sighed, and the tension in his shoulders eased noticeably. "We're not ready to make the official announcement yet, but we locked in Asher Price."

I lifted my chin and pressed my lips together. Well, shit. Mason might not need to carry the bats this season after all. Last season, Asher Price's batting average was the highest in the league. And the man was the angel of major league baseball. Smart and calm. A family man the media loved. The guy could do no wrong.

Wouldn't be the worst thing for the team. "Great." I left it at that, because I didn't have the first clue why he'd bring me in here to tell me this.

Wilson hit me with the glare he mostly reserved for me. "That said, pitchers and catchers will report for spring training a week early."

My stomach sank, but I locked my jaw to keep from cursing out loud. Not only was I supposed to go see my father before I left for Clearwater, but the puffin exhibit was set to open a week before spring training started. Avery had been floating on cloud nine as the date got closer, and my normally surly sister had even been relatively chipper. Not only had she designed the logo, but she'd been asked to create a lot of the art for the media blitz.

I could skip the Long Island visit if I had to, but there was no way I'd let Avery down. "Not going to work."

"I wasn't finished." He clasped his hands on his desk and glowered at me. "I called you in here to give you a heads-up, but also to let you know that you'll be given a two-day extension for your zoo appearance."

"Great." I nodded. At least he wasn't being a dick.

He huffed out a big breath and kept his intense focus locked on me. "You've done a lot for that bird."

I sometimes called Puff "that bird" too, especially since it made Avery smirk and roll her eyes. It made no sense that it put my teeth on edge when Tom said it, but I had to take a moment so I didn't say something I'd regret.

"I broke his wing. It's the least I can do." I shifted in my seat, holding eye contact, all the while wondering if he'd ask about Avery while he had me here.

"And the slider?" He cocked a brow.

That wasn't a question I liked being asked, but it was probably a better alternative. I lifted one shoulder. "Sucks less."

He sat back in his chair. "Needs to be better than that."

"Yup." That was why I'd been working on it every day.

Neither of us spoke again for a long moment. We watched one another, him working his jaw from side to side and me ignoring the trickle of sweat that rolled down my spine as I waited for him to lose his shit about my friendship with his daughter.

Finally, after what felt like a lifetime, he tipped his chin. "Shut the door behind you. I have some calls to make before we make the announcement this afternoon." With that, he turned his attention back to his computer, dismissing me.

I left, simultaneously thrilled to be done with that awkward conversation and annoyed with myself, because it was probably the best talk we'd ever had. For the next two months, I'd have to double down on my efforts to get along with the man, because come March, I wanted to be dating his daughter.

I pulled out my phone and clicked on the *Messages* app, then tapped *Blondie*. She needed to know I'd still be at the exhibit opening before she heard about the change of schedule from her father. But mid-message, I stopped. I'd rather tell her in person, and based on the last text she'd sent, she was in desperate need of a caffeine fix. I deleted the message, then pulled up my dad's thread.

> Me: Coach says I have to report to spring training early, so I'll have to miss the clinic. I'm sorry. I know the kids will be bummed.

My heart felt heavy in my chest. This would be the first time in years that I'd missed the winter clinic my dad put on for his high schoolers. He'd been the gym teacher at the same school for forty-two years, and he'd been the baseball coach for almost as long. All the towns in the area came to his winter clinic.

> Pop: don't worry about it. You can't control your schedule.

> Pop: but COACH? You moved on from calling him Satan, I see.

I rolled my eyes.

> Me: for a few months now

> Pop: funny how the right woman helps settle a man.

> Me: we're just friends

> Pop: GIF of an old man slapping his leg and laughing.

Slipping the phone back into my pocket, I headed for the elevator.

"Hey, Damiano." Cortney appeared in the hallway. He glanced behind him, to where Liv was watching us and giving us a thumbs-up.

As he turned back to me, she stepped into Beckett's office and shut the door.

"Can we talk?" Cortney tipped his head to his office door, making his blond man bun bounce.

It was weird seeing him in a suit all the time, but now that he'd taken over as the team's GM, I'd have to get used to it. Seemed crazy to me that he'd gone from playing to running the team, but no one would second guess Beckett Langfield.

I stepped into the room I hadn't been in since Cortney'd had it redone. The shelves filled with books and even the table covered in a puzzle were on point for the man.

The jersey hanging on the wall, though, had my brows shooting up. That was a weird choice.

"Beckett." He shook his head. "He asked if I wanted a framed jersey, and for some asinine reason, he thought I'd want his."

The big double zero with Langfield on the back was centered on the wall for all to see.

I had to chuckle as I picked up a photo of Cortney and his future stepson, Liam, from one of his bookshelves. "Did you two finish the Porsche?"

They had been redoing a classic car together for the last few months.

Cortney beamed. "Yes, two days before his road test, so I'm officially his favorite."

The door behind me flew open, and I bobbled the framed photo.

"Are you having a meeting without me?" Beckett rushed into the room, but came to a stop and frowned when he saw me. "Damiano?" He turned and gave Cortney a similar hard look. "Why are we meeting with him?" He focused on me again, now full-on glaring. "What did you do now?"

I held up my hands but kept my mouth shut. I didn't have the first clue what was going on.

Cortney crossed his arms and rested his hip against his desk.

"Didn't Liv need something?"

"I know when my wife is distracting me. Is this about the puffins? Is there an issue?"

"No." Not as far as I knew. And there better not be an issue. I'd taken great care to keep things on track for both Avery and Puff.

"Not a distraction. It's probably just that bet Liv and Dylan have going." Cortney shrugged.

Beckett's eyes narrowed on the GM. Cortney's fiancée was Liv's best friend, and the four of them, plus their kids, lived with a couple other women and their families. Why Beckett and Cortney had moved in with them instead of insisting they leave the commune situation they had going on was beyond me. It was a crazy situation, but both men seemed to take in stride.

If it were me, I'd have lost my shit by now. I could barely handle living with Bambi. But they lived in a house with at least a dozen people and acted like it was no big deal.

"Didn't Liv tell you?"

"No." Beckett worked his jaw from one side to the other.

Cortney shrugged again, plastering on a smirk. "Ah. Probably because Dylan's winning."

"Winning what?"

Cortney cocked a brow. "Ya know…who has the *most* this week."

"Most what?" Beckett looked at me like I would know.

I shook my head and kept my expression blank.

Waving one hand, Cortney waggled his brows. "You know…most."

Oh. In most situations, I'd call bullshit, but with Dylan, it was hard to say. She was a total free spirit. I could see her deciding to have an orgasm contest with her best friend. I started to chuckle, but quickly covered it with a cough.

"He gets it." Cortney tipped his head my way.

The wheels in Beckett's head were turning now. He scanned the shelves behind us, then snapped his attention back to Cortney. "No ducking way is Dylan winning." With that, he spun, strode away, and slammed the door shut behind him.

Cortney brushed his hands together, then rounded his desk and sat.

"You're fucking with him, right?" I asked.

"Oh, 100 percent." Cortney laughed evilly, dropping his elbows to the desktop and steepling his fingers.

In this moment, I understood why Beckett Langfield had hired this guy. Although very few people would stand up to or give Beckett a hard time, Cortney had no issues. It was probably nice to have someone on the team who was more than just a yes-man.

"Are we having a meeting or what?" Or was Cortney fucking with me too?

His expression evened out into the supportive one he typically used with me during games. "Just a conversation."

I sank into the chair across from him. "Is this about Price?"

With a shake of his head, he sat back. "But if you have issues, my door is always open. He's a solid choice, though. I think you two will work great together."

I did too. "He's got big shoes to fill, but I'm looking forward to working with him."

"Not many of us wear a size eighteen." One side of Cortney's lips kicked up, but then he tempered his expression and sat up straight. "On a serious note, I wanted to check in and see if you had anything to declare for human resources before the season starts..." He let the sentence trail off as he studied me.

I surveyed him in return, at a loss for what he thought I'd want HR to know.

After several silent seconds, he cleared his throat. "I might wear the suit now, but when I was still your teammate, I heard all the rumors about you and Avery."

I shrugged. "We're friends, man." I tamped down on my annoyance that he was sticking his nose in my business, but I understood that, with any team, there were rules regarding fraternization.

He nodded once. "You'll come to me if that changes?"

With a huff, I stood, but I kept my anger in check. "Sure."

Behind me, the door flew open again. "Man Bun," Beckett growled, stomping into the room. "My wife has no idea what you're talking about."

And that was my cue to leave. With a chuckle, I sidestepped him and slipped out.

Avery
27

AT THE SOUND of my whistle, Sarge flew across the green screen and landed on my gloved arm. My stomach growled so loud Jana, who was on the other side of the room, laughed. We'd been at this for entirely too long.

This was our fourth and final set of photos today. We'd done a few with the giant condors, and then we popped in for some in the parakeet house. Wobbles, our favorite snow owl, was a natural in front of the camera. We'd started Sarge's session at three thirty so we could be wrapped by five, but Sarge had refused to leave the perch for the first hour. Winter was hard on most of the birds. They were all pretty mellow, but it made it almost impossible to get them to do more than just sit and watch what was going on around them.

Once the nearly ten-pound bald eagle was steady on my arm, I turned to Jana, who'd positioned herself behind the camera. "Did you get it that time?" Sarge was only cooperative to a point, and he'd about reached it.

"Um..."

Jana flipped through shots on the camera's small digital screen. Since she had been tasked with updating the zoo's website with information on Blondie's Birds, she'd requested action shots of the fan favorites. And the zoo's only bald eagle fit that bill. Everyone loved the big guy.

"Can we do one more?"

"Last one." I waited for Jana to agree before I put Sage back on his perch.

Just as I was getting back into my spot, the door behind me opened. I didn't bother looking. I was ready to get this done and get out of here. It was well after five, and most zoo employees had headed home for the day.

It was probably Dean. He was stuck here too, waiting for me to call him to come get the bird and take him back to his exhibit for the night. I couldn't blame him for being impatient. My poor tummy was screaming for food, and it was Friday, so that was North End Pizza day.

I brushed off the thought, because it would only make me hungrier, and focused on Sarge. Across the room, he cocked his head to the side.

I whistled, and on command, the bird took off. But instead of coming to the red glove on my arm, he soared over my head.

Shoot. What the hell was he doing?

I spun, tracking him, until my eyes landed on Chris, who was standing in the corner by the table. And Sarge was heading right for him.

"Holy fuck." Chris backpedaled, stumbling the whole way. He tripped on a chair and toppled over it, and in the next second, Sarge landed on the center of his chest. Chris's hat flew off his head and skidded away as his back slammed into the tile floor beneath him. With one ankle still tangled with the chair leg, he held his hands in the air, palms out, like he was trying to ward off the creature.

With my heart in my throat, I rushed over. Pale and wide-eyed, Chris stared at me. The bird was calmly standing on him, picking at its wing and paying him no mind. As I approached, a single feather fluttered from Sarge's wing and landed on Chris's red shirt.

"Are you okay?" I asked.

Sarge looked up at me as if he thought I was talking to him, then tilted his head and leaned in closer, studying the man he had pinned beneath him.

Chris blinked at Sarge, then at me.

Sarge edged in even closer and stuck his beak in Chris's hair, allo-preening him. Chris's eyes went wider than I'd ever seen them when Sarge brushed his big orange beak through the hair beside his ear.

"Shit." Chris's shoulder twitched. "What's he doing? Is he trying to eat me? Or spit on me?" His lips barely moved as he whispered, as if he were hoping the bird wouldn't catch on.

"It's okay. He won't eat you." The scene was adorable, but I wasn't sure Chris would be thrilled with the truth here. "He's grooming you."

His eyes widened and he choked. "Blondie, I'm trying not to scream like a girl. Can you please get this massive beast off me?"

Now he was just being dramatic. Sarge was a sweetheart. But I took pity on him since he looked like he was on his way to having a panic attack.

"Sarge." I whistled and held my arm out like I'd done before.

As the bird opened his wings, readying to take off, Chris's already pallid face drained of any remaining color. But he kept it together, and with two flaps, the eagle was resting on my red glove, his talons wrapped around my wrist.

Slowly, and without taking his eyes off the bird, Chris lifted to his elbows. "I'm not sure whether I feel better or worse that he's on you now."

Sarge tipped his head and danced along my arm.

"No," I clipped, ensuring the bird didn't take off for Chris again. Then I turned my attention back to my friend. "It's the shirt. He's trained to fly toward the red."

In one quick motion, Chris jackknifed to sitting, grasped his shirt at his nape, and yanked it over his head. Then he tossed it across the floor like it was on fire.

I wanted to laugh, but that desire quickly died out as the sight in front of me registered and my mouth went dry. Broad shoulders, high, defined pecs, and a ribbed six-pack.

Well, damn. I'd forgotten exactly how good he looked shirtless. Without my permission, my entire body lit up like I was seeing him for the first time. And yet memories of his chest pressing against mine as he moved inside me invaded my mind and sent a burning heat searing through me.

He tilted his head and studied me.

My body warmed another degree, and I may have let out a whimper in response to his attention.

"You okay?" His biceps bulged as he pushed himself to his feet.

I nodded as he stepped closer. When he stood in front of me, my senses were flooded with the rich scent of his cologne. I averted my gaze. His scrutiny was so intense I thought I might combust. He lifted a hand and ducked lower so I was forced to look at him. In response, a pack of butterflies danced in my belly. He ghosted the back of his pointer finger against my cheekbone, and I fought the shiver that tried to race down my spine.

With his eyes fixed on my mouth, he ran his tongue along his bottom lip, and I swore I felt the slow swipe between my thighs.

A cold nudge to my temple snapped me out of the trance, and the accompanying squawk made Chris jump back.

That was all it took to break the spell between us. With another step back, Chris ran his hand through his dark hair.

I cleared my throat. "I'll put him back. Give me a minute."

Slowly, Chris lowered his chin in acknowledgment. Then he backed up another couple of steps.

I needed a minute to get a grip. So I turned, careful to make sure Sarge was ready for the move, and took a breath. When I'd let it out, I eased my way across the room toward the large crate that Dean would use to move him back to his habitat.

Jana stood beside the crate, practically bouncing on her toes.

"Jesus, you two are fire." She clapped her hands softly in front of her lips. "I'm all hot and bothered just watching you."

"Don't make it awkward," I hissed. One day, my friends would move on and accept that Chris and I were not dating, but today was not that day. I bent and got Sarge back into the box and locked it.

"Me? Make it awkward?" She shook her head and flipped her phone my way. "Look at this and tell me again that you're only friends. You were totally eye-fucking each other."

In the photo she'd taken, I was facing Chris. The huge bird was perched on my arm, and Chris's back was to the camera, but my face was in focus. The flush on my cheeks was undeniable, as was the way my pupils had blown wide. My lips were parted, and Chris's finger was caressing my face. I could almost hear myself panting through the phone. My thoughts were written on my face like they were words on a page. Shit. He was probably mortified. He'd been clear about hating that kind of attention.

"You two need to come to your senses and start fucking the shit out of each other," Jana whispered.

I shook my head as my heart tripped over itself. "It's not like that."

"Oh, babe," she laughed. "It's definitely like that, and it's going to happen. Mark my words."

"No, it's not." My tone may have been a bit too sharp, but I didn't want her to make things awkward by pushing something I wasn't sure Chris wanted. Plus, he was leaving for spring training in less than two weeks. It wasn't a good time to broach the subject, even if he might want to. "Stop making it weird."

"Wow, harsh." Jana crossed her arms, tucking her phone into her side.

"Sorry." I sighed, shoulders slumping. "I'm tired. Between getting ready for the puffin opening next week and doing these shots, this day has felt more like a week. Never mind the constant interruptions. And I didn't even get lunch."

Behind me, and much closer than I realized, Chris cleared his throat.

My stomach flip-flopped at the sound. It had been doing that a lot lately, no matter how often I told myself to cool it. With another mental reminder to my stomach and my heart, I turned around.

His hat was flipped backward so that only a few wisps of his dark hair were visible. His jaw was locked like he was grinding his molars. But that broody vibe worked for the man. I knew him well enough to know that he wasn't upset with me, or even annoyed. No, he was much more likely to be annoyed with himself.

"I didn't mean to be an interruption." He rocked on his heels.

Instinctively, I reached out to reassure him that he wasn't. When my hand hit the warm, smooth skin of his chest, I dropped it and clenched my fists at my side. My cheeks heated with embarrassment, but I dipped my chin and continued on. "You aren't. I'm just hungry and cranky. I haven't eaten all day, and I haven't come close to getting enough caffeine to keep me functioning like a normal human."

"I can help with that." He tipped his head to the table he was standing by when I first caught sight of him.

On top sat a to-go cup of coffee and one of my favorite protein bars. A lump formed in my throat at his thoughtfulness. When he'd texted to see how the photo shoots were going this afternoon, I'd complained about the lack of coffee, and I may have mentioned how I'd depleted my protein bar stash and had forgotten to replenish it. And here he was with both. He didn't get nearly enough credit for being so thoughtful. I made sure he knew how much I appreciated him, but to the world, he was still just a hothead, despite all the work he'd done to change his image during the offseason.

"Maybe that will hold you over and we can order pizza."

"You are my favorite human today."

"Good." He chuckled. "Maybe one day I'll beat out the birds too."

"Shut up." I whacked his side.

This time when my hand hit skin, he snagged it and held it there against his rib cage. A ripple of need echoed through my body at the contact, igniting a low fire in my belly.

A small smile pulled his lips, and he angled in closer.

Behind me, Jana cleared her throat. "You might want to grab your shirt. Although half of Boston wouldn't mind the view, most restaurants in town require it. Plus, if you left here looking like that, you'd be accosted by women offering a hot night between the sheets at every turn."

Chris shook his head. "That's the last thing I want."

His words doused the flame flickering in my core. Right. And I needed to remember that.

Christian
28

Blondie: OMG. Did you see the design for the sign? We just got it. Gi crushed it.

Blondie: Picture of the puffin house sign

Me: Yeah I told you she's talented

Blondie: It's just so cute. I love the puffins. The zoo wants her to redo the signs for the other houses.

Me: Good. If they pay her enough, maybe she can quit that crappy job

Blondie: Stop being a grump. She might love it.

Me: She hates everything

Blondie: GIF of an eye roll

Christian
29

"THIS SIGN IS FREAKING AMAZING." Kyle tilted his head back and surveyed the puffin and the penguin. The birds stood back-to-back, with the Boston skyline behind them. Gianna had incorporated a baseball in front of the puffin and a hockey puck in front of the penguin. "I legit can't believe she drew it."

"Ya ever seen Dragon draw?" Emerson, who was standing beside me, slapped my arm.

Kyle turned to me and shook his head.

"He's pretty damn good," Emerson said, "but she's a million times better."

"I keep telling her that. And Avery raved about it." I took in the colorful sign again. I'd seen it several times, but mounted here, it looked even more incredible, and it fit perfectly with the zoo.

Gianna wasn't as excited with the results as I expected her to be, and I'd yet to figure out why.

A small group of zoo employees squeezed past us.

"Who are we waiting for? My dick's going to freeze off, and you know how much the women of Boston would suffer if that happened." Kyle held his fist up like he expected one of us to pound it.

With a *humph*, I took a step back, and beside me, Emerson shook his head.

Kyle dropped his hand and huffed a laugh. "Rough crowd."

"We're just waiting on Mason, and he's coming now." Emerson tilted his chin to the center fielder who was heading our way.

"Why are we outside?" Mason asked as he approached us where we stood in front of the black glass building that was Puff's new home.

The structure was modern and looked almost like black ice. Not that Puff cared about the outside appearance, but I was sure the little guy would be happy here.

"Where's Avery?" he added as he, too, assessed the new building.

"She has a lot to coordinate. Balloon animals and snacks and all kinds of other fun stuff, but when she was over last night, she said she'd be around and promised to say hi. I can't wait to help the clowns with the balloons." Emerson was all but bouncing up and down beside me. The extreme anticipation that was bubbling out of him over the idea of balloon animals was baffling. The man acted like he was four years old. Though I supposed I should be used to it by now. It was very on-brand for Bambi.

"Ooh, Avery was at your house last night?" Mason waggled his brows. "Like for a sleepover?"

"Why do you insist on acting like a child?" I scowled at him. With Emerson, Mason, and Kyle here, I felt like I was babysitting. Their maturity levels ranged from the ages five to fifteen.

"Clearly not. If he was getting some, he'd be in a better mood." Kyle slapped my back. "It's been what, eleven months now?"

I clenched my fists at my sides, ready to push him off me, when the sound of a throat clearing caught my attention.

Behind Emerson, Cortney and Beckett, both donning their Revs jerseys, appeared. Although they were coming as part of the team, the word was that they were bringing their families with them, yet they were alone.

"Eleven months for what?" Beckett took each of us in, his expression as intense as always.

Mason smirked. "Dragon's in the middle of a dry spell. He's gonna get carpal tunnel if he keeps working his hand the way he is."

Emerson fucking giggled. "I got him a pocket pussy for Christmas to help take the edge off."

"Hey, me too." Kyle held out his fist, and Emerson bumped it.

They both had, the fuckers.

"It's funny," Kyle mused. "He's baseball's most popular bachelor, yet he's been in a dry spell for almost a year. That shit's messed up."

"You assholes are free to go out and dick around," I snapped. "But I don't want just anyone. So until I get the right girl to realize she wants me, I'm content to be a moody motherfucker. Get used to it."

"Spoken like a man in love." Beckett stepped closer, scrutinizing me. "Who is she?"

Frowning, I eased back. What the hell? Since I'd known the guy, he'd had a good handle on personal space, but suddenly he was crowding my personal bubble.

"No, you don't." Cortney pulled on Beckett's arm. "Liv said you were done meddling in lives and fixing people up," he warned. "Plus, we need to make sure Enzo has Delia locked down before your mind wanders to a new project."

Delia was Liv and Dylan's best friend, and the only single woman left in their house these days.

Beckett scoffed and yanked his arm out of Cortney's hold. "Did you see the way they were dancing at the gala last week? Medusa is locked down." Beckett turned back to me. "Give me a name. I have the Midas touch when it comes to matchmaking."

"For the love of God, leave the poor man alone." Cortney huffed. "You are not a matchmaker."

"Um, remind me again who set you up with your beautiful fiancée?" He broke out in a smug grin. When Cortney didn't respond, Beckett shoved a finger in his chest. "Me. It's me."

Cortney cocked a brow. "You know the next line."

Beckett only narrowed his eyes and crossed his arms.

"I'm the problem."

Around me, the group broke into fits of laughter. But I was anxious to avoid any talk of Avery around the Revs' owner—a.k.a. the man who could shut shit down between us in a heartbeat—so I pulled the door open and waved the guys over. "Can we please stop dicking around?"

The addition made the place twice its original size, and the ice, water, and rocks behind the floor-to-ceiling glass looked brilliant under the bright lights. The place looked perfect, and the birds happily moved through the water.

I scanned the large space until I found Puff. He was on a rock, jumping around with four of the other puffins. My heart floated in my chest at the sight. He'd found his group of friends. He still had the sad, dark face and dull beak, but Avery promised that in another month, he'd be back to the white-faced clown that I first met.

My dad and sister stood with a group of people near one corner of the room. Gianna had met with the zoo's director to talk about doing more work for them, so she'd already been here for a couple of hours. My dad tipped his chin and gave me a thumbs-up. The signal could mean one of three things: good luck, be good, or the meeting went well.

I returned the gesture, then continued scanning the crowd. When I caught sight of Avery, all the air rushed out of my lungs. She was always pretty, but on occasion, looking at her was like getting punched in the gut. When she was dressed up, yes, but even more so when she stood with her shoulders back, confident and proud, and when she was excited. Today, she'd mastered the trifecta. Her hair was down and wavy, and she wore just a hint of makeup. Her gorgeous face looked fresh and natural, but her normal look was enhanced by whatever she'd done. The navy dress brought out her blue irises and clung to her curves. Fucking stunning.

I roughed a hand down my face and cupped my mouth, unable to pull my eyes away.

"Oh, duck me," Beckett said beside me, startling me enough to make me drop my hand and turn. "No, no, no."

He eyed me, then Avery, his green eyes full of curiosity and maybe a hint of warning.

Cortney loomed over him and pulled him toward the front doors. "We're supposed to be helping Liv and Dylan."

"No, we're not." Beckett yanked himself out of the giant blond's grip for the second time since they'd been here. "Liam told us to go do our damn jobs and not make this worse by riling the kids up."

Cortney sighed and pointed to the door, and with a grunt, Beckett stomped away. Cortney shot me a warning look and followed.

"I don't think you need to give him a name anymore." Mason chuckled.

My stomach twisted into knots. But then Avery was heading this way, and all thoughts of the Revs' owner and GM dissipated. Thank fuck my friends let it go too. As much as they gave me crap about her, they kept their mouths shut in front of her.

"Hey, guys. Thanks for coming." She beamed at us, clasping her hands in front of her.

"Anytime, Blondie." I tugged the end of one of her long blond curls.

She swatted at me, then took me in from head to toe. Once she'd finished her perusal of me, she surveyed the rest of the group. Her lips were pressed together, making it hard to tell whether she approved. "Hannah and Liv went over the plan with each of you, right? After pictures with Puff, we're going to put you all at different stations to help run the activities and interact with the guests."

Hannah and I had met yesterday, and she'd filled me in. I was staying with Puff so I could show the kids how to do behavior call signs. Avery had agreed to help me. She'd be the one giving him the fish as treats because that crap wasn't up my alley. I had limits, even with Puff, and his love for dead fish was definitely one of them. Bird shit was another. We'd had a few heart-to-hearts about the time and place to shit—namely, when I wasn't around. The smell was something I wanted no part of.

Once the guys had all confirmed that they understood the plan, she moved us over to where we would pose for photos with Puff.

When she left to track down the marketing team, Beckett stepped up next to me, as if he'd been hovering, waiting to reprimand me.

In a voice so low I was worried he'd been possessed by a demon, he said, "Tom Wilson loves his daughter, and he hates drama. So be fucking sure of what you're doing. He won't hesitate to insist I send you back to AAA or trade you."

I wanted to call it a threat, but when I forced myself to meet his eye, what I saw there looked more like a concerned warning.

My stomach sank at the idea of being traded. This was where I was meant to be. Not because of my teammates—although as I watched them play with Puff, I had to admit I loved the assholes—but because of *her*. I couldn't help but seek her out. As if she were my true north, I found her instantly. No. I couldn't leave her behind. Even seven weeks in Florida seemed too long.

With a sigh, I deflated.

Beckett slapped me on the back, making me go rigid once again. "But I will say I've learned that certain things in life are worth the risk."

Huh. That sounded an awful lot like permission to break the rules.

As Beckett walked away, I took in the scene again. The full room of people, the face-painting and balloon animals. Avery's bright smile. I wanted this to go well for her, so that was all that mattered today.

Avery
30

BOTH GUYS DOVE for the white ball as it bounced. Emerson knocked Chris's paddle out of the way, and the ball soared past them and smacked the floor-to-ceiling window. Outside, the snow was coming down in puffy flakes, making it feel like we were in a snow globe.

"Great shot." Gianna and I tapped paddles. I had kicked off my heels when we arrived, and next to Gianna, who had to be close to five-ten, I felt like a little girl.

Bo had headed home soon after the exhibit opening so he could beat the snowstorm, but Gianna was staying the night since she had another meeting with the marketing team from the zoo coming up. They were working to incorporate more of the sponsors into the details of her designs, like she had done for the Puffin Penguin house, and wanted to review specifics before she sketched the initial mock-ups.

"What's the score now? Twelve to two?" Gianna asked, with a smug look directed at her brother.

Chris flayed her with a glower he typically saved for when he was pissed off on the field. It was one I hadn't seen in months. He was not the best loser.

Beside him, Emerson was all but giggling. "I can't believe we both missed that one."

Chris huffed. "Bambi, I get that you can't hit the ball to save your life, but stop blocking me." He tossed his paddle onto the table. "Time to switch teams."

"I think we've tried every combo at this point." Emerson waved a finger between Chris and Gianna. "And you two have hated them all."

"He doesn't want to team up with anyone but Avery, 'cause you and I both suck." Gianna rolled her eyes.

I wasn't all that great at ping-pong, but I was better than either of them. Even hampered by my tight navy dress, I had a better chance of getting the ball than they did. So although Chris was happier when we paired up, it made our teams grossly unbalanced.

Emerson was still as happy as a kid on Christmas morning. He was terrible at the game, yet he always kept his cool. Always had fun. In fact, I'd yet to ever see Emerson truly upset. If I could bottle whatever made him so freaking happy all the time, it'd be an instant bestseller.

"I think I've improved a lot." Emerson beamed like he hadn't just been insulted.

Chris rubbed his forehead. "I can't believe I'm saying this after this disaster of a game, but yeah, you have."

If this was an improvement—the guy had maybe hit one out of five shots—I couldn't imagine what he'd played like when they'd purchased this table last spring.

"Just takes practice." Emerson shook his empty beer and wandered toward the kitchen. "Who wants another?"

"Me," Chris called a little too eagerly.

"I'll take one more. It's only ten," Gianna said. "Although it feels like a million o'clock."

"Hell yeah, it does." Chris ran a hand over his face and sighed. His eyes were rimmed red, and his face sagged just a little.

He'd stayed for the entire opening event today, smiling and talking to every person who approached him. And afterward, his teammates came over for pizza, so the guy was exhausted. The day had been a huge success. The pictures were so cute, and several were trending all over social media.

The marketing team at the zoo had no doubt Puff would be a celebrity all summer. But though he'd played the part perfectly, Chris was the farthest thing from an extrovert. He'd done far too much peopling for one day.

That meant it was time for me to get out of his hair. I knew well enough to know Chris would insist on walking me home, and he didn't need to do that at midnight. Especially since the snow was starting to pile up.

"It's getting late. I should head out." I followed Emerson into the kitchen.

"Ugh." Gianna wandered in and propped herself up against the island. "You are not leaving me with these two idiots." She pointed at Chris as he appeared behind her. "I thought you were staying the night. Weren't we going to watch *Schitt's Creek*?"

"I love that show." Emerson slid a beer to her along the granite, then set a second one in front of Chris. "When Alexis pretended to be a lawyer"—he waved both hands—"gold. Let's watch that one."

"No," Gianna huffed. "We have to start at the beginning."

"So we can watch it all together?" He waggled his brows. "Like from top." He paused. "To bottom."

"What does that even mean?" Sighing, Chris sank onto a stool.

I wondered that too. From here, it looked like Emerson was trying to flirt but had missed the mark. But he knew how to flirt. He was damn good at it, in fact.

Chris shook his head and twisted the cap off his beer.

"You'll just have to do it without me." I shuffled toward the door.

Before I'd gotten more than a couple of steps from the island, Gianna latched on to my wrist and glared at her brother. "You're letting her walk home in a blizzard?"

The snow had started this afternoon, but this was by no means a blizzard. At least not by Boston standards.

"I don't make Avery do anything," Chris growled.

"So she can stay?" Gianna almost smiled.

I wasn't sure when she'd decided she liked me. On Christmas day, I could have sworn she had only put up with me. But today, she acted like we were friends.

Chris ground his teeth together. "You aren't allowed to make her do things either, Gi. And if she stays, there's nowhere for her to sleep."

Gianna picked up her beer and shrugged one shoulder. "I don't see why she can't sleep on the sofa with you."

Chris's eyes practically bugged out of his head.

Did he hate that idea that much? Or was the response just one of surprise?

"Or one of you can sleep with me," Emerson offered.

"No." Chris shot up to his feet, and the stool clattered behind him. "Absolutely not."

"Why?" Emerson smirked.

"Because I am not sleeping in the same bed as you."

Chris was more frustrated than he had been at his sister, and she was an expert at pushing his buttons. Though I wasn't sure if it was because of Emerson's suggestion alone, or because the guy seriously wanted Chris to explain why he thought it was a shit idea.

With more emphasis than was strictly necessary, he pointed at me, then at Gianna. "And neither are *either* of them."

"I really don't have to stay…"

"Please," Gianna begged.

I studied Chris, hoping to get a read on his true feelings.

He met my eyes, and sincerity echoed across his every feature. "You can do whatever *you* want. You're always welcome to stay here, but I'm equally willing to walk through a fucking blizzard if that makes you happy."

"*Aw.*" Emerson tilted forward, planted an elbow on the island, and rested his chin in his hand, beaming at Chris.

Chris pointed at his roommate, his face a stony mask again. "Don't start."

"So?" Gianna looked so hopeful, and Emerson was smirking. Chris looked ready to pass out for the night. It didn't seem fair to make him walk me home.

My chest squeezed tight. "I can stay."

"Slumber party!" Emerson laughed.

Gianna shook her head at him, but she was almost smiling. He had that effect on people. No one could stay cranky long around him. Even Chris struggled with it.

"I can sleep on the sofa so you two can have the bed," Gianna suggested, eyeing me, then her brother.

My heart skipped, and then I was inundated with one vivid memory after another. His lips moving down my body. Writhing against his tongue. Pounding desire, burning need. The look in his eye as he moved inside me. The sound he made when he came. My breath sped up, and heat pooled low in my core.

My cheeks flamed, and suddenly, it was hard to pull in a full breath.

"No," Chris snapped. Like he was angry that she'd even suggest it. But of course he was. Our relationship wasn't like that.

I shook myself out of the memories.

"The couch is fine really," I assured them, though as I did, I ran my hands over my hips, remembering the short navy dress I was wearing. Even without the stockings, it would be wildly uncomfortable to sleep in. "But maybe I could borrow sweats or something."

All three piped up at the same time.

Chris lifted his hand. "I've got clothes," he said to me, then he glared at Gianna and Emerson. "Please stop being weird."

Part of me wanted to agree. Since I mentioned leaving, every moment had been awkward.

Without another word, Chris righted the stool he'd knocked over, then stomped out of the kitchen.

"He doesn't express it well, but he's thrilled you're staying. Really." Emerson rounded the island and looped his arm over my shoulder. "And I'd hate seeing you wandering in the snow. So you want a drink?"

"Nah, I'm good." I rested my head on his shoulder and felt some of the tension that had taken over in the last few minutes ease from my body. Since Chris and I had become good friends, his teammates had all developed this older-brother type protectiveness when it came to me. And I couldn't say I hated it.

I peeked up at Emerson. "Are we really watching *Schitt's Creek*?"

"I don't know. Chris hates it."

Tilting my head back, I frowned at him. "Really?"

"It's, like, impossible to believe, right?" Gianna shook her head.

Footsteps echoed through the foyer, and then Chris appeared, holding a bundle of clothing.

"You hate *Schitt's Creek*?" I asked.

With a long breath through his nose, he glared at his roommate. "Stop telling people that."

Emerson dropped his arm and reached for his beer, but he didn't respond.

"He probably says it because it's true." Gianna shrugged.

"Do not gang up on me." Chris hadn't glared this much in weeks, but his roommate and his sister had obviously made some kind of pact to press every one of his buttons tonight. "Just because I don't love it like you do doesn't mean I hate it. If it's what you want to watch, then we'll watch it." Though his words were harsh, when he turned to face me, his expression was gentle. He held out a Revs T-shirt and a pair of black sweats. "These have a drawstring, so they should work."

"Thanks. I'm going to change before we start it, if that's okay."

"Better use the hall bathroom. Gianna's shit is all over mine."

"There's a pack of extra toothbrushes in there," Emerson said.

"Why?" Gianna asked, one brow raised.

"For the same reason no one is sleeping in his bed tonight." Chris rolled his eyes. "He hardly ever sleeps alone."

Without responding, Gianna lowered her chin and picked at the label on her beer bottle.

"Dude, don't be a dick." Emerson frowned at Chris. "I don't have women over more than a couple times a month."

I'd never seen the happy-go-lucky guy look so upset. But what was even more surprising was the way he side-eyed Gianna with a look of uncertainty.

Hmm, that would be something. I could see it. She was gorgeous. But I could guarantee Chris wouldn't be happy if he saw the interest in Emerson's eyes.

I didn't want to give my thoughts away. Too often, they just showed up on my face, and I could be way off in my assessment of his sister and his best friend. So I hurried out of the kitchen and headed down the hall.

I changed quickly and used a spare toothbrush that Emerson had stocked in the closet. When I reemerged, it was to yet another argument.

"Babe, rom-coms are the best." Emerson shifted his attention to me. "Tell her. We love them."

I shrugged. "We do."

"I don't." She slumped back into the couch and crossed her arms.

I curled up on the chaise end of the couch. "I thought we were watching *Schitt's Creek*."

"That was the plan, but then he turned on the TV and saw that." She pointed a red nail at the screen, where the information page of Netflix's newest release was pulled up. "And he wants to change the plan."

"It was just a suggestion." Emerson shrugged.

"A bad one."

"See? This is what I was talking about."

Chris came out in nothing but a pair of gray sweats and his dark-rimmed glasses, holding a toothbrush in one hand, and my heart tripped over itself at the sight of him.

"I told you that the two of you would fight and make it miserable."

"Fine." Gianna held both hands up. "Fine. We'll watch whatever you want."

"Exactly. It's my house, so I get to pick the movie." He stomped over to Emerson and snatched the remote out of his hand. Then he dropped it into my lap. "Avery, put on whatever you want." With that, he spun and strode back to his bedroom.

Emerson and Gianna both laughed, but neither commented.

I arched a brow and pointed the remote at the TV. "So *Schitt's Creek*?"

When Gianna and Emerson both nodded, I navigated to the correct screen and found episode one.

Chris reappeared, snagged a blanket from the back of the recliner, and settled on the sofa next to me, propping his feet up on the chaise.

He was so close I could feel the heat radiating off him as he spread the blanket over our legs.

Not even halfway through, my eyelids were feeling heavy.

I tipped toward him and rested my head on his shoulder. "Can I?"

"Sure, Blondie." He lifted his arm and draped it along the couch behind me. "Use me as a pillow anytime you want."

He tucked me into his side so my head rested on his chest. Cocooned in his warmth, sleep pulled me under almost instantly.

Christian
31

CUPCAKES. Something tickled my nose, and it smelled a lot like cupcakes. That had become one of my favorite smells over the last several months. Though I could bask in the scent all day, the room was stifling. It felt like I was wrapped in a blanket fresh from the dryer. I turned my head, searching for cooler air. Instead, my chin brushed against a warm surface.

Finally, I forced my eyes open, blinking several times to bring the world into focus. I'd come out to watch TV wearing my glasses since my sister was staying in my room for the night, but apparently, they'd gone missing. Even so, it was clear that the object I'd brushed against was the top of Avery's head.

The sight sent memories of last night flooding back to me. I'd spent the night on the couch with Avery, who was like a little heater, pouring out warmth. At some point, we had shifted, because instead of being propped up against each other, she was now laid out across my right side and snuggled into my chest. Her lips were millimeters from my bare skin. My muscles tightened at the sight of her so close to my bare torso.

I was hard—of course I was; it was morning—but when I caught sight of her hand resting on my upper thigh less than an inch from my cock, all the blood in my body surged south. My dick throbbed, pushing against the gray material and practically tenting my pants. It took a concerted effort to lock my hips in place, because I desperately wanted to shift so her fingers would brush against me.

And what kind of a creepy fuck did that make me? The poor woman was asleep.

Yesterday had been the longest day of my life, but last night had almost broken me. From the moment I walked into the room and saw her curled up on the sofa, my body came alive. I'd had to grab the blanket to cover what my gray sweats couldn't. Then Avery had snuggled into me and dozed off. Instead of being relaxed by the contact, my body had been a live wire. I'd spent two hours listening to David Rose say and do stupid shit just so I could focus on things other than the woman in my arms. Otherwise, I never would have settled enough to sleep. And now, once again, I had a raging hard-on.

Damn, what I'd give to stay like this forever, cuddled up with the woman who took up three-quarters of my thoughts every day. But the last thing I wanted was for Avery to wake up and catch me hard and gawking at her. Or for Gi and Emerson to come out and find us entwined like this. Not after the way they had acted last night. The two of them so badly wanted us together, and fuck, so did I, but based on the frowns Avery kept sending their way when they'd made veiled comments, the pushing made her uncomfortable.

That was unacceptable.

I desperately wanted more with Avery, but if she never felt the same, then I'd take the friendship and hold on to it forever. Because the smallest piece of her was better than none at all. So I refused to let anyone mess up what we had. Including myself and my massive boner.

I slipped off the couch, careful not to wake her. She groaned in protest, but settled again when I carefully covered her with our blanket. She tucked a hand beneath her cheek and shifted at the loss of my body. A wisp of blond hair fell over her face, so I carefully pushed it behind her ear again. Her lashes fluttered, but she didn't wake.

God, I'd never get used to how naturally beautiful this amazing woman was.

She mumbled incoherently, then let out a little moan, making my cock once again stir to life.

With a sigh, I forced myself to walk away. My bathroom was connected to my room, since I had the master, and my sister was worse than a grouch when woken up, so I settled for Emerson's hall bath. It was a standard tub with a shower, and at my height, it wasn't my favorite. But I needed some relief. It didn't even matter if I got my hair wet.

I pressed my hand against the gray material of my pants, putting a little pressure on my cock. I almost groaned when the image of her smaller, softer hand appeared in my mind.

While I waited for the water to heat, I left my palm in place, even if it only eased the ache slightly. When I slipped out of my pants, my dick jutted out, hard and angry. Holding my breath, I stepped under the spray, then I wrapped my hand around myself, remembering the taste of Avery. How her body quivered every time my tongue teased her clit. The way her legs locked around my head as she bucked against my face.

I squeezed the head tight, swallowed, then thrust my hips forward. Images of her beneath me, her legs wrapped around my waist. God, she was so tight. She'd felt like a vise around my dick, milking me while her breath ghosted over the side of my face. That night had been entirely too short.

I pumped harder and faster as my imagination played out a different ending to our one night. An ending that wasn't an ending at all. A scenario where we woke up together the next morning. And every morning after that.

My hand on her neck and her exhales on my cheek. The warm, soft press of wet lips against me. I imagined feeling her mouth running across my jaw, down my neck.

My throat got tight when her blue eyes appeared in my mind. Avery peering up at me as her mouth made the painstakingly slow journey down my body, trailing down my chest, teasing me, creeping down my stomach, heading to exactly where I needed her.

My dick pulsed in response. I squeezed hard, then pumped faster.

Her pink lips parting in an *O* before they surrounded my cock and sucked me in. Her mouth a hot, wet heaven.

I slammed one hand against the wall in front of me, and my legs threatened to give out. With a groan, I forced my eyes open and watched my release spill out and hit the gray tiled wall. It didn't even come close to what I craved. It hardly took the edge off, but after almost a year, I was used to it.

Five minutes later, I was out of the shower, and although my pants were comfortable once again, I was antsy. I was leaving for Florida in just a few hours, and considering the snow, it would be smart to check on my flight before I got Avery up and walked her home. But I had no idea where I'd put my phone. With Avery here, I hadn't even looked at it after Pop had texted that he'd made it safely home.

The living area was bright this morning. The eight inches of snow that had fallen made the world outside sparkle with that clean white energy that reflected onto all the surfaces.

Avery groaned from where she was still tucked under the blanket on the couch, stealing my attention from the winter wonderland on the other side of the glass.

Once again, my cock jumped. I forced myself to think about bird shit, since it was the fastest way to get myself under control.

"You showered already?" Her voice was garbled, the morning still caught in her throat.

I ran my hand through my damp hair. "I gotta finish packing and stuff, so I figured I'd do what I could out here before I had to wake Gianna." It wasn't the truth, but it wasn't exactly a lie either.

"Oh. I should get out of your way." She stood up and stretched. Her shirt—*my* shirt—fell halfway down her thighs, and she had rolled the waistband of the sweats, despite the drawstring. She swam in the oversized clothing, yet the sight of her like this was a punch to the gut. Because she was wearing *my* stuff, like she'd been marked by me, and that made the caveman that I'd been trying to shove deep down inside my soul jump up and scream *finally*.

I'd never understood it until Avery. I'd never gotten why team-mates went on and on about their girl wearing their jersey. Or friends who went crazy over their woman in their coat. But in this instant, seeing Avery in my clothes, it all became clear. This season would suck if I didn't get to see her sporting my number at least a few times.

She dropped her hands to her sides. "Let me get dressed and—"

"Wear my clothes," I blurted, interrupting her more than a little rudely. But I couldn't help it. The words had flown out of my mouth without my permission.

She tilted her head and frowned at me. "What?"

I sighed. Now that I thought about it, this wasn't even the caveman. This was just common sense. "Blondie, I'm not sending you home in a dress and heels. You can stay in that. Give me a few, and I'll grab a pair of socks and my snow boots."

She turned and shuffled to the window. The sigh that escaped her as she brushed her fingers over the glass hit me square in the chest. With a soft smile on her lips, she took in the snowy wonderland that Boston had become overnight.

"It's always a mess, but I love a good snow day."

I nodded. Not because I agreed, though. No, not at all. But because that sentiment was 100 percent on par for her.

"You're right. I should probably borrow your clothes. I'll freeze in my dress."

"Exactly. And if you froze, then what would Puff do?" *What would I do?*

She laughed, but she didn't turn away from the Boston skyline.

"Okay, I'll grab a couple of things. Give me a sec." I turned in a circle, searching the main area of the apartment for my phone. It only took two rotations to locate it where I'd left it on a stool by the ping-pong table. I pocketed it, then I headed back down the hall to my room. I knocked softly, and when Gianna didn't respond, I tiptoed in.

I wasn't a total dick, so I left the light off, but that meant I was forced to rummage through my drawers blindly. Once I'd found what I needed there, I slipped into the large closet and closed the door. In here, I could get away with using the light, so I flipped the switch, then searched for my Timberlands. I slipped into a pair of wool socks, then stuffed my feet into the boots and tied them tight. I tossed a hoodie over my head and grabbed what I needed for Avery, then slipped back out of the room. Thankfully, my sister didn't so much as stir.

In the living room, Avery pulled the sweatshirt I'd given her over her head and then put on the socks.

"I don't know about those." She eyed the boots I'd set in front of her. Although they'd be enormous on her tiny feet, they were tall, so they'd keep the snow out.

"Just tie them tight."

A crease formed between her brows as she pulled them on. She yanked on the laces, but struggled to get them tight enough, so I dropped to my knees on the rug at her feet. After tucking the black sweats into the top of the rubber, I tightened the duck boots as far as they'd go.

I sat back on my haunches and fought a laugh. She looked like a clown wearing shoes ten sizes too big.

She stood and lifted one foot awkwardly, taking a single step. "These suckers are half the size of my leg."

"My feet aren't *that* big." I frowned at her.

Her eyes went wide. "Are you kidding? Fourteen is huge."

Objectively, I was tall, yes, but in the world I lived in, a world full of athletes, I was hardly average.

"You should see Miller's eighteens."

"I have, and what he wears can't even be considered shoes. They're skateboards." She took another step, but the toe of the boot caught, and she stumbled. "There's no way I can walk in those things."

I roughed a hand along my jaw and chuckled.

She zeroed in on me, and her eyes went soft.

"What?" I asked when she only watched me silently.

"I love it when you smile."

Damn, that sentiment made my chest feel weird. I rubbed a circle over my heart and cleared my throat. "What can I say? You make me smile."

She tilted her head to the side, and the ends of her loose ponytail fell over her shoulder. Damn, she was cute.

More than anything, I wished I didn't have to say these next words. "Grab your stuff. We gotta get you home so I can get to Florida."

For the first time, I found a positive side to leaving for spring training. There wouldn't be any snow to greet me when I landed in Tampa.

After we bundled up, we rode the elevator down to the lobby.
While the car descended, I pulled out my phone, opened the white and
red app, and tapped the appropriate button, then tucked the device
away again.

We'd made it four steps out the front door when she teetered
forward and threw her arms out.

I grasped her wrist to keep her from going down and steadied her.

"Your giant shoes are even harder to manage in the snow."

Pressing my lips together, I took her in. Just standing still, she was
wobbling again. And her only other option was dangling off her tiny
pointer finger. "Give me those." I pointed to the heels and the dress she
had thrown over one arm.

She cocked her head but did as I asked without argument.

I zipped the shoes and the dress into the front of my coat, then
spun around and bent at the knees. "Hop on."

"What?"

I glanced over my shoulder and held my arms out at my sides.
"You can't walk in those boots, and we'll freeze if we stand here all
day. We've already been through this. Puff needs you, and I have a
plane to catch."

She rolled her big blue eyes, but she held her arms out for balance
and shuffled closer. Once she was directly behind me, she grasped my
shoulders and launched herself up as best as she could in all her oversized attire. I gripped her under her thighs to help, and she wrapped
her legs around my hips.

"Am I too heavy?"

She asked the question every woman in the world uttered when a
man lifted her off the ground. More women needed to realize men
knew how much we could carry, and if there was any doubt, then we
wouldn't pick a girl up. Holding Avery in my arms was a privilege,
and it was not one that I'd take for granted. I would never drop this
woman. Hell, if it were up to me, I would never let her go at all.

"Don't be silly, Blondie."

I trudged down the street through the icy mix. Some sidewalks had been cleared, but most were still piled with snow. The air was crisp in that just-snowed way, but I loved how it muffled the noise. The city was blanketed in a cool hush that made me want to stay out here forever.

"I love how pretty everything looks," she mused, the white fog of her breath floating around my face. "Especially this early, when most people haven't come out yet."

Even I couldn't deny the beauty of a snowy morning.

She waved to a few people as we walked. "You know, I could get used to this kind of chariot service."

Chuckling, I hefted her higher and shook my head. But the truth was, I'd happily carry her anywhere she wanted to go. "That mean you're gonna miss me when I'm gone?"

She was quiet for a minute, and when she finally spoke, her voice was hushed, her usually cheerful tone muted. "More than you know."

Those words burrowed into my skin, dropped into my gut, and tugged hard. I wanted to spin her around my body and pull her tight against my chest. Tell her I felt the same way. That one phrase gave me hope that when I got back from Florida, things would change between us.

As we rounded the corner to her building, a guy in a puffy jacket and beanie jogged to my side and held out a take-out bag and a white cup.

"Chris D?" he asked.

I made eye contact with him and lifted my chin, then to Avery, I said, "Grab that for me, would ya?"

"What's this?"

"Your breakfast." Turning my attention back to the guy, I added. "Thanks, man."

"Wait…" He pointed at me. "Are you Dragon Damiano?"

During the offseason, this happened less. Especially when I was wearing a winter hat and a giant coat. But I'd never take for granted my ability to play a game I loved. And regardless of my talent, the fans were what made it possible. So I always had at least one rose-gold Sharpie in my pocket, and even in moments like this, when I didn't love being stopped on the street, I would give them a few minutes of my time.

"Yeah."

His eyes lit up, and he lifted a fist to blow into. "No freaking way."

Avery slid off me, already knowing what was coming. And I had to give her credit. The girl hadn't once complained.

"Could we get a picture, man?"

I'd mastered the art of the selfie by now, but Avery reached out for the bag, her coffee, and his phone. "I'll take it."

She took a few, like always, and the dude thanked us repeatedly before finally leaving us alone to go inside.

"You DoorDashed breakfast for me?" She smirked at me, then eyed the bag. She only let the expression drop when she brought the to-go cup of coffee to her mouth.

In an ideal world, I would have made breakfast for the two of us and forced her to stay and snuggle on the sofa all day. Maybe put on another movie. Spend some time exploring the side of her neck with my lips, especially that spot right below her ear. The spot that made her breath hitch. But in that scenario, she was mine, and I had the apartment to myself and I had nowhere to be. In real life, I had to DoorDash coffee to her place and then get on a plane.

I cleared my throat. "We all know how you get without your coffee." I gave her a hard time, but I'd never seen her all that cranky. I was the cranky one in this relationship.

"Ha ha." She turned and came dangerously close to wiping out because of the damn winter boots.

Somehow, she saved her coffee from a sudden death, even as I scooped her up into my arms.

"Chris," she shrieked as I cradled her against my chest.

"No face-plants in the snow today. I don't have time for an ER trip." At this point, I was already cutting it close. I'd have to leave for the airport in an hour, and I still had to hoof it home and pack.

"Do you have time to come up and eat breakfast with me?" She rested her head against my shoulder.

My heart sank. Dammit. "I wish I could, but I gotta leave at nine."

Her lips turned down in a pout. "You have to come up to get your boots, at least."

I chuckled. Although I wouldn't need them in Florida, I'd appease her and take them with me. As we stepped into her lobby, it was as if the peaceful, happy bubble we'd existed in the whole way here popped. Now goodbye hung heavy in the air between us. Spring training was full of long days and lots of practice. The seven weeks would go fast, but that tingling idea that a lot could change in seven weeks hovered in my mind.

The silence in the elevator was deafening and the jingling of the keys in the lock too loud. The way the door creaked open was almost ominous. Neither of us rushed in. Maybe because she was as acutely aware of these last few minutes together as I was.

Finally, I forced myself to step inside, and I was instantly enveloped in the smell of vanilla cake that always clung to her. I'd have to find a candle to sniff while I was away so I could pretend she was close.

Wow, that sounded pathetic, even to me. I shook off the ridiculous thought and took in the space. I'd been here plenty of times, but I needed a distraction from my wayward thoughts.

Her apartment was homey. Small and cozy and so much like her. Framed photos and knickknacks cluttered every surface. The big puffy couch took up most of the living room, and her only dining area was a bar-height bistro table in the kitchen. She wobbled her way to the table and heaved herself onto a stool, and I followed.

Avery toed off the oversized boots while I took her dress and shoes out of my coat and placed them on the stool opposite her. When she'd finally extricated herself, she pushed to her feet and watched me. Her gaze was intense as she moved closer. My heart hammered louder with each step she took. Instinctively, I sensed the slight change in her. A hesitation, like she was nervous.

When she was standing directly before me, she wet her lips, never breaking eye contact. Her expression was open, needy, as she watched me.

Never in my life had I seen a woman looking more kissable than Avery did at this moment. Finally, she was putting out the signals that I had literally been waiting months for.

I snaked an arm around her waist and tucked her in close. She came willingly, even eagerly, slipping her hands under my coat and clinging to the fabric of my sweatshirt. My hands trembled, and it was suddenly hard to breathe. Bowing my head, I pressed my lips to the top of her head.

She sagged against my chest, whether in disappointment or relief, I wasn't sure.

Regardless of the thoughts running through her mind, and regardless of how desperate I was for more, Avery was a once-in-a-lifetime woman. She deserved so much more than a rushed kiss right before I left for seven weeks.

"Good luck in Florida," she mumbled against my chest, clutching my shirt tighter, like she didn't want to let go. "Have fun. And." She paused, swallowed hard, and looked up at me from beneath her lashes. "Miss me a little, okay?"

I smirked to hide the way my heart cracked just then. "I'll try." The truth was I'd miss her a whole hell of a lot. And when I got back, her year would be up.

Me: Whatcha doing for the big day?

Chris: Big day?

Me: Valentine's Day! How did you forget already? You sent Puff his favorite sand eels yesterday so he could pass them out to his potential spring flings.

Chris: I do not call them spring flings.
That's you

Me: Well, yeah. But whatcha doing?

Chris: Worried I have a date?

Chris: I don't have a date, Avery. You don't have to be afraid

Me: I wasn't afraid. Lol

Chris: So the hour-long silence was…?

Me: Work. I do that even if you have the day off.

Chris: Sure. You going out with the girls?

Me: No. Wren's out of town and Jana has an actual date. So I'm doing a rom-com marathon. Too bad Emerson isn't here. He'd love it.

Chris: What about me?

Me: Are you saying you're sad that you're missing the movie marathon?

Chris: That's exactly what I'm saying

Me: You could watch them too.

Chris: Like together on FaceTime?

Me: Sure. We can do that.

Chris: How bout I call you at 7?

Me: okay

Me: I just walked in from work. Why were there three DoorDash delivery people waiting on me when I stepped off the elevator?

Chris: Hmm. I couldn't say. Did they bring you anything good?

Me: Sushi, popcorn, an Oreo milkshake, and runts.

Chris: Wow lucky girl. All your movie favorites

Me: You never stop surprising me.

Chris: I just want you to have a good night, Blondie

Christian
33

Blondie: Picture of banana pancakes

Me: Are you bragging that you're at our favorite place without me?

Blondie: No, I'm showing you how sad the pancakes are. I think I saw a tear of batter drip down one because they're being ignored.

Me: You could eat them...

Blondie: They like you better than me. They just push my fork away and refuse to jump on.

Me: You are ridiculous, but I miss your face

Blondie: Pic of her face.

Christian
34

"YO, YOUR DAD BEING FUNNY TODAY?" Mason snapped a towel at my shoulder.

Brows pulled together, I popped out an AirPod and eyed him in silent question.

"You never laugh at him."

"Laugh?"

"Yeah. You're locked and loaded. No one gets through to you on game days but Pop. That's what you always say." Mason shrugged.

"Oh." He was right. That was my normal pregame ritual. But when I turned on my music and sat back to get into the zone, the text that made my phone buzz didn't come from my father. Avery's ridiculousness about pancakes was exactly what I needed to ease the tension creeping over me.

Our first spring training game was today, and my slider was doing better. I was ready and focused. Even Tom Wilson and I had been getting along mostly okay for the last few weeks.

"I'll bet ten to one he's talking to Blondie."

I glared at Emerson, who was standing in front of his locker, wearing just his girdle. Although they had all taken to calling Avery

Blondie so that Wilson didn't clue into who they constantly razzed me about, their use of my name for her was getting annoying. More so from Emerson than anyone else, though, because somehow, he could always tell when she called or texted.

"Ooh, I'm not betting against Bambi." Mason chuckled, throwing an elbow into my side. "But damn, that girl's gotten past the Do Not Disturb filter. That shit sounds serious."

They all knew nothing had changed. I simply shook my head and turned back to my roommate.

"How do you always know?"

Two lockers over, Asher Price, our new catcher, snorted. He'd been fitting in well with the team, and I had no complaints about him squatting behind the plate. He possessed this naturally chill aura that was contagious. So far, he and I had clicked well. "It's not hard to tell when you're talking to her."

I pivoted and narrowed my eyes on the new guy.

"You get that look." He shrugged, then dipped his chin and went back to buttoning his jersey.

"Right." Emerson whacked Price's arm twice.

Our new catcher's eyes went a little wide, and he stepped away from the mostly naked dude touching him.

"He totally does." Emerson shook out his pants and stepped into them. "Like you don't get why you're smiling, but you don't give a shit that you are."

"I think it's more like you're staring at the most precious thing in the world, and you can't believe your luck that she's smiling back." Asher dropped into his chair and untangled his socks.

"The right woman, man." Eddie, our shortstop, added with a slow nod. "Makes you feel all kinds of lucky."

"I don't think I want that." Kyle kicked one foot out and hooked Mason's vacant chair with the tip of his shoe, then pulled it closer.

With an aggravated sigh, Mason yanked it back. And the fight for the chair would continue.

"I don't want to be tied down or forced to stay in one place," Kyle went on. "I like freedom."

On either side of me, Eddie and Asher shook their heads. A year ago, I would have agreed with Kyle, but the truth was, spending time with Avery was the farthest thing from a chore, and I'd never once felt stuck or tied down. It was my favorite pastime and what I looked forward to most every week. But they'd given me enough shit, and I needed to get back to my pregame routine and focus.

"I'm in the zone," I reminded them, jamming my AirPod back in. Then I pulled up Avery's messages and got back to the conversation about whipped cream and pancakes.

It wasn't until it was almost time to head out that I realized Pop had stopped answering me. He was normally quick to give me a full rundown of every batter and what he thought I should do, so it was strange that he'd gone radio silent. Quickly, I fired off a message.

> Me: You okay, Pop? You didn't finish your take on Arizona bats

He hadn't replied by the time I had to head to the field, so I put my phone in my locker and forced myself to push away the echo of worry in my mind. My father would want me to focus on my game rather than stress over what was probably nothing.

The second I stepped onto the mound, I tapped my wrist twice and let it go.

Four innings later, I was in the zone. Our bats were on fire and we were leading six to nothing. My fastball was hitting, and even my slider wasn't shit.

Price tapped the inside of his thigh and flashed four fingers.

Nodding, I rose for my windup. I released the ball and watched as it soared to the plate and dropped into the dirt at the last second, just as the batter swung.

"Strike."

Asher tossed the ball back, but as I caught it, he turned to the dugout. I followed his line of sight and frowned at Tom Wilson, who was heading my way. Why the hell was he coming out to lecture me? I'd just nailed that fucking pitch.

"Damiano."

"No."

He and I had been doing okay for the last few weeks. But if he was going to start this *I'm the coach, bow down to me* shit and all of a sudden revert back to distrusting his players, we weren't going to make it through the season.

"Listen."

"No, you listen. My arm is on fire. I don't need to rest. I need to pitch a full game and get into the cycle again."

He regarded me, his expression stoic, and nodded. "I understand how you feel."

"So?" I gripped the ball tighter. I was not fucking turning it over. Routines were important for pitchers. So were arm workouts and resting periods. My body needed to get back into the groove of the constant pitching schedule I'd have to maintain for most of the year. If I didn't get that, I'd struggle for the start of the actual season.

He cleared his throat and ducked his head, but then he focused on me once again, and this time, when I really looked at him, I could see the concern etched on his features. "It's personal."

My chest constricted, stealing all the air from my lungs, and my mind whirled. All I could think was that he'd found out about Avery. Or had something happened to her? No. I couldn't finish that thought. I needed her smile and her crazy stories and her fucking birds that I didn't want to get close to but loved because she did.

I swallowed my panic. Locking my knees, I stood ramrod straight, hoping it was anything but Avery. "What's wrong?"

Turned out it *wasn't* Avery. But the words that came out of his mouth almost sent me to my knees.

No. Not my dad.

My legs wobbled and my head spun as I took in the details he'd given me. As if my body had taken over because my mind couldn't compute, I held the ball out to him.

He took it from me and tipped his head toward the dugout.

On autopilot, I walked across the grass and down the steps. "I need to get to New York," I said to no one in particular.

"I know."

Startling to a stop, I came face to face with Beckett Langfield.

"My pilot's prepping the plane now. I'll get you there." He patted my shoulder.

I flinched away from the touch, but I muttered a "thanks."

Continuing to the locker room, I rubbed at the ache in my chest, fixated on the possibilities of what I might find when I got to New York. Heart attack. A bad one. He'd been rushed into surgery already, but that was all the information Coach had.

I needed to call Gianna.

Shit. Gianna. She'd be devastated too.

I swayed a little on my feet. I needed to sit down. I just needed...I just needed him to be okay.

Avery
35

I WASN'T sure I should be here, but what I did know was that I couldn't stay in Boston. When Gianna called me in a panic because she couldn't get ahold of Chris, I did the only thing I could think of. I called Dad. I didn't explain how I knew or why I was so upset. Just that Chris's dad had had a heart attack and that he needed to get to New York.

Two minutes later, I saw the clip of Chris on the mound. I watched the color drain from his face as he swayed on his feet. He needed a hug. And support. So I couldn't stay in Boston and hope for the best. And a five-hour drive wasn't that big of a deal.

I stepped up to the nurses' station and rested my hands flat on the cool surface. "Um, I'm looking for Bo Damiano."

She assessed me, her expression full of compassion. "Are you family?"

"Yes." The lie slipped easily from my lips.

Her nod was slow but unquestioning. "Give me just a minute to get someone out here to walk you up. Why don't you have a seat while you wait?" she asked, holding a hand out to motion to the waiting area behind me.

I'd only been settled in an uncomfortable plastic chair for a few minutes when a man dressed in all green appeared and told me to follow him. Silently, I did. Down a hall and up an elevator. Then down another hall. Finally, he stopped in front of an open door.

I leaned forward and glanced inside.

Gianna was sitting with her feet propped up on her chair in front of her and her forehead pressed to her knees. Chris was in a chair nearby, eyes closed and leaning back, resting his head against the wall.

When the man who'd led me up here knocked on the open door, Chris's eyes shot open and instantly fixed on me.

He swallowed hard and blinked rapidly, as if fighting back tears. Without hesitation, I hurried for him. He didn't stand, but he held his arms out, his chin wobbling as he watched me cross the room. His arms were around me and squeezing tight before I even finished moving.

I dropped my purse onto the chair beside him and stepped between his legs. When he pressed his face into me, I grasped the back of his head, threading my fingers through his hair and wishing I could take on some of his pain for him as his body shook with a single sob. That was all he let out before he turned his head to one side and took a deep breath. He continued holding me tight, pressing his cheek against my abdomen. Settled only slightly now that I could see him and touch him, I kept that one hand on his arm and rubbed circles on his back, just holding him.

"How is he?" I asked, though I was afraid of what the answer might be.

Two chairs over, Gianna sniffed. "He's in recovery, but we don't know much."

"The next few hours are critical," Chris muttered against me. With a deep breath in, he finally pulled back. Then he yanked me down onto his lap and held me close.

I wrapped an arm over his shoulder and squeezed, soaking in his warmth and willing him to take the comfort I was offering.

"Can you just stay?" The words were a whisper into the side of my neck.

"For as long as you need," I promised.

Christian
36

"HE'S AWAKE?" I blinked twice, unsure that I'd heard my sister correctly.

A few hours ago, a nurse had informed us that he was stable. According to her, his vitals were looking good and they expected him to wake up at some point during the night. The relief was like a ton of bricks falling off my body.

My sister and I had always joked that Pop could never die. The reality was that he would one day. But I wasn't ready for that yet. I still needed him.

Once I knew he was stable, I had moved across the room to a double chair so Avery could lie down. I sat upright, closing my eyes and tipping my head back, keeping one hand on her hip as she rested her head on my thigh.

Her appearance last night would have brought me to my knees had I been standing. It was everything I needed and didn't know how to ask for. She'd shown up, and she'd let me hold her. She'd curled up in the chair beside me and laid her head on my shoulder, intrinsically understanding that I didn't want her to go. And fuck if she wasn't the calm I needed to get through these last few hours. She was my peace in the storm.

Thoughts of her must have finally settled my mind enough to allow me to doze off, because suddenly, Gianna was standing over me, shaking my arm to wake me.

"He's up. The nurse came in and said one of us can go back."

"You want me to go first?" I asked. Gianna struggled with new things. Anxiety would claw at her. She hated the unknown.

With her lower lip pulled between her teeth, she nodded.

I shifted, hoping to slide out from under Avery without waking her.

She stirred, and then her eyes popped open. "Everything okay?" She sat up, her eyes rimmed red and her hair a mess, looking from me to Gianna and back again, studying us for clues as to the news she was about to hear.

I stood, then squatted in front of her. "He's awake. So I'm going back to see him."

"You okay?" she asked, squeezing my hand.

I nodded, but in truth, I wasn't sure. A few hours ago, when she walked in, I'd almost lost it. I wasn't in that bad place anymore. My dad was stable and awake, and she was still here. Even so, I felt unsteady, like I was balancing on the edge of a cliff. All I could hope was that seeing Pop would help.

With a brush of my thumb against her hand, I pushed to my feet. Then I followed the nurse to his room.

The smell of disinfectant stung my nose, and my ears rang with the beeps and buzzes of machines. As we approached the nurses' station, I saw him. In a room across the hall. Behind a large window, he lay in a bed, hooked up to all kinds of wires and tubes. He was pale and gaunt, nothing like the man who was constantly laughing and teasing.

I swallowed, choking back the wave of fear rising up inside me. "Is he going to be okay?"

"He's got a long recovery ahead of him, but the odds are looking good." With a nod, she waved to the door, silently giving me permission to enter.

His eyes were closed as I stepped into the room, but I called out to him anyway. "Hey, Pop."

He cracked open his big brown eyes, and his lips twitched.

I cleared the emotion from my throat. "You gave us a good scare."

He nodded faintly. "Who's here with you?" The words were a breathy whisper.

"Just Gi and Avery and me."

His lips twitched again. "Good." Like they were too heavy for him to keep open, his eyes drifted shut, then his head sagged to one side. "Go home and rest."

My heart lurched. He was so weak. "No, Pop. We're not leaving."

He grunted, and the lines around his eyes deepened as he forced them open again. "You rest. I rest. Come back tomorrow." He wiggled his fingers at his side.

I slid my hand over his, clutching him tight. His hand was icy. Fuck. It was one more reminder of how close we'd come to losing him.

Closing my eyes for a moment, I willed the tears that stung my nose and the backs of my eyes to abate. When I opened them again, his eyes were closed, but he was squeezing my hand lightly.

"Go home," he repeated, his head lolling to one side.

"Pop." He didn't respond. He didn't move. I scanned all the medical equipment surrounding him, worried. But the beeping of the machine next to him showed that his heart rate and breathing were steady.

"He'll be in and out for the next while." The nurse patted my arm. "And he's not wrong. You should go home and get some rest yourself. You'll be more help to him once you've gotten some sleep."

With a small nod, I gave his hand another squeeze. "Love you, Pop."

In the waiting room, Gianna and Avery were huddled together on the double chair where I'd left them.

"He's sleeping again, but go see him. It's okay. He's pale and weak, but he's as stubborn as ever, so that's a good sign."

Wiping at her eyes, my sister stood and followed the nurse out of the room.

Avery rose from her chair and wrapped me in a hug. Locked in her arms, I took another breath. The cliff's edge felt farther away in this moment. Dad would be okay, and she was here with me.

When Gianna came back, we made plans to go to his place to sleep for a few hours. Avery's car was here, but we were all too exhausted to drive, so I ordered an Uber.

His house smelled like him. Like it always did. Automatically, my attention shifted to his chair in the corner. As always, there was a coffee cup on the table next to it, along with a book. Probably a mystery. He spent a solid 50 percent of his time at home in that chair. The leather was worn and molded to his frame perfectly. Fuck, my chest ached once again at the sight of the empty seat. He wasn't there. He wouldn't be walking into the room to give me shit about my pitching or Avery or anything else.

"I'm going to bed," Gianna said. Shoulders slumped, she shuffled to the stairs.

My poor sister was exhausted. She had come home from the store and found him on the floor. Her quick thinking, calling 911 and starting chest compressions, had saved him.

For hours before I arrived, she'd sat at the hospital alone and terrified. Where the fuck was Jake? Until this moment, I hadn't even thought about the asshole. I opened my mouth and inhaled, ready to ask, but snapped my jaw shut. Now wasn't the time.

"Let me know if you need anything," she added, heading up the stairs.

"Come on." I pulled Avery up to my old bedroom. "You can stay in here. I'll take the sofa." I pulled the top drawer of the dresser open and pulled out two T-shirts. I held one out for her, then I shuffled to the bathroom, leaving her to change in my room. When I returned, she was sitting on the far side of the bed with the blankets pulled over her legs.

"Stay here, Chris," she said, patting the mattress beside her. "You're exhausted. You don't have to sleep on the sofa."

It was exactly what I needed. She was exactly what I needed. Without argument, I slid under the covers beside her. When she lay beside me, I wrapped an arm around her torso and tucked her into me, inhaling her sweet scent and soaking in her warmth. Her body molded against mine, and wisps of her blond hair floated against my lips.

"Thank you, Avery." It didn't seem like enough, but it was all I had for now.

"Anything," she answered.

That single word settled deep in my heart, giving me permission to rest.

Avery
37

"I'M FINE. STOP HOVERING," an oddly grumpy Bo snapped at his daughter. In all my interactions with the man, he'd never been anything but pleasant. But now that I was seeing this side of him, it was obvious who his kids had inherited their narrowed-eyed glare from.

Two days after his heart attack, Bo had been moved to a regular room, and he was already getting stronger. He'd had a double bypass and was understandably weak, but with some changes to his diet and time for healing, the doctors were hopeful that he'd make a full recovery.

"I was just trying to fix your pillow." Gianna sat in the seat she'd claimed and shifted uncomfortably.

"My pillow is fine." He frowned at his daughter, then raised a shaky hand an inch off the bed to point at his son. "And before you suggest it again, I am not moving to Boston."

"Pop." Chris sat forward, dropping his elbows to his knees. "It makes sense for you to be where I can help—"

"You—" He gritted his teeth, and a shot of pain flashed across his features. Closing his eyes, he took a small breath. When he opened them again, he was calmer. "You are going to be in Florida for another three weeks."

"I'm not going back yet—"

"You are." His father nodded almost imperceptibly. "I'm fine. Weak, yeah. I won't argue that. I can't really lift my arms, and my chest is on fire, but I will not allow you to sit here spoon feeding me pudding when you should be pitching for the team you've been dreaming about being a part of your whole life." He regarded his daughter warily. "And you're working on the biggest project of your career. One that you're afraid to get excited about because you're worried that it'll be ripped away from you. Keep your chin up and get it done. You're talented. You deserve this. I won't let you sit here putzing around either."

Both kids opened their mouths, but Bo didn't give them a chance to argue before he went on.

"We'll hire a nurse to shovel god-awful pudding into my mouth while you go back to being the stars you are."

Both Gianna and Chris looked miserably torn. Guilt pressed down on their shoulders, and I could see their minds working on new arguments.

Bo, though still drawn and exhausted, looked resolute.

"I can stay."

Maybe. There was an issue at work, but I could continue handling it remotely if I was needed here.

Bo turned his steely expression on me, though his tone when he spoke to me was far softer than the one he'd used with his kids. "Avery, dear, you have a lot of responsibilities too. Plus, if you're here, then who will take care of my grandson?" One side of his lips pulled up in an almost-smirk.

"Fuck's sake. You can barely sit up, and you're already giving us shit," Chris muttered, dragging a hand down his face. "I don't want to leave Gi at home alone either." He side-eyed his sister, keeping his expression neutral. "What about Jake? Where is he?"

I winced, because I'd been wondering the same thing. Gianna had spoken to her boyfriend on the phone multiple times since I'd arrived, but he'd yet to make an appearance.

It broke my heart. She, like her brother, was carrying the weight of the world on her shoulders, and she needed someone here to help hold her up.

Gianna looked away. "He's been busy this week."

Chris clenched his jaw and tightened his grasp on the arm of the chair, but he kept his comments to himself.

My phone buzzed in my hand, pulling me away from what could still turn into a brawl between the two hotheads on either side of their dad's hospital bed.

> Dean: I know you're busy, and I hate to say the B word, but Sarge is feeling worse today.
> We're going to test for the bird flu. The clicking sound is more pronounced, and his eyes don't look good.

My heart lurched. Shit. We'd quarantined two peacocks who'd tested positive last week, but we were optimistic that we'd caught it before it spread.

We still weren't sure whether we were dealing with a low-pathogenic strain or a high one. A low strain, if it did spread, would require a lot of work and quarantining. We'd find ourselves in an all-hands-on-deck situation for the next few weeks. A high strain would decimate our avian population.

The difference in treatability was drastic. Both peacocks seemed to be responding to antibiotics, which was a good sign, but if it turned out that Sarge, or any other bird, was also sick, we would need to test all 407 of the birds in residence and lock down any that were positive to keep our animals safe.

> Me: Call everyone in and get all the birds tested in the next twelve hours. And call the lab. Tell them to rush the pathogenic testing. Let me know as soon as you can.

It hurt that I wasn't there to help my team. They could use the extra hands, and the guilt of not being there to oversee the situation was eating at me. Not to mention that, because I was gone, my team was constantly calling or texting me to check in, wasting valuable time and making the already challenging job that much harder.

A large palm covered my thigh, sending a wave of warmth through me.

"What's the matter, Blondie?" Chris squeezed my leg and lowered his head to study me.

"Nothing." With a shake of my head, I looked away from him and set the phone down. I had no poker face, and the last thing I wanted to do was give him more to worry about.

But with every hour, anxiety was building up inside me. It wasn't only the workload that had me feeling bad for not being there. Sarge was a fan favorite, and I'd worked with him longer than any of the other birds in residence. The idea of losing him was enough to make my eyes sting with tears.

As covertly as I could, I breathed deep once, and then again, searching for calm. Chris needed me here.

"We're going to grab coffee." Chris stood and loomed over me until I tilted my chin up and acknowledged him. He tilted his head toward the door.

Swallowing thickly, I stood too. Then I followed him out.

We'd only made it a few steps down the hall when he stopped. "What's the issue?"

I lowered my focus to a spot near the base of his neck, unable to maintain eye contact, and shook my head. "Just work."

He dipped his chin, catching my eye, and squinted.

"It's not a huge deal." With a long breath out, I stared at my UGGs, scuffing one, then the other, on the white tile.

It was the biggest issue we'd had at the zoo since I'd taken over as the head of avian medicine, so that was a lie. It was a big deal. But he'd almost lost his dad this week. A heart attack was a bigger deal.

He tucked a hand under my chin and pressed lightly, making me look at him. His dark eyes demanded answers.

"It's just bird flu."

He cocked his head and blinked several times. "Wait…" He searched my face, frowning deeply. "That's the one…that…kills birds." He went ramrod straight and grasped my wrists.

"I don't think it's that strain." With the way the peacocks were responding to treatment, it was likely the low-pathogenic strain. The lesser of two evils. So staying here for a few more days might be okay.

"Avery." He shook his head. "You're their doctor. If you have sick birds, you need to be there."

"It's—"

"Stop." Chris cut me off, squeezing both of my wrists gently in emphasis. "If we were talking about a disease in humans and you were their doctor, there would be no debate."

I couldn't disagree. And if I were on vacation, I'd already be on my way home. But that wasn't the case. I was needed here too.

He sucked in a harsh breath, and his eyes went wide. Sliding his hands down to mine, he laced our fingers and clutched them tight. "Puff is okay, right?"

"He's not sick. But we'll have to test all the birds now."

"If you're not there, that means there are only six people available to do that?" he asked.

"Seven," I corrected. "One vet, the five zoologists, and an intern."

He nodded. "Okay. This is what's going to happen. We're going to say goodbye, and then you're going to go back to Boston. They need you."

I sank my teeth into my lower lip to keep it from trembling. "I thought." I swallowed, considering him: the frown on his face, his low brows. "I thought you did too."

His lips pulled up into an almost smile, a rare sight, and he cupped my cheek. "More than you could ever know. But I'm good now. It's time for you to go take care of our little guy and his feathered friends."

I coughed and reared back, a little shocked. "Did you just call Puff *our little guy*?"

With a sigh, he lowered his hand from my face. He grasped my hand again and tugged me back toward his father's room. "Come on, Blondie."

Stumbling behind him, I replayed his words and considered how passionately he'd fought to convince me to go home and help. God, this man was incredible. And I hated that so few people saw the real him.

"Avery has to go back to Boston," he announced as soon as he stepped into the room. "She's having a vet emergency."

Gianna crossed her arms and tilted her head, as if she was miffed that I'd bail.

"What's wrong?" Bo croaked.

"The birds have the flu. We don't want Puff to get sick, so she's saying goodbye and driving home. They need her. The birds can't die." Chris tugged me to the chair where I'd left my purse.

Gianna's eyes widened, and she bolted upright in her chair. "What?"

"Hopefully it's not that bad," I rushed out as Chris shoved my purse into my arms. "Really, I can stay. They've got it covered—"

"We just had this conversation," Bo gritted out. "Everyone is going back to their important lives and leaving me be. Remember?" He shot each of us a glare. "Because I am fine."

"It sounds like they need you, Avery," Gianna added.

My heart felt like it had cracked in two, but I'd go. It was clear they supported the decision, and there was a lot to get done at the zoo. I stepped up next to the bed and patted Bo's hand. "I'm glad you're doing better."

"We'll see you soon." He flipped his hand over and gave mine a light squeeze.

Gianna appeared beside me and shocked the hell out of me by throwing her arms around me. "Thanks for being here for my brother," she whispered. Then she pulled back and glared at Chris. "Come back with actual coffee after you walk her to her car."

With a shake of his head, Chris herded me from the room. He was quiet as we rode the elevator to the ground floor and as he guided me to the parking garage.

"Are you sure you don't want me to stay?" I asked, frowning up at him.

"Your job is important." He opened my car door and put gentle pressure on my lower back. "And we're good now."

Still torn, I held my breath, but I climbed into the driver's seat.

He rested a hand on the door frame and leaned down. "Drive safe, okay?"

All I could do was nod.

"Text me."

I nodded again, feeling like a bobblehead.

He swallowed and shut his eyes. When he opened them again, an intensity I hadn't seen in forever shone brightly in them. "I can't tell you how much it means to me that you came. Or how much I needed you these last few days." He cleared his throat. "You showing up, being here for me without me having to ask?" Ducking his head, he went silent for several heartbeats, but then he swallowed, his throat working, and fixed his gaze on me again. "It means so much."

We were frozen like that, neither of us moving, the air around us charged in a way that buzzed almost audibly.

On impulse, I leaned up and pressed my lips to his. He jerked back like I'd shocked him, bumping his head on the doorframe in the process. He cupped a hand over his mouth and stared at me, wide-eyed.

And my heart sank, along with my stomach. Shit. I had thought...

"Sorry," I said, whipping my head around and studying my hands in my lap.

"No, Avery, it's not..." He trailed off.

"I should go." I swallowed back the tears threatening behind my eyes and blinked rapidly.

He sighed, his shoulders slumping. "Text me when you get home."

"Yup." I nodded, but I couldn't bring myself to look at him.

He cupped my cheek and gently turned my face so I was forced to look at him. "After Florida, we're going to talk."

I nodded again, not trusting my voice.

And with that, he stepped back and shut the car door between us.

Great. That was just great.

Christian 38

Me: Did you get home okay?

Blondie: I ended up going straight to the zoo

Me: How is everything there?

Blondie: Just busy. They had 8 more positive tests already. Puff was negative, though, so you don't need to worry.

Me: I'm glad the little man is okay. But listen...I don't like how we left things. I know you're busy, but we need to talk about that kiss. I don't want to do it on the phone, but when I get back, we need to talk, okay?

Blondie: Sure. Great.

Me: Ok

Christian
39

"SIT," Tom Wilson barked at me.

Holding back a grunt of annoyance, I dropped into the black chair in his office at the training facility. This space was smaller, more efficient than his space in Boston. Pretty much black and white. Not much personal shit. Just a phone and computer on the desk. A stack of binders and a few books on the shelf behind him. A white board with notes on the opposite wall. The man was pretty streamlined.

His fists clenched on top of the black desk and he angled closer. "I thought I told you a few more days."

He had, but my dad was doing better. His only issue when I left was that he was aggravated with Gianna and me for being around constantly. And if I couldn't be at the hospital with him, then there was no point in staying in New York.

I fully intended to bring him up to Boston as soon as I was back home, but Gianna and the two lovely nurses we hired would have it covered when Pop transferred to a short-term care facility. So I was back in Florida.

"It's been four days. I'm ready to pitch."

He narrowed his blue eyes, the ones he'd passed on to Avery, at me. Automatically, my hand lifted to tap my wrist in what had become my heartbeat of calm over the last year.

I took a deep breath and racked my brain, searching for words I could string together coherently. Avery and I were not in a great spot, and it was my fault. I owned that. She had shocked me when she kissed me, and I'd reacted like an asshole. I'd been waiting a year for that moment. I'd planned and thought about every detail of how I'd finally kiss her again. And nowhere in the grand scheme I created did I intend to give her a quick peck in a hospital parking lot before parting ways yet again.

Maybe I should have opened up to her then. And I definitely should have gone in for another kiss. But even if I had, we'd still be ten states apart and probably even more unsure. Because I wasn't in the right head space to have the conversation we needed to have.

Our texting for the last few days had been shit. She'd been busy with the sick birds, and I'd been dealing with setting up care for Dad, so our only communication had been limited to quick check-ins that revolved around those two topics.

I swore I almost passed out from relief when she told me the puffins and penguins had tested negative. But then I'd wished I could pull her in close and hold her when she mentioned that Sarge was getting sicker. That was really weighing on her. But I wanted to give her space to deal with that, and I was making an effort to be here to listen when she needed me.

Plus, I couldn't dive into my feelings about her through text message. It was a *look her in the eye, slash my heart out of my chest, and hand it to her* type of conversation.

"Does this mean you think you don't have to listen to me?" Tom Wilson's words jarred me back to the present.

Clear the air with him. That was my goal.

"Sir." I swallowed. "I know I need to listen to you, and I respect that you have more knowledge and experience than I do."

He cocked his head to the side, his lips parting slightly.

"But," I continued, resting my elbows on the armrests of the visitor chair and lacing my fingers, "it's a two-way street."

He reared back in his chair and crossed his arms.

I held out a single hand. "Please let me explain."

He gave a clipped nod.

"I want you to hear me, so that means I need to stop yelling. I get that. I need to stop acting like an ass, because no one takes a person like that seriously."

His brows were practically in his hairline now.

"This season, I'm going to work on being calm, but I also intend to work on clearer communication."

Not only with the Revs coaching staff and my team, but with this man's daughter. And as soon as I was back in Boston, that would be my top priority.

"In that regard. I want you to hear me out. I appreciate the time you gave me to take care of my dad. It means more than you know that no one questioned my need to leave and no one expected me to rush back. So thank you."

He nodded and steepled his fingers in front of him. "You're welcome. We understand family comes first."

"Now," I said, "I'm telling you that my dad is stable and cared for. And for me to be a successful member of this team, I need to start pitching. I'm ready."

He glared at me for a good minute before he finally huffed a big breath out of his nose.

"You've grown a lot this last year. I see that. When you showed up, you were a hothead who couldn't control himself. But the man sitting here today is one who's obviously making smarter choices." He leaned his forearms on the desk. "And I will do my best to listen when you talk and hear what you are saying."

"Thank you." I lowered my chin and left it at that.

For a long moment, neither of us moved.

He raised a brow like he wondered if I had more to say. But I didn't. And after another minute, he gestured to the door. "If you're playing today, then you better warm up and get dressed."

I almost smiled, but instead stood and held out my hand. "Thanks, Coach."

He sighed but stood and took it. "Now shut the door on your way out."

A huff of a laugh worked its way out of me at that. Some things would probably never change.

Avery
40

Chris: You okay?

Me: Yup

Chris: You're really quiet

Me: Just busy with the birds. It's been a long three weeks, but I think we finally have the bird flu problem under control.

Chris: I'm glad they're all getting better, especially Sarge

Me: Me too

Me: You pitched a good game yesterday.

Chris: Thanks

Me: Did you land in NY yet?

Chris: Yeah in the Uber on the way to Pop

Me: Give everyone a hug for me.

Chris: They would all think it's weird if I hugged them. I don't hug

Me: You hug me

Chris: You're different

Avery
41

I SET my phone down and sighed. Yeah, I was different. But what did that mean to him?

Kissing him had been a colossal mistake. Since that moment, things had been weird. We were both trying to be normal but doing a terrible job. The proverbial ostrich in the room made our conversations stilted and awkward, which meant we'd been talking less.

What I'd hoped would be an opening to explore our relationship had instead had the opposite effect. The moment I kissed him, Chris slammed that door between us shut. I could have sworn he had been sending signals for a while. Like maybe he was hoping for more from our relationship, like I was. But his reaction was in direct opposition to that. I was confused and couldn't say I was thrilled for the *I think we should be friends* conversation that we were going to have when he got home. I had no idea how I'd misread everything so badly.

"Babe, you still pouting about the not-boyfriend boyfriend?"

I glared at Jana.

"I'm telling you, I have the solution." Wren sat on the stool at my little table, legs crossed and a stiletto dangling from her foot.

My best friends had come straight from work, so Wren was dressed to perfection in high-waisted pants and a tight white button-down, and Jana and I were in jeans. But while Jana was wearing a cute sweater, I'd thrown on a worn T-shirt today. At least it was clean. For the last few weeks, while we'd been working to stop the spread of the flu, I had been showering and disinfecting at work.

"It's not the worst idea." Jana shrugged, propping herself up against the counter.

"I don't want to go out on a date. Even if I did, who would I go out with?"

My friends, in their never-ending quest to try out every bad idea in existence, had decided that the answer to my issue with Chris was to go on a date with another man.

"Then why not talk to Chris about trying for more?" Jana tapped her black nails on the granite next to her. "I don't get what the issue is."

"What if I feel this way about him because he's what I'm used to? What we have is easy, yeah, but maybe it's because we know each other so well. Because we've spent all our free time together since last summer." I shrugged. "And dating has always been intimidating for me. That's why I'd just force myself to fit into the mold of whatever my boyfriend at the time was looking for in a woman." My stomach knotted. "Maybe I should take another year off. I'm clearly not any closer to being comfortable out there again."

Wren blew out a harsh breath. "If you want to know whether you just like the idea of dating *someone* or if it's Chris in particular, then go out with another guy. What will it hurt? Either it'll feel like it does when you're with Chris, or it'll be totally different. Then you'll get your answers."

"But what does it matter when he made it pretty clear that he didn't want me kissing him?"

"What if you just caught him off guard?" Jana asked. "Actually talking to him would probably go a long way in solving the issue."

I didn't disagree, but he'd told me twice that we'd talk face to face. And I wasn't going to rush the weird *hey, I love having you as a friend, but that's it* conversation.

At the sound of a knock, I hopped off my stool and headed for the door, thankful for the interruption. If that conversation had gone on too much longer, one of them would've decided they had the perfect friend to hook me up with.

I pulled the door open, and a smile split my face. "Dad?" I asked, throwing myself into his arms. "What are you doing here?"

When I stepped back again, he tucked his hands into the pockets of his jeans and rocked back on his heels. "Got in today and wanted to take my daughter to dinner. Is that wrong?"

I led him into the apartment and closed the door quietly. "No, but Wren and Jana are here. Would it be okay for them to come along?"

"Ooh, look. It's big daddy." Wren smirked at my dad from where she was still perched on a bistro stool.

My father's jaw ticked as he glared at her.

"Hi, Mr. Wilson." Jana waved.

He gave her a quick nod and a small smile, then cocked a brow at Wren. "See how easy that was?"

She let out a breathy laugh. "So much less fun."

"Wren." I sighed. "Dad wants to go to dinner. You can come too, but only if you can behave."

She rested her chin on her fist and batted her lashes. "I can behave. Scout's honor, Mr. Wilson."

I couldn't even look at my father. Wren was gorgeous, and if he noticed, I might puke.

"I'll go pull the car around, then," my dad said as he backpedaled.

"Great," I chirped, ushering him to the door. Once he was gone, I stomped back to the kitchen and pointed at Wren. "If you make me want to throw up at dinner, I swear that will be the last meal you'll ever eat with us."

With a chuckle, she hopped off the chair. Then she wrapped an arm around my shoulder. "I'll be good. And honestly." She rested her head against the top of mine. "The solution to your problem is simple. If you'd talk to Chris, I think you two would realize you want the same thing."

Maybe, but I had no idea what that was. For now, I'd push thoughts of Chris to the back of my mind and enjoy dinner.

Dad's favorite pub, O'Hannigan's, was only a couple of blocks from the stadium, so the ride was an easy one. Particularly since Wren had stopped trying to annoy him. And when we stepped inside the place, we were immediately seated.

"Oh, Avery, I forgot to tell you." Wren clapped once our drinks had been brought out. "You know that Stonehenge print on the wall in your bedroom? The one by John Constable?"

I nodded and picked up my beer. "It's Dad's favorite." I tipped my head his way.

I wasn't into art the way he was. Or like Wren. She was obsessed, hence her career as an appraiser.

She sat a little straighter and turned her attention to my dad. And for maybe the first time in her whole adult life, she spoke to him like she did the rest of the population. "Really?"

He cleared his throat. "Just before I was drafted into AAA, I spent some time traveling around England. Salisbury was one of my favorite stops." He stared off into the expanse of the bar, his expression far away. "Stonehenge fascinated me, and I fell in love with that painting. I'm a fan of Constable in general. I have a few of his prints."

Wren rested her elbows on the table and tucked her hands under her chin. "How did I never know this about you?" She shook her head and waved the thought away. "Anyway, the original was delivered to the auction house today."

"Isn't that at the MET?" Dad lowered his chin and focused on his beer. He was acting weird.

She smiled. "The family wants it priced. They aren't sure they want to sell, but..." She shrugged. "Who knows."

"Hmm." My dad still didn't look up. Not until his name was being called across the restaurant.

"Wilson." A tall, good-looking man was heading toward our table. He wore a gray cashmere sweater and slacks that were tailored to him perfectly. His brown hair was crafted into the perfect side part. He looked like a shiny penny. Almost the opposite of Chris, who was a backward hat and ripped jeans kind of guy.

"Jude." My dad stood and shook hands with the man. Then he turned to us. "Jude, this is my daughter, Avery, and her friends Wren and Jana."

I held out a hand to shake his, trying not to compare his warm palm to Chris's as it wrapped around mine.

"Are you here with anyone?" my dad asked.

"No." He waved a hand dismissively. "I just ate at the bar."

"Want to join us for a drink while we wait for our food?" My dad slid into the chair next to where he'd been sitting so he was closer to Wren, and Jude dropped into the one next to me.

Jana lifted her hand and waved it between Jude and my dad. "How do you two know each other?"

"I'm the sports editor for the *Boston Globe*." Jude paused and scanned the table, wearing a smirk, like he was waiting for us to be impressed. He looked to be in his thirties. He was probably on the young side for such a prestigious job. I guess it was something to be proud of.

"Cool," Jana finally said.

"Do you know that Mr. Wilson coaches the team?" Wren's comment was pure sarcasm.

He chuckled and ran a hand over the front of his sweater. "Really? I hadn't heard. Just like I hadn't heard that the Revs are sniffing around UConn."

My father chuckled. "No work talk tonight."

Jude nodded and put both hands up. "Heard."

The waitress brought out our burgers, and Jude ordered an IPA. Then he focused on me and asked what I did.

"I'm a vet at the Boston Zoo."

He sucked in a quick breath. "That must be rough, at least lately."

I glanced at him out of the corner of my eye, surprised by the interest I saw in his expression.

"I follow the Instagram page and saw you guys have been dealing with a lot of sick birds for the last few weeks. I was worried about Wobbles."

Our snow owl had spent two weeks in the animal hospital.

"Yeah, I can't tell you how much time I've spent reassuring people on social media that Wobbles and Sarge are okay." Jana shook her head. "It's become my full-time job."

"Well, Boston loves them." Jude laughed.

"Both are doing better now." I picked up a french fry. "We actually got Wobbles back in his exhibit today."

"I saw." He smiled. "Are you all worried about any of the other animals?"

"Do not say that online." Jana pointed a fork at him, and he held both hands up.

"Luckily, we don't have a strain that spreads to other animals, so they should all be okay. And we've pretty much got it extinguished at this point."

We all fell into an easy conversation about the birds at the zoo, and before I knew it, dinner was over and the waitress was dropping off the check.

"I got it," Jude said, swiping the bill and standing up.

"You don't have to," my dad insisted, but Jude waved him off.

"I want to, but be prepared to answer my questions in the locker room," he joked. Then he turned back to me and handed me a black business card. "Call me, Avery. I'd love to hear from you."

Without another word, he walked away. When he was out of earshot, my friends broke out in a fit of giggles.

"That right there is the perfect solution to your issue." Wren waggled her brows at me.

"Huh?" I asked.

"That man clearly wants to take you out." Jana rolled her eyes.

"*What?*" My dad frowned at Jude where he stood at the host stand with his back turned to us. "You're not dating."

"It's been a year, big daddy." Wren smirked and tapped his upper arm with the back of her hand. "Keep up with the times."

He spun to me. "Already? I thought you started this no dating thing during the summer."

I shook my head. It was the night before opening day. As I walked home from Chris's apartment. One year ago tomorrow.

My heart ached at the memory. At the thought of Chris and the way he'd reacted to my kiss. I sighed and rested my chin on my hands, reading over Jude's business card.

"It has been a year," I confirmed. "But I'm not sure he's who I want to date." He seemed nice. And the conversation had been easy. But—

"How will you know if you don't try?" Jana asked, angling forward and giving me a genuine smile.

"Plus, no one will know but the four of us. If you hate it, then you'll know. No harm, no foul, right?" Wren cocked a single brow in challenge.

"I guess." My shoulders drooped, like the weight of the moment was threatening to pull me down. I wasn't sure, but I tucked the card into my purse anyway. Maybe they were right. Maybe I should see what it felt like to go out with someone who wasn't Chris. Even if I kind of hated the idea.

Avery
42

Blondie: Good luck! Opening day is a big one

Me: thanks. You coming?

Blondie: Not this time. I have a thing.

Me: What kind of a thing?

Blondie: Just a dinner.

Me: Like for work?

Blondie: Not really. But text me after the game and let me know how it went.

Me: Sure, have fun

Christian
43

I SCOWLED AT MY PHONE. I was an idiot for assuming she'd come to the game tonight. I should have invited her. Now my stomach was sinking and my heart felt like it had been pummeled by the news that she wouldn't be here. I rolled my shoulders back, mentally berating myself for reading too much into it. She had only been to a few games last season. But it was opening day, and I was pitching, so I'd honestly thought that she'd want to be here.

With a grunt, I tossed my phone into the locker. My dad was still recovering and didn't text the way he used to. Not often, at least. He and I had talked a few minutes ago, so I wouldn't hear from him again. And apparently, Avery had a thing.

And was it just me, or had she been cagy about what her plans were? It wasn't my place to demand details, but her short responses had a knot forming in my gut. I sank into my white folding chair and glared at the Revs logo in the center of the floor. Most of my teammates were chilling on the sofas surrounding the space, but I had no interest in being social.

I hadn't seen Avery since that stupid goodbye at the hospital because I'd only gotten back from New York a few hours ago. The trip had been successful, and my father would be moving into a small apartment near mine and finishing up his rehab here. I wanted him close, and we both agreed that it would benefit Gianna if we relieved some of the stress she'd been under. Over the last month, she'd been more down than normal.

Still, I had hoped to see Avery after the game was over. I'd envisioned bumping into her in the team room and asking her to hang out after. We were only here for another day before we left on a four-game road stretch, but I desperately needed to talk to her face to face.

"You good, Damiano?"

I snapped my head up and zeroed in on Wilson, who was standing in the doorway to his office with his hands resting on either side of the frame. He assessed me with a wariness I didn't quite understand. Not only had we not had any issues for weeks, but I hadn't had a single problem with fans or the media during spring training. I thought I'd finally found his good side. The running joke was that I'd been reformed during the offseason. Hannah liked to take credit. It was all stupid.

I cleared my throat. "All good."

He watched me for a long moment, not speaking. Then, with a nod, he turned and disappeared into the recesses of his office.

Weird. Although maybe it wasn't. Normally, I had a routine. And today, I wasn't on my phone with AirPods in. I sat forward, resting my elbows on my knees and running my hands through my hair, willing the trepidation that had been eating at me to fuck off so I could get in the right headspace for the game.

Price pulled up a chair next to me and dropped into it, legs spread wide. "Worried about the arm?"

I shook my head.

"Good." He reached out to pat my shoulder but stopped himself. "Sorry. No touching." He crossed his arms and leaned back. "Don't stress. Your fastball only improved this year, and your slider is exactly where it should be."

"No, I'm good." Standing, I snagged my AirPods from my locker and popped them into my ears. Then I slumped back in the chair again and closed my eyes. I didn't cue up a playlist, but my teammates didn't need to know that. Normally, this was the only signal they needed when I wanted to be left alone.

After I pitched a ho-hum first inning where we almost hadn't kept the Rockies from scoring, Emerson slid onto the bench next to me.

"You freaking out about..." He glanced over at Wilson, like he was making sure he was out of earshot, then lowered his head. "Avery."

I kept my face set in a blank mask and focused on Eddie Martinez as he stepped up to bat. "I don't know. It just feels weird."

"I bet it does." Emerson snorted.

The crack of the bat echoed through the stadium, and Eddie's bouncing grounder slipped between first and second, putting him on base easily.

Emerson scratched his head. "I don't know why she's going out with him."

The words registered slowly, but when they did, my stomach dropped to the floor. I turned to face my friend, feeling like I was moving through thick putty. "What?"

He shrugged and frowned, which was an odd expression for my always jovial roommate. "I know. It's been a year, yeah, but did she have to go out with someone on opening day? Come on. Even Wren realized it would fuck with your head, so she told me to keep an eye on you."

I opened my mouth, but nothing came out. I blinked. Then I did it again. The world around me went blurry, and suddenly, I couldn't feel my face.

Was he saying that Avery, *my Avery*, was currently out on a date with another man? My hands shook so violently I had to fist them against my thighs as I cleared my throat and searched my brain for the right words to ask.

"She's dating?" I growled.

He turned and finally really looked at me. His eyes went wide, and he slid back just a little. "Uh. That's what I heard." Cracking his knuckles—a nervous habit of his, I'd learned over the years—he whirled around. "Streaks, come here."

Kyle slid down the bench. "You freaking out about Avery and that douchebag reporter?"

I blinked, and my already cracked heart split right in two. Did everyone but me know about this? My chest felt funny, and I thought maybe my hands were numb now, as well as my face. And my chest burned. Wait. Was I breathing? I sucked in a hard breath.

"How long?" I wheezed.

Kyle tilted his head to the side, and Emerson frowned again.

"How long has she been dating him?" I gritted out through clenched teeth.

"You didn't know?" Kyle lifted both hands and glowered at Emerson. "Why did we tell him *now*?"

Emerson shook his head. "I thought—"

A bat cracked, and the stadium went nuts. Vaguely, I was aware of Asher Price's hit going over the right field fence. The guys around me stood, clapping and hollering. Robotically, I forced myself to my feet too. There was a good chance I gave Asher a fist bump as he moved past me, but in reality, I didn't know how I'd found myself standing on the mound at the start of the second.

My hands had been checked by the umpire, and the guy was reminded again that I didn't put shit on them, because I was weird. But I didn't remember speaking.

Avery clouded all my thoughts. An image of her smiling at some nameless, faceless asshole who didn't deserve her was all I could see. I wanted to kill him. But what if she really liked this guy? What if he made her happy? My heart wrenched, crumbling further. More than anything, I wanted her to be happy. How could I wreck that?

I nodded, unseeing, at the sign Asher gave me.

The fucker better treat her like a goddess. She deserved that and so much more.

I wound up and threw the ball. And I didn't even wince when it hit the dirt a foot in front of the plate and bounced toward the away team dugout.

If he didn't treat her with respect and shower her with affection every minute of every day, I'd kill him. And he better be good to her damn birds too. Because she loved them. Her boyfriend should recognize and support that.

The ball hit my glove with a *smack*. I brought my glove in close and looked at Asher, nodding, though I hadn't registered the sign.

Maybe I shouldn't let her go so easily. I'd been such a fucking dumbass when she kissed me. Maybe she didn't realize that I wanted her to pick me.

I threw the ball at Asher.

A pained groan echoed around me. "Fuck."

That brought me back to the moment, finally. At the plate, the batter was limping in a circle.

Asher was standing at his full height, his mask pushed up on his head. Then he was trotting toward me.

"Dragon, you got this?" he asked.

I blinked. He was holding a ball out to me, but rather than take it, I spun around, bent at the waist, and took in a deep breath. No. I didn't have this. I felt like I was going to throw up.

Emerson came up, squatting next to me and putting his hand on my back. "Let's get through this. Then you can talk to her, okay?"

I swatted at his hand and stood up.

"Damiano." The bark was deep and harsh enough to have me spinning around.

Wilson stood on the mound with his arms crossed over his chest and a glower on his face.

With a thick swallow, I prepared myself. I had promised this man calm communication, and I owed him that.

"Pull me." The words slipped easily from my lips.

His brows jumped to his hairline, and his arms fell to his sides. He pursed his lips and scrutinized me, like he was getting ready to talk me off the ledge.

That wasn't happening. "You need to pull me. My head." I swallowed and made the admission. "And my heart. They aren't here. I love this game, but I might be losing the single most important thing in my life." I blinked hard at the sting in my eyes. "I have to go fix that. So yeah." I nodded. "You need to pull me."

Avery 44

"YOU REALLY DON'T NEED to walk me up." I pushed the button for the elevator to my floor.

"I was hoping you might want to invite me in for a drink." Jude smiled. "Especially since dinner was short."

Dinner was short because he showed up more than thirty minutes late. A "work thing" came up. A story needed to be changed or something. I wasn't sure. He had glossed over the details, then changed the subject by asking about my day. After I'd sat alone for so long, I was pretty sure the waitress had thought I was being stood up. When Jude finally did arrive, she hurried us through the meal. Probably because she wanted to turn the table over. Not that I was complaining about the quick meal.

Jude was an okay guy. He did an okay job of listening when I spoke, and he asked somewhat thoughtful questions. But he also ordered a bottle of wine without asking whether I'd like any or noticing the beer sitting in front of me. Then he'd told the waitress we were skipping dessert. Again, without asking me. I would have rather skipped the dinner and had dessert only, since they served my favorite Oreo cheesecake.

For a year, Chris had treated me better than Jude did tonight. Day in and day out, he was thoughtful and caring. Yet we hadn't once been on a date. Even so, Chris had set the bar for how I should expect to be treated. And this guy, nice or not, didn't come close.

The elevator dinged, and as the doors slid open, he placed his hand on my back and guided me into the stainless-steel car. I was hit with an overwhelming need to brush off his touch, but I didn't want to come across as rude, so once we were inside, I turned and leaned on the wall. This way I could step away from him without making it obvious.

"Maybe another time." Or not. Honestly, I wasn't interested in doing this with him ever again. I hit the button for my floor, anxious to get home so I could text Chris and see how his game had gone. I should have trusted my gut and gone to the game instead of this stupid dinner, but my friends had insisted I go when Jude suggested the date and time. So in the end, I'd given in.

"Are you busy this Saturday?" he pushed.

"It's my bestie's birthday, so we're doing that." We'd briefly discussed the possibility of a night at a club or something similar, but I'd run with that if it kept me from doing this again. Why had I even texted this guy?

The elevator jerked to a stop, and the doors opened. Across the hall, a man sat on the floor with his back to my door. I processed the long legs clad in ripped jeans and the white Nikes before I really saw him. He was hunched over, elbows on his knees, his head hanging and his hand tapping on his wrist.

"Chris?"

He snapped his head up at the sound of my voice, and for one second, a wave of relief washed over him. But then he looked past me, and his face hardened.

"Don't you have the stomach flu?" Jude's question shocked me.

"What?"

Chris was sick? Was he okay, and how didn't I know? Scratch that. Of course I didn't know. For weeks, I'd avoided speaking to him and had kept our text exchanges as short as possible.

My heart panged in my chest. Was it another emergency—wait. Was his dad okay?

Jude stepped up beside me and placed his hand on my arm. I had to fight the way my body wanted to recoil at his touch. Chris's jaw audibly clicked as he glared at Jude's hand.

Quickly, I stepped out of Jude's grasp. "Is it your dad?"

Chris shook his head and reached for the baseball cap on the floor next to him.

"He left the game during the second inning after he almost threw up on the mound. Coach said he has the stomach flu," Jude explained.

I barely heard the explanation. My focus was locked on the wisp of back hair that peeked out around Chris's backward hat. He didn't look sick, just pissed.

"That's why I was so late tonight. I had to get the story ready to print tomorrow and shift some things around, since it's going on page one."

Chris pushed to his feet. "Are you telling me you made her wait on you for a date?"

"You know how it is. Sometimes work—"

"Is less important," Chris finished, shaking his head. "Get the fuck out of here."

"Excuse me?"

Chris stepped closer and hit him with a glare that was reminiscent of the ones he had been so famous for months ago. "Turn around. Hit the button." He pointed at the elevator. "And leave. *Now*." He scoffed. "Anyone worth her time would show up early to wait on her."

I took in my very angry friend from head to toe. His jaw, dusted with a five-o'clock shadow, was locked tight, and his hands were shaking at his sides. As his words ricocheted around my head, I realized that I'd never once had to wait for him. He'd always shown up and patiently waited for me to finish work, or he'd hung out while I finished my hair or makeup before we headed out. If we were meeting up, he'd be there when I arrived.

I heard the elevator ding behind me, but I didn't bother turning to watch Jude leave.

"You okay?" I asked, taking a tentative step toward Chris.

He shook his head. "I'm not sick. But...Talk." He swallowed hard.

"We need to talk." His voice was laced with a desperation that made my chest ache.

"Okay."

"Can we go inside?" He tipped his head toward my door.

Right. The hallway outside my apartment wasn't the ideal place to have a conversation.

Nodding, I pulled out my keys and stepped up to my door, my knees wobbling as I went. Dread and anticipation mingled inside me. Was he going to tell me that I shouldn't have kissed him? He wouldn't be this desperate to talk to me if that were the case, right? Had he gotten suspended again? He'd worked so hard with Hannah for months, but had he slipped and gotten himself in trouble? Would I have to watch reports about it on the news? Would my dad be cursing his name for the next week and a half?

He stepped inside behind me, and as I closed the door, he strode to the family room and paced behind the sofa. He ran his palm over his face and turned back to me. Dropping his arms to his sides, he balled his hands into fists and scanned my face, but he didn't speak.

"What happened at the game?" I asked, stepping into the room.

He blew out a breath. "I asked your dad to pull me."

"What?" My breath stuttered out of me. That didn't sound like him at all.

Brows furrowed, he put his hands on his head, his arms out. "Yeah, he was shocked too."

I shook my head and slipped my coat off. I dropped it over the back of the sofa before I rounded it so I was looking at him head-on.

He took me in, starting at my ponytail and working his way down my wrap dress to my legs and the flats on my feet. "You look gorgeous."

My stomach jumped at the compliment. I hadn't ever paid attention to how much Chris complimented me. Not really. But it stood out in this moment. Especially since Jude hadn't said anything about how I looked, which was kind of shitty. Like he hadn't bothered to notice.

With Chris, I always felt seen.

"Thanks." I smiled, but the expression slipped instantly, and I shook my head. "Chris, wait. What happened? You spent all last season pissed off that you couldn't finish a game, and now you're telling me you asked to be pulled?"

He frowned. "Some things are more important than baseball, Avery."

Wearing a mask of determination, he closed the distance between us.

"You were on a date." He bit the words out. "With some guy. And I had to say this before you had time to decide whether you liked him."

He traced the line of my jaw with one finger, eliciting the same kind of spark inside me his touch always did. I fought the shiver that threatened to race up my spine.

I couldn't meet his eyes. If I did, there'd be no stopping that reaction. And I knew that buzz that heated my stomach would hit like it always did when he looked at me with a tender expression on his face. And then I'd want more.

He stepped impossibly closer, his gray Revs shirt pulling tight across his chest, the R and the S settling on swells of his pecs.

I desperately wanted to reach out and run my hands over his chest, rest my head against his sternum.

I wet my lips. "Say what?"

"Pick me," he whispered.

My heart flipped in my chest, and I snapped my head up. "*What?*" The word was barely more than a breath.

"If you're ready to date, if you're looking for someone." He cupped my cheeks and took in every inch of my face before finally meeting my eyes. "I'm right here. *Pick me.*"

I swallowed and grasped his wrists. "What?" Clearly, my brain was malfunctioning, since that was the only word I could form. I didn't understand. I'd tried to kiss him weeks ago, and he'd acted like it was the last thing he wanted.

"I'm probably messing up again. Like I did when you kissed me. I screwed up so fucking bad that day, and I waited way too long to fix it. Because now I'll have to contend with that jackass." He stumbled over the words. "But I've been waiting a year, Avery. *A year.*" His eyes flashed. "But if you're ready." He released his gentle hold and dropped to his knees in front of me. "I am literally begging you to pick me."

I stared down at him, all but gaping. How on earth could he think that I *wouldn't* pick him?

He squeezed his eyes shut, and a look of defeat overtook his features.

"Wait." I dropped down in front of him, mirroring his pose, and clutched my hands to my chest. I swallowed past the lump in my throat, searching for the words to explain it. "I thought you didn't want that."

He opened his eyes again and searched my face frantically.

"When you didn't want me to kiss you, I thought—"

"Avery." He cupped my cheek again. "I've wanted this since the night we met. I was giving you time to figure out what you wanted. You said you were taking time off to find out how you deserve to be treated. I respected that. I wanted you to know what you're worth, because you're worth everything."

My heart stuttered painfully in my chest. God. That was exactly how he made me feel. Worthy. Deserving. And I hoped I made him feel that way too.

He leaned forward and pressed his lips to my forehead. "I hate the way I reacted to your kiss. I was surprised. That's all. And reeling. I had pictured that moment for eleven months." He brushed his lips down my nose, making my heart rate speed up and my breaths come faster. "That second I'd get to press my lips to yours again. When I could taste you again." He hovered over my cheek, moving slowly toward my ear, his mouth brushing against my skin as he spoke.

My lips parted, but I was speechless. Frozen.

"When you'd wrap your arms around me." He pressed his lips against my neck just below my ear.

A shiver raced down my spine, and a moan escaped me.

"I was shocked," he said against my skin. "But only because I wanted so much more, and you were about to drive away." His breath skated along my jaw as he moved closer to my mouth.

My heart hammered, and my body throbbed as he paused no more than a centimeter from my lips. Goose bumps broke out across my skin.

"Chris." I whimpered. If he didn't kiss me in the next ten seconds, I might explode.

"Kiss me again, Blondie," he whispered.

Without reservation, I pressed my lips against his.

He eagerly responded, his mouth moving against mine. A current of electricity shot down my spine, and I shivered.

I'd almost forgotten how it felt to kiss him. But just like last time, every cell in my body zapped to life. He groaned as his tongue swept into my mouth and tangled with mine.

Pressing closer, I wrapped my arms around his neck. His hands were running down my back, then they were at my waist, pulling me in tight. With my body locked against his, he spun. Suddenly, I was on my back, and his body was covering mine, pressing into me. He ground his hard cock against my hip, and my body responded, arching into him. I clawed at his back, knocked the hat from his head, raked a hand through his hair.

He pulled back, panting. "We should slow down." The passion swimming in his eyes was powerful enough to set me ablaze.

I didn't want to slow down. I wanted to be owned by this man. Dominated. It had been a year. And finally, I was ready for more. I *needed* more.

"We've been slow enough," I said, bringing my mouth to his.

He ran a hand up from my hip, over my breasts, then down my stomach to the tie that held my dress in place. With one hard tug, it came loose, and then his palm was on my bare skin, and my body lit up. He splayed a calloused hand over my ribs, brushing the underside of my breast with his thumb.

"I need to taste these tits again, Blondie." Deftly, he unsnapped the front clasp of my bra, then backed away. Heat flashed in his eyes, and then he was there, lapping at my pebbled nipple and giving it a hard pull. The rough stubble of his jaw sent tingles radiating through me as he continued his exploration. Need swamped me, heating my veins and my core. Whimpering, I arched into him, pressing my breasts against him. The floor was hard under my back, but I relished the pain.

It only amplified the pounding between my thighs. The ache only he could ease.

"Chris," I panted, thrusting my hips against him but not finding relief. "Please."

He released my nipple and pushed himself up to his knees. With one hand, he yanked his shirt over his head. Then he was back, his lips skating down my body. "Do you want me here?" He kissed just under my breast, then worked his way lower. "Or here?" He peppered kisses across my stomach, then ran a line from one hip to the other with his nose, his hot breath teasing a path back and forth. "Or here?" He dropped lower, and on cue, my knees dropped open. "Or maybe you want me to clean up the mess I know you're making right here." He pressed his lips to the lace covering my pussy.

I moaned. "Yes, there."

He pulled in a hard breath, inhaling my arousal. "You're soaked, and I fucking love it. I can't wait to feel you come on my tongue." He hooked his fingers into the lace of my panties and pulled them off, then he was back, settling between my thighs. With a groan, he lapped at me. "My favorite flavor." He licked my sensitive skin again, humming as he went.

I whimpered and rocked against his mouth, desperate for more.

He draped his forearm over my belly to keep me from bucking. "Settle down. I've waited a year for this. I'm going to take my time, and enjoy every single drop of you." Then he got back to work, licking, sucking, nipping, until I couldn't take it anymore.

In record time, an orgasm ripped through me, and I came with his name on my lips.

He worked me through the release before taking one long, slow lap against me. "You're fucking perfect. I can't wait to be inside this beautiful pussy. Look at how you're dripping for me." He pulled back, once again on his knees, and studied my face, one side of his lips tipping up just a little. "Can I fuck you, Blondie?"

Spent, yet desperate for more, I nodded, slapping my palms to the floor on either side of me. "Yes. *Please.*"

He hauled himself to his feet, undid his pants, and shucked them and his boxers off in one yank. Then he was on his knees before me, gripping his long cock in one hand while digging through his pants pocket.

"I'm on the pill," I blurted.

He froze and blinked at me, his lips parted and his chest heaving.

"I want to feel you, Chris. Just you. I know I'm good."

He swallowed but gave his dick a rough squeeze. "I've been dreaming of this moment for so long, fucking my hand, pretending it was you."

The images of him getting himself off to the idea of me made my core throb.

He pressed one palm into the floor beside my head and rubbed the tip of his cock through my pussy, covering himself with my wetness. I tipped my head back, my body pounding with desperate need as he teased my clit with his tip.

"Please." I arched up to him.

"I'm good too. I've never not used a condom. But are you sure, Blondie?" His fingers bit into my hip like he had to physically hold himself back from slamming into me.

When I nodded, he pressed himself into me slowly. "*Fuck*. You feel so fucking good." With a groan, he thrust forward until we were fully connected. He dropped his other hand and buried his face in the crook of my neck, groaning against me. "I need to move."

"Yes," I begged, wrapping my legs around his waist and pulling him tighter against me.

He pulled back and thrust into me again and again, all the while murmuring filthy words in my ear. Faster and more frantic with every thrust, he took me higher and higher. I arched into him, needing to take him as deeply as I could, wanting to stay like this forever. With that small movement, he hit a spot that made my vision blur. Over and over, he continued until my legs were quivering and I was getting dangerously close to falling into oblivion.

"Come for me, Blondie," he growled in my ear.

Those words, that tone, were all it took. As if on command, I exploded, pulsing around him, squeezing him.

He let out a guttural groan and buried his face deeper in my neck. "Avery," he grunted. "*Fuck*." His arms shook as he came inside me. His breath pounded against my neck and his body trembled with aftershocks.

With a harsh breath in, he spun us so he was lying flat on his back. He settled me on his warm chest and held me tight. "You're fucking perfect, Avery. I can't wait to do this at least ten more times."

Christian
45

MUTED LIGHT FILTERED in through the window, dancing over the blue floral bedspread. I wasn't sure what time it was, but morning had definitely come too soon. Mostly because I'd spent half the night inside Avery.

I couldn't stop my smile. Fuck, it had been a good night. One that I couldn't wait to repeat. Hell. Why wait? We could relive it right now.

I rolled over and stretched out my arm, ready to pull her to me just like I had in the middle of the night. Only instead of her soft, warm body, I only felt cold sheets. Dread knotted in my gut. No way. This was her apartment. There was no way she'd ghosted me again. I flung the quilt back and scanned the room for my clothes, rubbing at my itchy eyes. Dammit. I'd slept in my contacts. It took a minute for me to remember that I'd ditched my clothes in the living room.

Images of Avery on the ground beneath me flashed through my mind and sent a tingle down my spine. I licked my lips, swearing I could still taste her. So where the fuck was she?

"Blondie?" I called as I hauled myself out of bed.

No response.

"Avery!"

Still nothing.

I stomped into the living area and swiped my boxers off the ground, then stepped into them. Her apartment wasn't big, so she clearly wasn't here. But why would she flee this time? I was holding my jeans and digging out my phone when the door opened and Avery appeared.

At the sight of her, I released a harsh breath. Fuck. My heart was beating out of control, and not in a good way.

When she noticed me, her eyes went wide. Her hair was pulled up in a messy ponytail, with several strands escaping, and she was wearing what looked like pajama pants under her coat and her UGG boots.

"Oh, shoot. You're already up." She shut the door, then she balanced the brown bag she was carrying in one hand while she shook her free arm, attempting to take her coat off.

I hustled to her and took the bag out of her hand. Then I helped with her coat. Her cropped tank gave me the perfect view of her creamy skin. I couldn't stop myself from pressing my lips to her shoulder.

She hummed and shivered in response, tilting her head to give me better access.

With a smirk against her skin, I wrapped my free arm around her waist and pulled her back so I could nestle my cock against her ass. "Hmm. This is how I wanted to start my morning."

"How are you possibly hard again? We barely slept." Avery giggled and ground her ass against me.

"Because I'm looking at you, and both my cock and I know where we belong."

"Good, because I definitely like having you both around." She spun and gave me a quick kiss.

And fuck if the naturalness of the moment didn't settle deep in my bones. I was still a little stunned when she snagged the bag from me, but I snapped out of it and hung her coat, then followed her to the kitchen.

"Where did you go?"

"Did you miss me?" She tipped her chin up as she set the bag on the counter.

I propped myself up on the doorjamb between the kitchen and foyer and watched her unpack plastic containers. From this point on, I'd ensure that we communicated better, so I was going to say all the things, even the ones that made me nervous. "Actually, I was worried you might be having doubts."

She stopped and frowned at me, her brow furrowed. For a heartbeat, she just watched me like that. Then her eyes widened and she dropped the container onto the counter and moved to me. She cupped my face with both hands. "None." She slowly shook her head. "No doubts, Chris."

My lips pulled up at the corners. "Good." I skimmed the bare skin of her waist, then leaned in to cup her ass and give it a squeeze.

"As much as I'd love to let you make me come a few times, I'm starving. And your omelet will be cold if we don't eat now."

"Aw, Blondie. Did you pick up breakfast at Mama P's?"

She smiled proudly and skipped back over to the counter. "You're always doing all the nice stuff. Now it's my turn." She picked up the three containers she'd set on the counter. "Can you get the coffee and the utensils?"

With a nod, I shuffled closer and pulled the beverage holder out of the bag.

"I wanted to feed you before you had to be at Lang Field."

The reminder hit me like a slap to the face. Dammit. I had to be at the stadium before noon. We had a game tonight, then an overnight flight to San Fran.

"What time do you have to leave?"

Fuck. I'd had less than twelve hours with her, and already, I had to leave her and fly across the country.

I pushed away the annoyance, committed to enjoying what little time we did have together. "Not for a couple of hours."

Pressing her lips together, she nodded, but she averted her gaze.

"What's the matter?"

She took a breath, and my stomach sank.

"Nothing," she finally said, focusing those beautiful blue eyes on me. "I was just thinking about what would happen when you got there. Whether Dad would ask questions. And I'm worried that things could get complicated from there. I don't want him and his stuff to mess anything up before we have time to just be us."

"It won't," I promised. "I won't let anything mess this up. And we don't need to say anything today, Avery."

She blinked at me, a little line forming between her brows. "You don't want people to know about us?"

I set the coffee on the counter and cupped her neck. Beneath my palm, her pulse hammered. For a moment, I just soaked in how good it felt to touch her like this.

"Baby." I dropped a kiss to her forehead. "I would scream it from the rooftop, post it on social media, tell the entire planet you are mine."

Her lips lifted, and her cheeks went pink.

But I would own the problem that she was referring to. "All that said, I get that your dad and I have a not-so-great history. I've been working on it. And there are the no-dating rules." He paused. "I think it's in our best interest to not break the news to him today. Let's do it together, and let's come up with a way to talk to him without making it a big, dramatic thing. You know he'd hate that. I'm good with waiting for a bit if you are."

The tension in her shoulders eased, and the worry lines around her eyes smoothed out. "Are you sure you don't mind?"

"He hates drama, Avery. So let's not be that. We can deal with it after the road trip." I pressed a quick kiss to her lips.

She smiled against my mouth, then pulled back and skipped to the sofa with our take-out containers in tow.

I followed her, watching as she sank onto the sofa. As I approached, she tracked my movements, her gaze raking down my chest. When it dropped lower, she wet her lips.

My chest swelled. I'd never get sick of turning my girl on.

When I was directly in front of her, she walked her fingers up my abs slowly, wearing a wicked grin, sending sparks through my body.

"Are you almost smiling again? Your cheek muscles are going to get worn out if you keep this up."

I chuckled. Hell yeah, I was smiling. She lit up every part of me. Every molecule in my being was relaxed and happy. Because everything that I'd ever wanted was in front of me right now. She worked her way back down my abs, and this time, my cock jumped.

I grabbed her hand. "If you keep going, my omelet will get cold, and then you won't get to enjoy it."

She sighed but pulled her hand away, then turned to the food on the coffee table. I dropped down next to her as she opened the first container. My omelet. Next were my potatoes. She opened her pancakes last and set the lid next to the black container before carefully pulling the bottom cake from the stack and placing it on the lid. She slid it to me, and I handed her a coffee.

I'd just gone back for mine when she stuck her fork in my omelet and stole her first bite. My heart settled in a way it never had before. If every day was like this one, I'd never have anything to complain about again. She took her usual three bites, then turned back to her whipped cream breakfast. She was shoveling in the first dollop when she reached for the remote.

The TV was tuned to ESPN, and there on the screen was footage of me bent in half on the mound. Emerson was squatting next to me as a commentator explained how I had been pulled from the game due to the stomach flu.

The screen went black, and the room fell silent.

"Sorry." Beside me, Avery's shoulders were hunched and her head was bowed low as she dragged her fork through the whipped cream on top of her pancakes. "I should never have gone out with him," she whispered.

"Hey." I grasped her chin and turned her head so she was forced to look at me. The sadness in her eyes made my heart hurt. "I hate that another man had the chance to take you out," I said, sticking to my new motto and being open with her. "But what happened yesterday taught me a valuable lesson. I should have made it clear to you long before last night how much you meant to me."

She swallowed, but she kept her focus locked on me.

"And I guarantee, Blondie, that from this point on, you won't ever question how I feel about you."

Her eyes misted, and she blinked rapidly.

I pressed my lips to hers, willing her to believe every word. She went pliant in my arms and sighed into my mouth. With a swipe of my tongue along her lips, she opened for me, and I dove in, tasting her natural sweetness mixed with the whipped cream. I dropped my hands to her waist and pulled her onto my lap. Then I pressed her against me and thrust my hips into her warm pussy.

She broke the kiss. "What about breakfast?"

I slid one hand along her waistband and slipped it into her pants. Palming her ass, I squeezed. Then I moved lower until my fingers ran along her slit, where she was already warm and wet for me.

She moaned softly.

"You got your warm omelet already. I couldn't care less if my eggs get cold." I sank a finger into her as I sucked on the sensitive skin just below her ear. "And there's something much hotter I need to taste."

When I pulled back to give her a wicked grin, she grasped my neck and pulled me close. And I let myself get lost in her, knowing this was exactly where I was always meant to be.

I knocked on the door and was immediately met with a pair of icy blue eyes. After being upstairs for thirty minutes and then spending another fifteen getting cleared from my "stomach flu" with the trainer, I got a message to report here.

"Shut the door," Tom barked.

I dipped my chin and stepped in. Shit. What were the chances that I could make it through this conversation without having to bring Avery into it? Although eventually we had to face her father, it made sense to give it a little time. She'd struggled through relationship after relationship with men who were only with her to get closer to her dad. Now she wanted to give the two of us a chance to settle in before he inevitably got tangled up in things. Her connection to him didn't matter to me, but the man was my coach, so whether we liked it or not, there was no escaping his involvement.

Plus, I wanted to give her time to build confidence in our relationship before he caused waves.

"Sit."

I dropped into the chair, used to this routine we had created. Him barking at me. Me trying to act like I didn't hate it. But I owed the man an apology.

"My freak-out yesterday was unprofessional, and I appreciate you covering for me." I shifted in my chair.

He sighed and ran a hand down his face. "It took a while, but I've come to terms with it. You'll always be an emotional player."

I blinked and reared back. "I'm sorry?"

He frowned but shook his head. "I'm not saying it's a bad thing, Damiano. You feel things big, and you're passionate about them." He focused on something behind me for a beat and let out a breath. "And since the two of us are very similar in a lot of respects, I expected less explosiveness, more analytical control."

I winced.

He held up a hand. "You're working on being more controlled, and I respect that. I've also learned that you need a style of coaching that differs from my norm."

I frowned, forcing air into my lungs. What the fuck was happening right now? "What?"

"I tried to box you in, but that wasn't the best approach. Because I want you to be passionate. About some things, at least."

I sat a little straighter, trying to process everything he was throwing my way.

"Winning, for example. You want the team to win, and you're self-aware enough to know when you aren't going to help us get there. Your slider. I thought pushing you to throw it would help, but you weren't avoiding the pitch. You knew it wasn't there."

"I did tell you that," I mumbled.

I'd been honest with him from the beginning. He'd just had a stick up his ass and refused to listen. A year ago, I would have pointed that out. A year ago, I did point it out. But in all the wrong ways.

He chuckled and leaned back in his chair, the leather creaking beneath him. "Not many people are honest enough to admit their faults, but you don't have that issue. You recognize weakness and you work to be better. You worked that pitch obsessively in the offseason, and it shows. It's stronger than ever. And although I didn't always believe it, I know you're an asset to this team."

"Thanks."

He pressed his hands together and tapped his chin with his fingertips, all the while watching me carefully.

I didn't shift or break eye contact. I just waited.

Finally, he let out a breath through his nose. "So you keep working on control and communication, and I'll work on listening and being the coach you need." He dropped his palms to the desk and pushed to his feet. Then he held a hand out to me.

As I shook it, I kept my jaw locked tight. He was right. I was honest to a fault, and right now, I wanted to tell him that I loved his daughter, and that I'd prove to him that not only was I an asset to the team, but that he'd never find a man who would treat her better than I intended to. I couldn't say any of that. Not yet. And leaving the office with the lie of omission hanging in the air was unsettling.

Christian
46

Blondie: I don't know if you get texts on the plane, but OREO CHEESECAKE? My doorbell just rang and this was waiting for me.

Blondie: Pic of a full cheesecake in a to-go box

Blondie: How?? they don't do takeout

Me: First, it's the Rev's plane. Of course Beckett has WI-FI. Second, I will always make it happen for you, Blondie. And thank your doorman. I heard he and his wife had a lovely dinner and took dessert to go

Blondie: You are my favorite human

Me: Someday I'll beat the birds

Blondie: GIF of an eye roll

Me: What are you wearing?

Chris: You know I'm about to play a game, right?

Me: You asked me first!

Chris: You're going out clubbing with Jana and Wren. I'm going to be stuck sitting on a bench, watching a baseball game while picturing men hitting on you

Me: Nah. Jana and Wren will get all the attention. People don't notice me.

Chris: Trust me, Blondie, everyone sees you. You're gorgeous. Have fun

Blondie: I'm sitting on the sofa in the exact same spot you made me come on your tongue, missing you desperately.

Me: I'm sitting two rows behind your dad on this flight. NO SEXTING

Blondie: pic of a sad face.

Me: You're beautiful, even when you frown, but I prefer a smile

Blondie: I'll smile when you're home.

Me: I'm on my way home. After the game, we'll go back to my place to make up for the five days we've been apart

Avery
47

I COULDN'T HELP but smile down at number thirty-five. His back was to me, but I was enjoying the view. The way his royal blue jersey pulled across his broad shoulders and how perfect his ass looked in white pants. Other than on TV and FaceTime, I hadn't seen him in days. So I'd soak in the sight of him for as long as I could. The national anthem ended, and we all clapped and lowered into our paddle seats.

"I love it when they wear the white pants." Smirking, Jana rested her booted feet on the railing in front of us and sipped her High Noon.

"I like the pinstripes better. Makes their asses pop. But it's hard to pick a favorite ass out of that lineup, isn't it?" Wren lifted her chin and scanned the guys. "Not for Avy, though. She has her favorite."

Jana leaned forward and waggled her brows at me. "Are you ready to thank us yet?"

I frowned. They'd told all of Chris's friends on the team about my date, and I was still irked by it. Chris had been distraught that day, and I hated seeing him like that. "Just because it worked out doesn't mean it was a good idea. You two caused a whole load of trouble."

"Ooh, I love trouble." Dylan, Cortney Miller's fiancée, peeked over the railing separating the owner's box from ours. "Can I help?" She was a gorgeous, bubbly redhead with curly hair and a bright smile.

Next to her, Liv Langfield inhaled deeply and held it, then blew it out slowly. "She means can she help solve the problem, not cause trouble."

"Right," Dylan chirped. "That's exactly what I meant." The way she pursed her lips and rolled her eyes, though, gave her away.

"Firefly, are you about to cause chaos?" Cortney Miller walked out the glass door clad in a pinstripe Revs jersey and holding a pink bundle.

"Oh my gosh." I hopped up. "Willow's here!"

Chris had sent me photos of the two-week-old, but I'd yet to meet her. A very proud daddy turned and tipped forward carefully so we could see her big blue eyes as she looked around. She had a full head of red hair and the chubbiest cheeks I'd ever seen; she was an angel.

"Can I hold her?" I asked.

Cortney frowned and took a small step back, but then Dylan was by his side and plucking the baby out of his arms. "She's not made of glass, Samson. Let her experience other people's energy, or she'll never grow into a well-rounded member of the greater we." She spun, her red hair flapping around her, and handed me the baby. "And we really want Willow to experience all those pinks that Avery channels."

Even wrapped in the thick pink blanket, the little girl hardly felt like anything in my arms. I bowed my head so I could get a good whiff of that baby scent and gave her a small squeeze. When I looked up again, Cortney was stepping up to the half wall, asking for her back. I couldn't help but chuckle at the overprotective dad as I gently placed her in his arms.

Once he had his daughter securely against his chest, he took a step back, and his eyes widened. "Oh, wow." He smirked. "This is the first time I've seen you in a jersey that wasn't two decades old."

Shit. With my heart lodged in my throat, I tugged at the blue shirt I'd pulled on over my hoodie and shifted on my feet, scuffing my Converse on the ground. I hadn't thought through an explanation, although I should have known someone would notice that I wasn't wearing Dad's number 49 and comment. "Yeah, I uh—"

"Lost a bet." Wren waved a hand in the air, saving me from stumbling through a nonsensical reason. "Whoever got the most guys to buy them drinks on my birthday got to pick the jersey for the loser." She smirked. "Why she thought she'd beat the birthday girl, I have no idea."

I rolled my eyes at her. She had tried to get us to bet her, and though I'd resisted, I had been the one to drag her drunk ass home on Saturday night.

"Huh." Cortney looked out at the field and watched Chris walk out to the mound. "We should get Willow in. It's cold out here. Come on, Dylan." He tipped his man bun toward the glass door, and the two headed inside, with Liv on their heels.

I let out a breath.

"Thanks for covering," I said to Wren. "I didn't think about who'd be sitting in the box next to us." I leaned against the railing.

Chris was standing on the mound, but he was looking my way. A thrill shot through me at the attention. Slowly, I turned in a circle, showing off the jersey he didn't know I had tucked into my drawer before spring training started. A smile pulled at his lips as he dug his foot into the sand beneath the mound. He watched me for a long moment, then tapped the fingers of his right hand on his left wrist.

My heart flipped in my chest, and I couldn't hold back the smile creeping over my face.

"What?" Jana asked.

"Nothing." I sat back down, adjusting my denim skirt.

Chris nodded at the sign Price gave him, then wound up. The way he lifted his arm and snapped the ball toward home plate was fluid, like a choreographed dance. The ball traveled so quickly it was hard to see before it slammed into Asher's mitt.

"Strike!"

The 105 flashed on every Jumbotron in the stadium.

But Chris just tapped his left wrist twice and went on.

My guy was on fire.

Christian
48

ADRENALINE POUNDED through my veins as I swiped the ball out of the air. We were at the top of the ninth, and this next pitch would hopefully end the game. My shoulder burned, but I relished the pain.

This would be my first complete game of my major league career.

It was part of what was causing the thrill that was currently ripping through me. But a large part of this incredible feeling could be credited to the blond up in the stands wearing number 35.

Fuck me. The moment she turned and showed me the number emblazoned on her back would go down in history as one of the best of my life.

I bent down and took the signal from Price. Then I stood and worked the ball between my fingers. I tapped my left wrist again. Avery probably didn't understand what it meant. But that small movement was all for her. That spot on her wrist was the first place I'd ever touched her.

I wound up and threw the knuckle ball.

It soared over the plate perfectly, and when the batter swung, he caught only air.

"Strike."

As I headed off the field, my teammates crowded around me, offering me fist bumps and head rubs as I moved past them. I might shy away from physical touch, but it was hard not to get into it with the guys I trusted most after a game like today's. Tons of reporters stopped me, and I answered a few questions before moving on. Although I gave them the time, there was really only one person I wanted to see. A blond in a blue jersey who owned my soul. The guys were rowdy as we headed toward the locker room, and no one noticed when I hung back and slipped into the empty training room. I waited a solid minute, then snuck out the side door and back into the hall.

Eventually, my job required me to go back in and talk to the reporters who would flood the locker room, demanding to know how it felt to pitch my first complete game of the season.

Good. That was the answer. They would roll their eyes and make comments about my lack of words. But that's how I felt. Good.

I only had to wait a few minutes before Avery, Wren, and Jana were dancing down the hall, laughing. I heard them before I even saw them.

"Blondie."

At the sound of her nickname, she turned, and when she caught sight of me, her face lit up. After she murmured to her friends, she skipped my way.

I opened the closet door beside me and yanked her inside, and my lips were on hers before either of us had said another word.

Finally, we came up for air. "You in my jersey is the best kind of hello," I muttered against her mouth.

"I missed you," she whispered.

With a groan, I pushed her up against the wall and claimed her mouth again.

Her lips brushed mine as she broke out in a smile. Damn. The sight of this woman in my jersey brought out a deep need to own her. I ran a hand up her inner thigh beneath her denim skirt. When I found my warm, wet target, I couldn't hold back a groan.

"Mmm, someone is as eager as I am."

"I missed you." She moaned. "Please don't tease me. Touch me."

Her breath skated across my lips as she pleaded with me. And fuck, was I more than willing to accommodate her request.

I slipped my fingers under her panties, teasing her slit, then sliding into her. Her pussy sucked me in, gripping my fingers tight as she rocked against me.

My cock throbbed against the cup in my girdle, desperate to get to its favorite place in the world.

"God, I should be embarrassed by how wet I am."

"Never," I demanded as my body heated further. "I love that you're drenched for me, Blondie."

I yanked my hands from her, and she groaned her protest. But I needed them both to free my cock from my pants and jock. I made quick work of them, then grasped her hand and brought it to me.

"Feel this. See how hard you make me." I groaned in her ear. "I'm not the least bit embarrassed, so you shouldn't be either."

While she stroked me over and over, her hand warm and soft on my rigid length, I yanked the hem of her skirt up around her waist. Then I snaked my hands around her hips and under her ass so I could lift her up. When she wrapped her legs around my waist, I rested my forehead against hers and heaved out a shaky breath.

"I need to feel that bare pussy milking my cock."

Whimpering, she reached between us and shifted her panties to one side. When she lined up my cock with her pussy, I thrust home. The second I was fully seated inside her, we both groaned.

Eyes locked with hers, I pulled out and slid inside her again, and I swore I could see into her soul. With every thrust, a small part of me left my body and moved into hers. Like we were being woven together so deeply it would forever be impossible to tell where she started and I stopped. I pressed her hard into the wall, slamming into her, desperate for a deeper connection. As the pounding pressure spiked in my blood and need raced through me, my breath came faster.

"Don't stop," she said. "Harder, Chris. Please."

With my lips over hers, I quieted her sounds as I buried myself as deep as I could go again and again until, finally, her tight pussy pulsated around me. I swallowed the moan that worked its way from deep inside her. The sound and the way she trembled in my arms sent me into a frenzy. I thrust faster and harder until euphoria swamped me. It hit with so much force I had to lock my knees to keep us upright.

"Avery." Her name left my lips like a prayer. I pressed her hard against the wall, needing the extra support. My arms shook as I buried my face in her neck and inhaled that heavenly scent of cake and her. Neither of us moved for a long time. We stayed wrapped together, breathing hard, soaking in the moment for as long as we could. That hard yank that I'd been feeling so often in my chest pulled at me. I wanted to stay like this forever.

"I didn't hear anything at all." Emerson's voice broke through my haze of pleasure. "I very much doubt anyone is in the closet."

Fuck me. A new kind of adrenaline kicked in then. Maybe we were louder than I thought.

I swallowed thickly, focusing on holding her up and keeping us still. Avery looked at me, wide-eyed and released her legs from around my waist. Gently, so as not to make any noise, I lowered her to her feet, but I kept her pressed to my chest.

"Sometimes we get rats down here. But I'm good at scaring them away. I'll check it out."

"Have you seen Dragon?" one of the assistant coaches asked. "He isn't at his locker, and Coach is pissed."

"No, man. Haven't seen him," Emerson called from just outside the door. "If I do, I'll let him know he needs to hit up his locker and that the reporters are waiting for him."

"Why are you out here with all the tunnel lights off?" The man's voice sounded closer too.

Avery's body went more rigid in my arms. But I wasn't worried. My teammates would cover for me. They had all season.

"I just like being in the dark, man. It's cool and quiet out here. It helps my Zen." There was a long pause, then, "I'd get my pants on and get into the locker room if I were you, Dragon. I might be able to convince that dumbass that it's rats, but Wilson isn't a moron."

I shook my head at my roommate, but I couldn't help but chuckle.

Avery buried her face against my chest and giggled. "You better go."

After one more slow kiss to her lips, I pulled up my pants and adjusted myself in the girdle. "I'll make sure Emerson lets you know when it's clear."

And with a smile stuck to my face, I slipped out the door. Today had been fucking perfect.

Avery
49

I TRIED to shimmy to the edge of the bed, but the heavy arm wrapped around my waist pulled me tight against the solid chest behind me.

"No," Chris mumbled into my neck. "Five more minutes."

"You've said that three times already."

"I've been back for four days, and this is the first time I haven't had to be at the stadium by seven. Give me a few more minutes to enjoy all this smooth skin." He buried his face in my hair and splayed a hand over the bare skin of my stomach.

I spun to face him. "I've got to get a few hours of work in before we meet my dad for lunch."

A trickle of dread ran through me at the thought of talking to Dad today. He'd be annoyed that I'd broken his rule about dating a player, but my hope was that he'd take it in stride once I assured him that this wasn't a fling, and it wouldn't cause drama for him or the Revs.

"You may have a day off, but I didn't get that lucky," I reminded him.

He frowned but leaned in and gave me a quick kiss. "Fine. We'll get up."

When I'd finally gotten out of bed, I swiped a pair of his sweats off the floor. "I'm stealing a shirt."

"Good luck. It's laundry day. I'm not sure I have a single clean shirt in the place." He laughed as he headed into the en suite bathroom.

I yanked open his T-shirt drawer, only to find it completely empty. Shutting it again, I moved on. When I pulled open the top drawer, my stomach lurched, and I froze. It was full of underwear and his wallet. Plus three boxes of the rose-gold Sharpies he always carried nowadays. And folded beside the box was what looked like a woman's shirt.

What the heck was this?

With trembling hands, I picked it up and held it out in front of me. It was a blue crop tank top. And in the drawer below it? A lace thong. It only took a second before I was hit with a memory of our night together a year ago. I'd worn these out that night, and I'd left them behind in my rush to get out of here. It was months before we bumped into each other again, and yet he'd held on to them?

Beneath the thong was a white slip of paper. No. It was a napkin.

No freaking way. Gently, I pulled it out and set it on the dresser. It was my awful drawing. The map I'd made of all my favorite places. The coffee shop with the best almond milk vanilla latte. Arti's famous Thursday special—North Side roast beef. My favorite Hawaiian pizza place that does North End pizza on Fridays. And Mama P's banana pancakes. At the top right corner was another drawing. A pair of love-birds, and beneath it, the word *Blondie*. It was the only part of the map that didn't look like a kindergartener had drawn it.

I startled as a solid arm banded around my waist.

"You kept this stupid drawing?" I asked, resting my head on his shoulder.

"It's not stupid." He pressed his cheek to my temple. "For a while, it was all I had of you, and then it was insight into how to help you realize that I saw you."

My eyes widened. He'd told me that he waited a year, and I believed him. But every day, he surprised me with the small clues that showed me how serious he'd been from day one. My eyes tracked over the blue and silver drawing.

"I asked you for a rose-gold Sharpie that night." I surveyed the boxes.

He nodded. "And that's all I carry now, because if you ever asked for one again, I was going to have it on me."

The sentiment made my chest tight. I turned and pressed my lips to his and slipped my tongue into his mouth. He tasted like toothpaste and him and a future only he could give me. One that I'd always dreamed of, even if it had felt out of reach. At least until Chris had come into my life. I wrapped my arms around his neck and pulled him closer.

"Blondie." Groaning, he gripped just below my ass and lifted me so I could wrap my legs around his waist. "If you're teasing me, you better stop now."

I smiled against his full lips. "I think we have enough time."

"Hell, yeah." With a quick squeeze to my ass, he carried me back to the bed.

Dad: Time totally got away from me. Sorry, Avy, but I have to cancel lunch. I'm still at UConn and won't be back until tonight.

I sighed at the message. I was used to it. His life was hectic during baseball season. The Revs were after a twenty-two-year-old senior from UConn who was killing it at first base. But Dad had promised that he and Cortney would be back by one today. As usual, baseball had taken over his life. He'd always been there for the things I needed him for, but often, if it wasn't a necessity, he didn't have time for it. I probably should have emphasized that I wanted to talk about something important. Then he would have made it happen. But I hadn't wanted to answer questions until we were face to face, so I hadn't even mentioned that I'd be bringing someone with me to lunch.

> Me: Okay. Can we do breakfast Sunday morning? I really want to talk to you.

The team had a doubleheader on Saturday, and they were leaving for Seattle on Sunday afternoon. I didn't want another week to go by without talking to Dad. Chris had let me lead when it came to him, but he was an open and honest guy. He didn't like keeping secrets, and it would ease his nerves if we could get everything out in the open. I was the nervous one, but I also knew it was time.

> Dad: Everything okay, Avy?

> Me: No problem. But I want to catch up, so I'm enacting our non-cancel clause.

I stood from my desk and headed to the Puffin Penguin house, where I was meeting Chris. When I arrived, he was inside the exhibit, hanging out with Puff. He was sitting on a towel to keep his ripped jeans from getting covered in bird poop.

With one wrist resting on his knees, he had his head bent low, and he was talking to his bird. "You're looking sharp again now that the colors on your beak are back. Puffette over there keeps looking your way. I think it's time to make your move." He glanced over at the female. "Don't wait too long. I know from experience that you'll regret it if she ends up looking at someone else."

Chris held up a finger and twirled it, and in response, Puff twirled around on the rock next to where he was sitting. When the bird stopped, he waddled over to him and nudged his knee.

"He wants his prize," I said, wandering their way with the small bucket that Chris never brought in with him.

Puff's head snapped up, and he was in the air, then perched on my shoulder before I made it to Chris.

"I'm trying to talk him into going after the prize." Chris tipped his head toward the female puffin with the pink band. Somewhere along the way, Chris had decided that she was Puff's mate. Whether Puff was totally on board remained to be seen. He pushed to his feet and took a few steps away from me. He knew what came next and preferred not to linger too close.

Shaking my head, I snagged a small fish from the bucket. Then I tossed it into the air. Puff launched himself off my shoulder, caught it in his beak, and dove into the water. Within seconds, all twenty of the birds in the room were swarming my feet. I tossed them all a few fish each before Chris and I left them to enjoy their lunch.

After washing our hands, Chris reached for mine. "Nervous?"

"He canceled," I admitted.

He pulled me to a stop and frowned. "What's he got going on that's so important he had to cancel on his daughter?"

I shrugged. It wasn't a big deal. "Barring an emergency, unless I specifically tell him I really need him, from February until November, baseball trumps all."

Chris ran a hand down his face, and the backward hat on his head shifted slightly.

I sagged, suddenly feeling weighed down. "Sorry."

He pulled his hat off his head, then repositioned it. "No. Don't be sorry. He's *not* going to cause stress for us." Looping his arm around me, he tucked me into his side and brought his lips to the crown of my head. "I promise."

Maybe not for *us*, but keeping our relationship a secret was eating at Chris.

"We rescheduled for breakfast on Sunday. I made it clear that he can't cancel, so he understands that it's important."

His chin bumped the top of my head as he nodded. "So now that we have an unexpectedly free afternoon, what do you want to do?"

"Its March in Boston, besides depression, which shuts down half the city, there isn't much else going on." I stepped out of his arms and turned back to my office. "Let me get my stuff and we can figure something out."

Walking beside me, Chris pulled out his phone. He opened the door to the cool spring afternoon, but his focus was still set on his device. Once we'd collected my things from my office, we headed out through the zoo's exit and onto the streets of Boston.

"Since we still have the reservation at O'Hannigan's, want to just eat there? We can hop on the green T line. It's two stops from here."

"Sure." Chris nodded, his thumbs flying over his phone screen.

He pocketed it just as we hit the bottom step and swiped his card for both of us. It wasn't until we were on the train that he took the phone back out, and then he was tapping away once again.

"Is there another name for it?" he asked, scrolling. He let out a huff, then typed something else.

"For what?"

He glanced up at me. "This depression festival or event or whatever. I can't find any info on it."

I frowned, lost. It took me a solid ten seconds to process his words, and then I had to bite back a chuckle. He was so damn cute. "Are you really googling depression festival?"

He sat a little straighter beside me and blinked slowly. "You don't want to go?"

This time there was no stopping the laugh that bubbled out of me. "I was making a joke. March in Boston is cold and dreary and *boring*. That's what I meant by depression. Everyone has winter sadness."

"Oh." His brow furrowed, like he was still trying to figure out what the hell I was going on about.

I clapped a hand over my mouth to stifle another laugh. "Sorry, I can't help but wonder what a depression festival would look like."

"Shut up, Blondie." He tilted closer and tickled my side.

Rather than jerking away, I jumped toward him.

He bowed his head and kissed me quickly before pulling away. "We probably shouldn't do that in public yet."

He was right. Even with a ball cap pulled low, people recognized him. That only made me more eager to break the news to my dad.

Christian
50

"DRAGON."

At the sound of my name, I clicked out of the message thread between Avery and me and pocketed my phone. When I spun around, I found three reporters descending on my locker. I'd had an average game. Nothing like last week's complete game, with a few fastballs clocking in at 105 miles per hour. I hadn't hit that mark today.

I'd considered giving Avery a hard time about not being here, like her absence was the cause of my shortcomings. But if I did that, she'd probably decide she couldn't miss another game. And her job mattered as much as mine did. Tonight, she was attending a donor event at the zoo, which was definitely more important than sitting in the stands watching me.

Still, seeing her in my jersey, cheering for me and the rest of the team, fired me up. Tomorrow's breakfast with Tom couldn't come fast enough. I was sick of sneaking around. Unless that sneaking around consisted of sex in a storage closet again. Anytime she was up for that, so was I.

I smirked.

"Good game today, but how'd ya feel about the fifth?" A guy from ESPN shoved a mike in my face.

I fought my natural tendency to glare and instead forced an almost smile onto my face. As the pitcher, I was always getting shit from reporters. What did they think I would say about the two-run homer I gave up that inning?

Oh, best moment of the game for me. Thanks for asking.

I wanted to roll my eyes. But I'd make Hannah proud and not piss off Tom. Fuck no, I would not upset him the day before I planned to tell him I was dating his daughter.

"Probably spent too much time on the slider this offseason. I'm sure Wilson and Price will be riding me about the knuckle ball for the next couple of weeks. Luckily, Martinez's catch and that quick double play got us out of the inning quick."

"You seem to be happier this season."

I spun to address the man who'd asked the odd question, and my stomach knotted when I zeroed in on him. It was the guy Avery had gone out with. From the second they'd stepped off the elevator that night, I'd known who he was. Yet he wasn't a reporter. This guy was the sports editor for the *Globe*. So why was he here?

Keeping my cool, I took a breath. "The season has started off well. You all know my pop had a heart attack while I was at spring training. He's improved a lot since then, and that has been a huge boost for me."

He cocked a brow. "Nothing else?"

My heart thumped harder against my chest, but I kept my composure, even though I didn't like what he was implying. Typically, the reporters kept our personal lives out of the locker room interviews.

"Life is good in general." Leaving it at that, I turned away from him and happily answered several questions that were relevant to the game. After I'd given them an ample amount of time, I tilted my chin. "All right, guys. I'm gonna hit the showers."

The group dispersed from there. All but Jude. Fuck.

"In a rush to get home?"

This time, I couldn't help myself. I sent him a smirk. "Wouldn't you be if you had someone to get home to?"

He stepped closer and lowered his voice so his next words were just between us. "How long have you two been hooking up?"

"Don't know what you're talking about." I shrugged and turned back to my locker, hoping like hell this dude would take the hint and get out of here.

"Come on. Man up to it at least," he goaded.

While I unbuttoned my jersey, I scanned the area around us to make sure the other reporters were focused elsewhere. "Respect the space, man. We don't talk private business here. This room is for baseball." I shucked off my jersey and tossed it onto my chair.

"That sounds like confirmation to me." He smirked.

"Take it however you want."

Jude kept his focus locked on me as he called out. "Coach."

My heart stuttered and sank. Shit. There was no doubt in my mind that I wouldn't like what he said next. I had promised Avery no drama, and this was the definition of locker room drama.

Almost in slow motion, Tom spun and stalked toward us.

Jude finally broke eye contact when Tom was standing beside him. Then he dropped the bomb. "What do you think about your daughter dating your problematic hothead?"

Ever in control, Tom kept his expression even. The only sign that he was pissed was the way his jaw ticked almost imperceptibly. His attention shifted from Jude to me. The look he gave me seared like a branding iron. "Seems like its settled him a bit." His jaw tightened again. "Excuse me."

With that, he strode into his office and shut the door behind him.

I was so fucked.

Avery
51

I GAPED AT THE TELEVISION, barely hearing what the commentators had to say over the blood rushing in my ears.

"That was a dramatic end to a somewhat quiet doubleheader. If Tom Wilson wasn't aware of his daughter's dating status before today, he definitely is now." The commentator laughed uncomfortably after the feed in the locker room cut off.

They continued talking about whether our relationship could be credited for the change in Chris's attitude this season and whether my father's response could even be considered confirmation that a relationship existed.

This was exactly why my father didn't want me dating his players. Now that the news was out, all the media would be talking about was my connection to Chris when they should be reporting on the game.

But Chris was more than just a guy I was dating.

My heart hammered in my chest so violently I pressed a hand to my sternum to ease the ache. Chris hadn't wanted to wait so long to break the news to my dad. What if this messed up what we had been building?

I shook my head. No. It couldn't. I wouldn't let it. He mattered too much to me.

He was the person I wanted to talk to first when I had a story to tell, and his arms were the ones I craved when I needed a hug. When I wanted to cuddle on the couch and watch a movie. When I was snuggled in bed. He stole my breath and made me laugh, especially when he pretended he was nothing but a grump. The man who knew exactly what I needed without having to ask. He understood me on a level that no one else could.

He wasn't just my boyfriend or my best friend; he was my person. My other half. Dad would have to understand that. I needed Christian Damiano in my life in a way that I'd never needed anything before.

I snagged my keys off the counter and stepped into a pair of shoes I'd left by the door. There was only one place I could be right now, and it wasn't at home.

The whole way to the stadium, I reminded myself to relax. That Chris and I were fine. There was nothing my dad could do to mess that up.

Except...What if he traded Chris? He wasn't that serious about his rule against me dating a player, was he? I didn't work for the Revs, so our relationship couldn't be considered fraternization, but what if Beckett Langfield had more defined policies that I hadn't asked about? What if one of them had to go? Chris or my dad. I'd never thought beyond my dad's rule to what the repercussions could be.

My heart pounded and I blinked hard, holding back tears as I parked. Barely holding it together, I rushed into the stadium. I flashed the badge my dad had given me, then rushed past security and down the concrete tunnels to the team room, where I hoped Chris would be.

I rounded a corner of a somewhat full hallway just in time to see Chris heading out of Dad's office.

"Chris," I cried, launching myself at him.

He caught me and pulled me into a fierce hug. "Avery, what are you doing here?" Holding me at arm's length, he scanned my face. "What's wrong?"

How could he ask that?

My heart cracked open, and tears escaped, despite my best efforts.

"If they trade you to Minnesota, I'm coming too. I want to be wherever you are." I burrowed into the crook of his neck. "We're meant to be together," I cried, my words muffled. "You are my person, and I love you more than even my birds."

For one beat, his body went rigid, but then he tightened his hold on me.

"I love you too, Blondie." He kissed the top of my head. Grasping my arm, he held it between us, pressed to his chest. He tapped my wrist twice as he whispered in my ear. "Blon-die." He repeated the word, tapping in time with the syllables.

I reared back so I could study him, though I didn't pull away.

"When I'm upset, angry, or even feeling out of control, your name and the reminder of the first time we connected settles me. Reminds me to work to be the person you need me to be."

My heart skipped, and a rush of love washed through me. In the last year, I'd seen him do that so many times. And all along, he was thinking about me?

"We've got this," he said. "I'll protect our relationship. Don't doubt that."

"Damiano," my father growled behind us. "I swear we just had this conversation."

Chris let out a low sigh, his shoulders sagging.

I spun out of his arms. "We tried to tell you but—"

"My office," he snapped, waving us both in.

I reached for Chris's hand, and he gave mine a squeeze. That connection alone eased my fears. And when I looked into his eyes, relief swept over me. This man loved me, and I loved him. That was all that mattered. And we could handle whatever came next.

Inside Dad's office, Cortney was leaning against a wall and Beckett sat on the sofa with one ankle crossed over a knee. Both men were dressed in suits and wearing serious expressions.

The instant the door was shut, I said, "If you trade him, I'm going with him."

My father frowned like he was confused rather than angry.

"I'm not trading him." Beckett scoffed. "You know how many people can throw a 105 mile-an-hour fastball accurately?"

"Uh?" I looked from one man to the next while my mind tried to catch up.

"Pretty much only your boyfriend." Cortney chuckled and waved at Chris.

"If someone's going, it's your father," Beckett said.

My stomach sank. "Wait." I held a hand up. I didn't mean for that to happen.

"Not Funny," Chris snapped, stepping closer and rubbing my back. "No one is getting fired or traded."

My father sighed and dropped into the chair behind his desk. "I've had a suspicion that there was something going on between you two since you called in the middle of a game practically in tears over his father."

"And I've been aware of the situation since Chris came to me the day after his 'stomach bug.'" Cortney used air quotes on the last two words.

"Keep rubbing it in that he came to you, Man Bun," Beckett grumbled.

"You told him?" I turned to Chris, clutching the front of his shirt.

"He came to me in confidence. He wanted to clarify that the two of you would be protected, along with your dad and the whole team. To ensure there would be no fallout that could hurt you," Cortney explained.

Chris's lips pulled up slightly. "I keep telling you, Blondie. I will always protect you and our relationship."

"So, no one's in trouble," Cortney confirmed.

"We were here to confirm that there would be no drama." Beckett laughed. "We'd succeeded just before you threw yourself at him and implied that he was going to be traded while you declared your love in the middle of the hallway in front of about twenty-five reporters and most of the team."

The knots that had formed in my stomach the moment I watched the clip of Chris and my dad after the game tightened.

Chris draped his arm around me and glared. "That was the best moment of my life, so don't mock it."

Beckett put both hands up.

"Okay." My father pounded on the desk. "Team shit over. Now I would like to talk to my daughter." He met my eye, his frown smoothing out just a fraction. "And her boyfriend."

The acknowledgment was step one.

"All right, Man Bun, our work here is done." Beckett pushed to his feet. But he paused beside Chris. "All kidding aside, hang on to those moments that make life worth living. Not everyone is lucky enough to find them so early in life. For some of us, it takes forty years before we get to experience them."

He patted Chris's arm, and when Chris froze in place, trying not to flinch, Beckett chuckled. Then he was striding out the door.

"Good Luck." With a smile, Cortney pulled the door shut.

"Sit," my dad barked, tipping his chin to the chairs in front of his desk. That was the way my dad talked to his players, but long ago, I'd drawn a line with him. He could not speak to me in the same way.

Chris moved to sit, but I pulled on his hand to stop him and shook my head.

Dad closed his eyes and released a breath through his nose. When he opened them again, his features had softened. "Sorry." He cleared his throat. "Can we sit and talk about this?"

Chris almost reeled back at the drastic change.

"Dad doesn't talk to family the way he talks to his players," I explained, tugging Chris toward the chairs.

"I'm not ignorant as to what goes on in the locker room." My dad scowled. "For a year, I've been hearing about this girl that had my pitcher in knots. Often, the talk isn't great."

Chris worked his jaw from side to side but didn't speak.

"But the tone was wholly different when the guys talked about Chris's girl." Dad rested his elbows on his desk and clasped his hands. "He demanded a level of protection and respect for her. He was fine with his teammates mocking him, but they better respect this girl." Sighing, he glanced at the ceiling, then back at us. "It wasn't until January that I realized you were the girl everyone was talking about."

I took Chris's hand again and gave it a gentle squeeze.

My dad stared at the connection for a moment before he went on.

"I've always dreamed of the best for you. I can't say I ever imagined a hotheaded, explosive major league baseball player could fit into the future I hoped you'd have." My dad shook his head. "But when Christian looked at me and told me to pull him, I knew you'd found the best kind of man." Ducking his head, he swallowed thickly. "Because to him, you were more important than a baseball game."

"She always will be," Chris said, shifting to the edge of his seat.

Lips pressed in a straight line, my dad regarded me. "He loves you. And if I'm not mistaken, you just ran in here announcing that you loved him more than birds."

Chris huffed a laugh beside me and brought our joined hands to his lips.

"Happy and treated well. That's all I've ever wanted for you." Dad pushed to his feet and moved around the desk to stand in front of us. "And if you've found that with Christian Damiano, then he is one lucky guy."

With my heart in my throat, I jumped up and looped my arms around Dad's waist. Although I didn't need his blessing, it was nice to have.

"However," my dad said as he stepped back. "From this point on, all the relationship drama stays at home and out of my locker room and stadium."

"Yes, sir." Chris nodded.

"Hannah's already working on fixing all this"—Dad waved his hand—"mess of a night. But it *won't* be a constant issue. Understood? Cleaning up the fallout today is one thing, but we have no interest in making this a habit."

Dad continued to yammer on about rules and whatnot, but I just smiled at Chris. Looking at him, the only fallout I could imagine coming from the last year was a happily ever after.

Epilogue

CHRISTIAN
June

"It's dry." Avery was trying her best not to cringe. "What did you do to it?" She pushed the chicken around on her plate.

Although I agreed with her, I'd never admit it, and I'd already eaten every bite.

"What do you mean *do to it*?" Tom asked, stabbing a piece with his fork. "I baked it."

"Kinda badly." Avery frowned. "Do you have Nutella? That might help."

My stomach rolled, and I fought a shudder. Avery's food choices were always a bit weird.

"You mean to tell me you're going to put peanut butter on your baked chicken?"

"It's hazelnut butter." Avery hopped up from her chair and shuffled to the kitchen.

Tom looked from his plate to mine. "Was it really that bad?"

"Not at all," I lied.

As a guest in my girlfriend's dad's home, my job was to shut up and eat. We'd had dinner here a few times over the last couple of months, but it would take years for me to feel comfortable enough to tell Tom he was a terrible cook. Or maybe I never would.

On the mound and in the locker room, we had an open and honest relationship. At home, I kissed his ass. And that was fine.

Avery practically skipped back into the room with her nut butter. She'd just gotten the lid off when her phone buzzed on the table beside her plate.

We all froze as she read the message.

"It's time!" she squealed. "They're hatching." She dropped her knife and snapped to her feet again. "Are you coming, Dad?"

"Yes." He sighed. "I'll go see the damn birds." The man acted like he was put out, but he secretly loved Avery's birds almost as much as I did. There wasn't a single guy on the team, coaches included, who wasn't a big fan of Puff.

"I'll drive." I snagged the keys off the table next to the door while Avery slid her shoes on.

"I'm texting Gianna. She and your dad will want to come too," Avery said, already firing off messages.

I sighed.

My father had moved to Boston's Conran Center, the best cardio rehab in the world, to finish his therapy back in April. I was getting him an apartment that was finally finished at the end of this month, and he'd stay in town. It had been a struggle but Gianna and I finally got him to sell the house on Long Island. Puff was part of the reason.

Avery finally set the phone down. "I told Emerson too. And Mason and Kyle."

Oh, fun. We'd have the peanut gallery in attendance.

Twenty minutes later, we were in the puffin house at the Boston Zoo, rapt by the footage on a television screen that had been set up for the staff. Two of the three eggs rocked slightly. I could just make out the crack in one of the whitish shells with subtle black speckles.

"It's so close." Avery bounced on her toes, her palms pressed together over her heart and her fingers tapping together. "Puff's going to be a daddy, Chris."

"I knew Puffette was his girl." It was always going to be the bird with the pink band. Puff looked at her and knew. I understood that.

Avery rolled her eyes.

"Hey, all." Dean appeared, hitting me with a covert smile when Avery wasn't looking.

I nodded in answer to his silent question, and with that, he stepped away again.

"Enjoy the show," he said as he wandered off.

"Did we miss it?" I spun at the sound of Pop's voice. He was flanked by Gianna and Emerson, but even so, I headed his way, eager to help him. But he held his hand out quickly. "I can walk over to you. I told these two the same damn thing. I do not need help."

Being somewhat helpless these last few months had been hard for Dad. But he was getting closer to being back to normal every day. He'd been placed into a more self-sufficient apartment now that he was moving easier and able to shower without help.

"Dumpty and Bosco are on their way too." Emerson beamed. "Isn't it exciting?"

"You'd think it was your baby for how much you're bouncing up and down." Gianna rolled her eyes.

Emerson leaned close and whispered something that had her glancing away. Gianna had been staying at my place for a few weeks, since I was pretty much living with Avery, and things seemed off between her and Emerson.

I watched them both. Gi had sidestepped, and had her arms crossed over her chest, and Emerson was now ignoring her as well. Though maybe it was because he was fixated on the eggs on the TV screen. I couldn't put my finger on exactly what was off, but I trusted my best friend not to mess with my sister, so whatever it was, I wouldn't stress about it.

"Hey." Avery tapped my arm. "I'm going to head back and check on them." The nesting birds had been moved out of the exhibit to make them more comfortable, so they were all in the back. "You ready, grandpa and great-grandpas?"

Tom and I both groaned.

Pop, on the other hand, smiled and clapped his hands. "Absolutely."

Our responses made Avery's smile impossibly brighter. Spinning on her heel, she laughed and headed toward the employees only area, her blond ponytail swinging. Once she was out of sight, the door that led into the exhibit opened, and Dean stepped out onto the rock. In the space of one heartbeat, he was surrounded by hungry birds. It wasn't an easy task to get Puff out of there on his own. Not with all the attention Dean had garnered from the entire puffinry.

Tom cleared his throat. "You nervous?" He knew my plan because I'd swung by his brownstone on my way home from the game last week.

"He's depending on a bird. Of course he is." Gianna rolled her eyes. At this point, I was pretty sure Avery was the only person who didn't know what was happening today.

"Puff isn't going to mess up. I trust him." I shrugged.

Tom shook his head. "The damn bird could eat it."

"Our grandson is smarter than that," Pop joked.

I winced. Why hadn't I thought of that? It was too late now, because Dean was back, with Puff in tow. The white ribbon around his neck was in place and everything.

As soon as he noticed me, Puff hopped onto my shoulder.

"Keep a hold of this, and you'll be fine." Dean passed me the harness. "She thinks I'm bringing him back for when they hatch."

As if on cue, one of the eggs on screen wobbled, and the egg cracked, revealing a tiny black beak.

"Better get in there," Dean said.

I wrapped the lead around my hand and then, out of habit, I tapped my wrist twice. Was I nervous? No. Avery was it for me, and she felt the same. But those pregame jitters were hitting.

A chorus of good luck sentiments echoed behind me as I walked away.

Dean opened the door labeled employees only, and Puff and I slipped in. The room was all white, with six sets of half walls. Only a few housed actual bird's nests. Avery was leaning against the half wall at the one farthest from the door.

Puff, likely noticing her, squeaked, startling me a little and ramping up my heart rate more.

"Shh," she whispered. She barely glanced at us before turning back to the nest.

I settled in beside her and wrapped an arm around her waist. Two minutes later, the hole in one thin, speckled shell was big enough for the puffling's head to pop through. The tiny creature was squeaking and squawking already. Puffette hovered over it, instantly calming her baby. "Congrats, Puff," Avery murmured. "You're officially Puff Daddy now."

"And on that note," I whispered into her ear. "Puff has something for you."

Putting gentle pressure on her waist, I spun Avery to face us. She tilted her head, brow furrowed, and glanced back at Puffette and her puffling.

"Since we're grandparents now, I thought it might be time to officially make us a family." I tapped my chin, and Puff tilted his head back so his beak pointed to the ceiling.

The move exposed the diamond ring hanging from the white ribbon on Puff's neck.

Avery's eyes went wide, but she was frozen in place.

I dropped to one knee, careful not to jostle Puff.

With a squeak of her own, Avery covered her pretty pink lips with both hands.

"So what do you say, Blondie? Will you marry me?"

She blinked hard as tears pooled in her eyes, but she nodded vigorously.

On my shoulder, Puff mimicked the motion.

"Yes," she whispered, yanking my hand to pull me to my feet. "Yes," she said again, this time with her palms pressed to my face and her lips ghosting mine.

I slipped the string from around Puff's neck and slid the ring onto her finger. Then I let Puff off his harness.

He flew straight over to Puffette and landed just behind the nest.

"It's crazy how one slider led to the start of two perfect families." Avery placed her hand over mine on the half wall in front of us.

The sight of my ring on her finger ignited a round of fireworks in my chest. I pressed a hand to her abdomen and pulled her back so she was flush against my chest. "Can't complain about the fallout, though. Because Puff and I are both very lucky guys."

DEAR READER

First, let me just say a massive THANK YOU! Thank you for reading The Fall Out, especially since these two really took you for a ride. Yes we were all annoyed Avery went out with the dopey reporter. But it all worked out just the way the book universe wanted. And who didn't love getting to see more Cortney and Beckett, those two love to jump into every story and try to steal the show. But seriously, THANK YOU for supporting me. It's only because readers exist writers get to live out their dreams.

Some books are hard, and some are easy but Christian and Avery's story just flowed and hopefully you ended up loving them and Puff as much as I did.

And there is plenty more baseball fun to come! Yes, Emerson is next…. Who can't wait to see what goes on in that unicorn of happiness's head huh? Hopefully you'll join me on the entireBoston Revs ride because we have so many more to go this year!

Check out Mason's Story in Gracie York (My pen name with AJ Ranney) Together Again May 1 st . Then Emerson in The Fall Out this summer. Spend the fall with Kyle Bosco when the play boy finally falls, and then get snowed in before the holidays with Coach Wilson and someone…

Finally, remember: Live in your world, fall in love in mine.
Jenni

Acknowledgments

A big thank you my kids who have to hear, "Hold on a second, mom is writing." Or "I have one more signing this weekend." You big guys have become constant babysitters for lives, and have manager to learn to fend for yourselves while I'm at signing but you all always more excited than I am when the next book releases. I'm so grateful for all four of you!

Thank you to my parents, who support me in all I do all the time. I couldn't get through life without you guys. Being able to count on you both all the time for help or support, or encouragement, is the best gift. Thank you for being examples I can strive to be with my kids and being the best grandparents ever.

Beth, thank you for being you. Detailed, and organized because I am not. And your series bibles are amazing. You are friend and such an amazing supporter of me. I'm so excited to see you again soon. Finding you was the best thing that ever happened! I will never stop singing your praises from the rooftop. Don't doubt yourself because you rock at your job, and we all know it! Thank you for being the wonderful person you are.

Becca and the rest of the Author agency you all are the best. You keep up with me and always keep things under control. I'm chaos and I'm sure I make you nuts with the wait, when is the cover reveal messages, I constantly send your way.

Sara, thank you for adding me to your plate when it was already overflowing. Because I love you. Not just as a PA although you are amazing and your work ethic cannot be matched, but I love that you make me smile and laugh with me. And we have fun on this crazy ridiculously overly busy adventure we are on. I'm thankful for your friendship and support more than you have any idea. Your graphics are always better than I could have picture and your ideas are perfect. Your eye for design and detail is amazing, it inspires me. And I'm so proud of the amazing business you created and I cant wait to watch you keep flying.

Jeff, thank you for being the final nit-picky check to make sure everything is perfect. Becoming a romance reader wasn't on your to do list, but I'm grateful you did it anyway!

Britt, the rest of dedication...not just because you called him first because you did, but because you are always first. First to share your new great idea to help us both. First to drag me along with you everywhere. First to cheer me on. First help me with idea. First to text me pretty much every day. So if I have anything you want you know it's yours every time. Its crazy to think there were years before I knew you because now a day doesn't go by where we don't talk a million times. I love that every time we are together the laughs don't stop. Thank you for all your help making this story work and for adding into yours all the stuff I threw your way. Your ability to create the perfect story and characters is something that amazes me. You rock this author thing every day and inspire me by how hard you work. I love seeing your success!

Daphne thank you for being not only one best friends but my teacher. The amount of knowledge and insight you have given is something I am forever grateful for. And your friendship is something I don't want to do without. No matter how busy you are and how crazy your own life is you are always checking in on me because you are simply the best. Everyone should check out the Lovewell Lumberjacks by Daphne Elliot because this woman has too much talent to not be known to every reader.

Amy, thank you for being the organized one, the one that keeps us on track, and the one that makes sure we get it done. For putting up with my chaos and my next 'fun' thing. I'm so lucky to get to call you one of my best friends.

Amy Jo thank you for being a friend and an amazing talented merch maker! I love that you are always willing to do book therapy, which reminds me I need to chat....You always jump as soon as I need anything and a package is in the mail with amazing keychain, bracelets, mini and more! And your surprises are the best. You organize my drives and keep the TikTok teams running smooth.

Jess, best thing ever when Britt had you meet us in Salem, because I got to make a new amazing friend. I love that you are always there with your support and shot from the roof about my stuff. Having a cheerleader is great, but when the cheerleader is a friend who will chat more than books, and be there whenever you call is amazing. I cant wait for more fun time together and more thoughts on all the Revs from you!

Anna thank you for being a great friend and helping whenever I need beta reader. And making sure my zoo stuff tracked on this book. For having so many TikTok accounts that I cant even keep track and shouting to the world to read my books. I'm grateful for your support and friendship.

To all my author friends and beta readers, thank you for being supportive and inspiring writers. Haley Cook, AJ Ranney, Kristin Lee, Alexandra Hale, Amanda Zook, Kat Long, Bethany Monaco Smith, Elyse Kelly, and so many, many more.

And big thank you to the rest of my friends and family who have helped me with encouragement and feedback. I love you all and am so thankful for your support.

ALSO BY JENNI BARA

Want more Boston Revs Baseball?

Cortney Miller

Mother Maker

Christian Damiano

The Fall Out (The Boston Revs Three Outs Book 1)

Emerson Knight

The Fake Out (The Boston Revs Three Outs Book 2)

Kyle Bosco

The Foul Out (The Boston Revs Three Outs Book 3)

Coach Wilson

Finding Out (The Boston Revs Three Outs Book 4)

Curious about the baseball boys from the NY Metros

NY Metros Baseball

More than the Game

More than a Story

Wishing for More

Romcoms written as Gracie York

Goldilocks and the Grumpy Bear

Tumbling Head over Heels

Along Came the Girl

Peter Pumpkined Out

Made in the USA
Columbia, SC
15 November 2024

46603884R00165